Leonard Kip

Hannibal's Man and Other Tales

The Argus Christmas Stories

Leonard Kip

Hannibal's Man and Other Tales
The Argus Christmas Stories

ISBN/EAN: 9783744707701

Printed in Europe, USA, Canada, Australia, Japan

Cover: Foto ©Andreas Hilbeck / pixelio.de

More available books at **www.hansebooks.com**

HANNIBAL'S MAN

AND

OTHER TALES.

The Argus Christmas Stories.

By Leonard Kip,

Author of Aenone, The Dead Marquise, etc.

PREFACE.

The following stories were written, with a single exception, for the columns of THE ARGUS, of Albany, N. Y.

Four of them have already appeared in successive Christmas numbers of that well-known journal; the fifth — PRIOR POLYCARP'S PORTRAIT — now for the first time makes its salutation to the public, and in advance of any different form of issue. The remaining story — THE SECRET OF APOLLONIUS SEPTRIO — was published many years ago, anonymously, and under a less appropriate title.

INSCRIBED

TO

Edmund Clarence Stedman,

in token of

APPRECIATION AND FRIENDSHIP.

CONTENTS.

Hannibal's Man.

Hannibal's Man.

NOW that the earliest buds and blossoms of Spring are peeping stealthily above the more protected borders of the glacier, or from certain sheltered nooks of the surrounding snow-crowned slopes, it is one of my chiefest pleasures to wander forth and gather them as precious trophies, for the adornment of our mountain-cabin. This I do, not loving flowers for themselves. In my own land, the sweetest rose-buds, in the most romantic woodland nooks, would be passed by me unnoticed. But here, in the Alpine fastnesses, where for so many months the land lays fettered with snow and ice, and even chance passengers do not often journey by, those flowers are to me a type of coming Spring,— a joy, in that they speak of partial release from hyperborean bondage,—a memento of the softer climate of my own far-off country; and as such I value them, apart from any sentiment connected with their own mere intrinsic beauty.

Why then, since all the while my heart thus remains fixed upon the congenial memories of my native home, do I linger in this land of wintry captivity and cheerlessness? It is very easy to explain, indeed, why at the first I took refuge in such a lonely region. Disappointment in certain cherished hopes,—chagrin about baffled ambitions,—the inevitable sadness engendered through failure in a friendship where most securely I had learned to trust,—these several influences combined to create in me a temporary dislike of all the world, its society, restraints, and interests, and thereby drove me away to these Alpine wilds, where, more completely than elsewhere, I thought that I might avoid encounter with mankind. And yet, now that at last the morbid influence has left me, and once more I learn to pine after the pleasures and pursuits of the outer world, why do I linger longer in this enforced seclusion and only from the mountain heights gaze longingly into the sunny valleys through which so easily I might journey to my home? Surely I do not love the mountains. Their unchanging outlines weary me,—their passing lights and shades afford me no variety,—their wintry blasts enfeeble me,—their rude, uncouth inhabitants repel me. In the whole range of snow-crowned peaks I can gather no kindling of romance to inspire me with the least enthusiasm ;—for me the dearest place on earth must ever be my little dingy home in the narrowest of all streets in Heidelberg. Yet here, in this tempestuous spot, I have remained the Winter through ; and at last it has been impressed upon me with the certainty of fate, that I shall never leave the Alps again.

There is one prevailing reason for it all. Before I had remained many weeks in this uncongenial district, and while the freshness of the life of perfect isolation was still most powerful with me, I had

chanced to see and at once had loved Ursula. She
was a simple Alpine maiden of sixteen, —herself an
orphan, —brought up in kindly, loving charity
within the neighboring convent, and thereby naturally remaining almost a stranger to the outer world,
—knowing, indeed, no other home than that of the
circumscribing convent walls. I loved her, at the
first meeting with her, for the soul-lit beauty of her
face and the unapproachable graces of her lithe
figure ; and she, childlike and trusting, loved me in
return, inasmuch as she had learned to look upon me
as marked with something different from the gross
boorishness around her. Therefore, while yet the
world remained distasteful to me, I had yielded to the
impulse of my sudden love for her, and led her away,
as my precious bride, to that little cabin set apart
upon the mountain-side.

There we have lived in happy freedom from all
outward intrusion ; but now that there has come
again to me a yearning for the past and its familiar
scenes, it is mingled with a strange dread of making
the attempt to realize them. For how may I dare
to hope that Ursula can ever adapt herself to that
other and more artificial life, of which, as yet, she
has never even read ? And how,—more especially,
I ponder,—can I venture, with due regard for my
own peace of mind, to lead her into that outer world,
where she would see other men, between whom and
myself, so easily she could make comparison unfavor-
able to me ? For, in my heart there is an exceeding
jealous nature, which I never can subdue. I know
that she has chosen me because I am different in her

eyes from any of the rough, uncouth people around her. And yet I am not of stalwart form or of prepossessing mien. Much delving over hidden roots of dead languages has taken from me all possible graces of the body. I know that, in a different land, she could not fail to see many men whom, for their appearance, she would naturally prefer to me. While I reside upon the Alpine slope, apart from others of our race, I can remain to her ignorant, untutored eyes a god ; but among different men, how can I answer for it that her simple, childlike nature, thinking no harm, but merely influenced by her instinctive love for the grand and beautiful, might not become warped from its true regard for me? Better a life-long seclusion, indeed, than that this should happen. And so, while thinking upon my own country, with a longing that knows no rest, month after month, I find myself lingering among the sterile mountains. And telling Ursula that the world outside is very cruel, and, if possible, more forbidding even than among the avalanches, I press her close to my heart and glory in the pleasant deception which I feel would retain me ever constant in her sweet affection.

"And now, thinking only of our mutual love and letting the outer world pass by, unheeded, we will wander forth once more," I said to her this morning, "and search for early flowers. Last week, indeed, we looked in vain ; but since then the sun has shone

out warmly, and already I see signs that the buds
are sprouting below, against the glacier banks."

"Why should we go to-day?" she hesitatingly
rejoined. "For listen how the convent-chapel bells
are even now warning me."

"I hear the bells, far down the Pass, tolling a
requiem," I said. "It is the requiem of the chamois
hunter who was killed two days ago. But how can
that affect yourself?"

"I know not, except that these things always seem
to influence my lot, however they may seem to apply
to others," she responded, a shiver of apprehension
passing over her frame. "Do you not know that I
am the convent's child, and under its protection?
And so whenever I am about to encounter peril, a
kindly warning is sounded out to me from the bells.
While, if it is a coming joy, so do the bells announce
that, as well. Doubtless the bells are now ringing
for the slain chamois hunter; but if it was not also
meant as a warning to myself, I should not now be able
to hear them. The wind would carry the sound the
other way, or it would be deadened to my ears. But
listen now to the dirge, how close it sounds, even as
though the bells were just outside!"

"It is a foolish fancy, Ursula," I said; "and one
that would not now come to you, but for long confinement in the house. The purer air abroad will
dissipate such vagaries. Come,—let us depart; for
I know that since we were last at the Glacier, fresh
flowers have been born to greet and cheer us."

It was as I had supposed. Ere long, in a little
recess where the rocks receded from the icy abra-

sion, I found a tuft or two of grass amid thin layers of fast dissolving snow-wreaths; and in the center of all, a clump of pale lilly-shaped crocuses. I severed them carefully from the ground and first twined three or four in Ursula's thick tresses. Then holding the others in my hand for the decoration of our cabin, I turned with her upon the homeward path. Yet before departing, feeling moved by some indefinable curiosity, I approached the edge of the great Glacier and gazed down upon it.

The vast icy sea here and there was cracked and broken — roughened in wide portions as though, at one time, watery waves had been raised upon it by the wind, and frozen by instantaneous blast; and throughout its greatest extent, was covered with sheets of snow, laying many feet deep upon it. In certain spots, however, the snow had either blown or melted away, and in other places the surface of the ice had liquified and again been frozen with glassy smoothness. This happened to have been the case just where now I stood; and I could look down many inches into the clear, unruffled depths of the ice, almost with the same ease and distinctness with which one can gaze into a quiet pool belonging to a running spring.

"See, Ursula!" I said, after a moment, and pointing downward. "A log."

It lay, apparently, two feet below the surface of the ice, indistinct and shadowy in form, but evidently a log. What else, indeed, could it be?

"Yes,—a log," remarked Ursula. "Can it have been there very long do you think?"

"Who knows? For centuries, perhaps," I said. And then, a little proud, it may be, of my power to instruct, I told her all I knew about the theory of the glacial formations. How that this same river of ice had been forming from above for many generations and working downward upon its rocky bed, at the rate of a few inches every year, until at last it would decompose and melt away into the valley below. How that it had the faculty of grasping and concealing within its icy embrace, more securely than within miser's chest, whatever might cross its path; but how that after long periods, it might even be after many centuries, it was always forced to release its prey, which, from the melting of the surface of the ice and possibly from some inherent power of self-extrication, would gradually work up into the outer air and become forever free. How that this same log, imprisoned for so long, was now doubtless upon the point of attaining its release, and in a few months would float away on mountain stream, down to the sea itself.

"And we will watch it in its efforts after freedom, my love," I said, as we returned to our home. "It will be a pleasant pastime for us during the passage of the Summer."

A very little thing, indeed, for me to interest myself about, after my enlarged communications of the past with the outer world. And why, in fact, do I not only ponder long upon it after our return, but even write down the whole circumstance in exact detail? Hardly do I know,—or even whether it is one or several causes that impel me. It may be

2*

that I give heed to such a trifle simply because there
is no other way to occupy my time. It may be that
through want of proper exercise for it, my mind is
already losing its proper tone and attuning itself to
trivial things. And it may be, after all, that I am
influenced by the desire to make true record of
Ursula's superstitious fancies at the moment when
her very words are still fresh in my memory ; so
that hereafter reading them, and acknowledging that
no misfortune has come to her, she will learn to dis-
possess herself forever of such vagaries. It is not
pleasant to see her sitting beside the fire, her head
buried reflectively between her hands, and her whole
attitude that of one moodily brooding over a mystery. Rather should she learn to laugh merrily at
the whole conception of a warning from the convent bells.

A week has slowly passed away ; and this
morning we have repaired once more to the Glacier.
When there before, I carefully marked the position
of the log ; and from my close measurements, I now
find that the whole body of ice has moved one inch
along the bank. This, of itself, would make little
change. But meanwhile the sun has been hot, and
the sloping of the surface of the ice from the center
of the Glacier has allowed the melted portions to
run off, and I can now see clearly that the log has
been brought much nearer to the surface than before,
so that I can inspect it with increasing distinctness
of observation. And I now find that, though a log,

it bears something of the shape of a man; a branch, or that which might be a branch, being projected from the side like to an extended arm.

"And of course it must gather in interest for us, Ursula," I remarked, as I pointed out to her this fact. "For now we can plainly see that the log has some attempt at rude carving. In truth, I have little doubt that it is an old-world representative of a heathen god,— most probably a statue of Odin himself. Once honored as an idol, this log must have been accidentally thrown into some abyss, to become, after many centuries, a study for our profane gaze."

To Ursula, the theory seems to bring little interest. How could it be expected, when in all probability she has never even heard of Odin? But with myself, it fills the mind with strange speculation. Can it be that, after all, this apparently profitless existence in the Alps is destined to make me famous as the discoverer of a rare relic of an ancient race?

Again an interval of a week, and once more we have visited the spot. And now I find that I must alter my previous conjecture. All this while I see that the supposed idol has been gradually approaching the surface still nearer; and now that I can examine it more closely, I can detect that it is no mere rude carving of a savage age. A charming bronze statue, rather, of the highest type of art, so natural is it in its proportions and attitude. A

representation of a warrior in helmet, breastplate
and sandals, with shield upon his arm and short
sword at his side. One leg is thrown a little forward, and the shield is raised so as to cover the
head ; yet, not sufficiently to conceal a portion of
the helmet crest. For many minutes I gazed in
almost speechless admiration.

"A wonderful discovery!" I broke forth at last.
"And who can tell how valuable? To the archæolo-
gist, a revelation,—to the artist, an inspiration,—to
us, a possible fortune. Of the age of Augustus, it
may be,—or even earlier. And how came it here?
For how many centuries may it not have been
imbedded in this solid ice? Ursula, in another
fortnight, at the most, we can obtain possession of
our prize. Until then, let us subdue our impatience,
and watch to see that no one may spirit it from us."

And, that no possible precaution may be neglected,
I have sprinkled snow lightly over the spot, lest any
other person passing,—an improbable circumstance,
indeed,—may look down into the clear ice and claim
my prize. Each day, henceforth, will I sally forth
to watch for indications of intrusion. Yet all the
while will I struggle to subdue my own impatience,
and not look too prematurely upon the statue ;
preferring to wait until the elements may deliver it
up to me, and then to enjoy, in sudden and complete
fruition, the sense of its artistic loveliness.

Now let me strive to regulate my thoughts aright, to the end that I may set down everything in due sequence and in order, without confusion or exaggeration, and thereby, hereafter reading it with more collected brain, perhaps, may know that it was not a dream.

This morning the fortnight of probation that I had allotted to myself came to an end, and I could control myself no longer. Taking a shovel and pickax in either hand, and accompanied by Ursula, I proceeded to the spot where lay my treasure, gazed carefully around to see that even at that last moment there was no danger of intrusion, and then, hurriedly and with nervous hand, brushed away the light covering of snow.

The warm sun of the advancing Summer had well done its work. The statue was now within a few inches of the surface, and a portion of the up-stretched shield had even begun to obtrude slightly into the outer air. The covering of ice was now soft and brittle. Even the pick was scarcely necessary for its removal. Carefully scraping around with the shovel, I succeeded in removing most of the incumbent weight of ice; and at length, to my inconceivable satisfaction, the whole statue lay expose l to view.

I lifted it a few inches from the ice, to assure myself that all was clear and disconnected beneath, and then gently let it fall into place again. I could not but notice that it was scarcely as heavy as it ought to be, for a work of solid bronze; and yet, for the moment, I suffered my mind to dwell only slightly upon that circumstance. The rather did I ponder upon the position and attitude of the statue. It lay,—as I have already said,—with one leg advanced and the shield raised as though to cover the head. A striking pose, indeed; and yet there was something in it, that, from the first, instinctively confounded me. Then, after a moment, I saw that this arose from the attitude of the statue being such that, if placed upon its feet, it could not sustain itself without external support,—the center of gravity being too far forward and the feet themselves not adjusted upon the same level. Moreover, there were no appearances of outward fastenings, whereby it might possibly have been designed to rest against a column behind. Apart from these mysterious defects, it struck me as a marvelous work of art; the muscles of arm and leg being admirably defined, and the torso, wherever the termination of the armor allowed its display, being a wonder of correctly defined anatomy.

"What think you of it, yourself, Ursula?" I inquired, turning towards her. Her gaze was fastened, as mine had been, upon the statue; and I looked to see signs of admiration in her expression. But all at once I noticed that she turned pale, a startled gleam of terror shot across her face, she gave a broken scream and fell nearly fainting into my arms.

"Did you not see?" she gasped, partially recovering herself. "Look! The statue has moved! It moved while I was looking at it!"

I turned again, ready to smile at her fears, and

deeming her apparent impulse of imagination only a new test of the artistic excellence of the statue, thus enabling her to deceive her own eyes with the contemplation of its life-like truthfulness. But I myself almost gasped with terror when I saw that it had actually moved. The leg was thrown further forward, and the shield had dropped towards the knees, exhibiting what had been previously concealed,—a rugged and unexpectedly aged appearance of face, partially covered with curling gray beard. The face was bronzed, indeed,—yet of a different color from the rest of the body. And while I looked on with an indefinable apprehension of something, I could not for the moment even attempt to explain, the figure rolled its head slightly towards one side, the eyes opened with a tremulous movement, like that of a person exposed to sudden light,—and there came the convulsive quiver of a long-drawn breath!

"Merciful heavens!" I said, "it is really a living man!" And resting my wife in convenient position upon the bank, I hastened to the relief of the stranger. I took him in my grasp, placed my hand beneath his head, and so gradually raised him into a sitting posture. To this he submitted without resistance, appearing, for the moment, like one who had not sufficient perception to comprehend anything that might be done with him. But in a few minutes, his eyes becoming more accustomed to the strong sunlight, remained open with less strained aspect; a light of new intelligence—the birth of a living soul, as it were—began to glow in them.

changing their lack-lustre appearance into an animated sparkle of inner perception; he breathed tremulously once or twice again; then drew up one leg in more easy attitude between his extended hands, and gazed inquiringly at me.

"Who are you?" I demanded, with little hope, however, of being understood. And in this opinion I was correct, for he merely gazed upon me with puzzled expression, left his eyes to rove up and down my dress with something of a dawning smile, and answered me in certain uncouth sounds, which were as incomprehensible to me as mine had doubtless been to him. Meanwhile, Ursula, having somewhat recovered from her first fright, arose and approached us, her curiosity apparently overpowering any remains of fear.

"I see it all now, Ursula," I said to her, anxious not merely to give to the facts that sensible explanation which would remove from them all suspicion of the supernatural, but also not unwilling once more to exhibit my capacity to instruct. "I see it all. He is merely a man, like myself,—and not a statue."

"And he has come—"

"Who knows from where or how long ago? But that he is a living man, how can we doubt? You have never heard, perhaps, how that certain animals have been brought to life again, after long exclusion from the air. Or how that there are fishes that may be frozen, and, after months, thawed out alive. What is that secret power of retention of existence, which belongs to some brutes and seems forbidden to mankind? Or is there really any such power that we do not have as well as the brutes,—being, as yet, merely ignorant of its proper application? Some persons have conjectured the latter, indeed; and have long wearied their brains in efforts to solve the enigma and apply to the human race those principles which preserve the brutes. Once or twice it has been believed that the secret was really discovered ; but yet the result could not be tested, for want of some one sufficiently confident or enthusiastic to allow of the experiment being tried upon his own person."

" And you believe that here — "

" Here, Ursula," I continued, delighted to find that she had so readily grasped the idea, " here, it seems to me, that nature has at last taken the experiment into her own hands, and, by what we would call an accident, has fulfilled all the necessary conditions for the continued suspension of the existence of a human being. At some far distant time, this man must have been overwhelmed near the mountain-top in a sudden fall of avalanche,—the wreaths of snow gradually thereafter turning into ice and so begirting him as to retain his vitality in suspense, and thereby hinder corruption. He has formed a portion of the Glacier for many centuries, perhaps ;—and now, at the melting of the ice, near the mountain base, he is at last released alive, for our edification and instruction. Truly, he may yet prove of more value than many mere statues of bronze or marble."

Meanwhile, the man, gaining confidence in his powers during those few moments, had slowly gathered his forces together and now raised himself into a standing position. Tottering weakly, at first, indeed; but soon recovering more of his strength, so that, with all his ripeness of age, he was able to assume something of an erect and self-possessed posture, as of a soldier on guard. Little by little, and yet with such steady gradation that I could perceptibly watch its progress, full restoration to what must have been his former state came upon him. Some hitherto latent natural heat of the body evolved itself; and, in a moment, the moisture of his scanty dress—that unavoidable moisture with which his long detention in the ice must have imbued him — began to pass off in visible steam, and soon he stood dry and comfortable as though raised from flowery bank. The first pallor of his complexion, tinged with livid green, faded away, giving place to as ruddy a glow of health as old age can ever expect to exhibit, and evidently his blood commenced a new circulation after its long stagnation. Momentarily his eye grew brighter and more earnest in its intensity. I could not help marveling at the change. A few moments before,—and though recognizable as a human being,—he had lain at my feet, imbued with all the repulsive attributes of a corpse. Now he stood a well formed man, as athletic in appearance as might be consonant with wrinkles and gray hairs, — instinct with health and ambition, — animated with a certain pleasing dignity of manner which could not fail to impress me with a consciousness of what he might have been in the long past days of youth or even middle age.

"Come," I now merely said; and taking him by the arm, I led him away, while Ursula walked at

his other side, ready to give him her support, as well,
if his so recently recovered strength should chance
to give way. But that there was no danger of this,
however, I could soon observe. He had recovered
his forces not readily again to part with them. In
silence he suffered himself to be conducted away,
evidently mystified with the singularity of his situation, but not in the least realizing his true condition,
nor where he had been brought to life, nor, at the
moment, able to reconcile the present scenes with
the cloudy torrent of past recollections sweeping
through his bewildered brain. Most likely his latest
memories must have been about matters that seemed
not many hours old. How, then,—he must have
speculated,—did he come hither and among persons
so strangely clothed? I could see with what confused curiosity he glanced at the dress of Ursula
and myself; a curiosity which was not at all diminished as he surveyed, on reaching home, the architecture of our cabin, as well as the furniture and
implements within.

And there at last he sleeps,—lying across my
hearth, in curled up posture like a dog. I look down
upon his outstretched arm still grasping his shield,
his other hand wildly tossing to and fro, in the agitation of his broken slumber,—I listen to his loud
breathing,—and I watch the flickering firelight play
upon his wrinkled face and tangled gray locks.
And again and again I ask myself who he may be!
Of what nation and of what distant age? And
what must have been the dire extremity of that nation, that for its defence, even old age must thus

have been summoned to the camp and forced to
bear the sword and buckler?

We have given food and shelter to the stranger,
and now for many weeks he has been abiding with
us. At first I supposed that he would have taken
early opportunity to depart, as escaping from imagined captivity; but such was not the case. He
seemed, indeed, rather indisposed to suffer me to go
out of his sight, as though deeming himself lost
without me. Whether his long dormant system
needed repose of another kind, or whether he has
been uncertain whither he could betake himself if
he fled, I do not know. But for many days at a
time he has remained in a listless, indolent state, sitting in his armor at my cabin door,—with something of the same indifference for the future with
which an Indian, surfeited with the fruits of the
chase, will lie around his wigwam ; and if I move
away upon any exploration of the neighborhood, I
find him tagging at my heels like a dog, apparently
uneasy in mind until he sees me safely home again.

Little by little I have made my own discoveries
about him. And almost from the very first, I have
ascertained my error regarding his age. For after
all he is not an old man, tottering in enforced
military servitude, to assist the waning fortunes of
an imperiled state. Those earliest appearances of
decrepitude were nothing more than the natural
results of long confinement from the light and air ;

and under the new conditions in which he is placed, they have passed away almost like a morning mist. At first, with the influence of food and warmth, the gray locks seemed to gain life, and rapidly changed to a dark, rich brown. Then the complexion softened into the soft hue of youth, and little by little each ugly wrinkle cleared away. After that the form grew more erect, gaining at least three or four inches in height. And so, step by step, the seemingly old man has grown young, and in less than a fortnight, has recovered all his natural beauty and elasticity, and stands disclosed to us a glorious creature, strong, athletic and alert, with the air and manner of a god, every limb moulded with more than artistic excellence, the face radiant with intelligence, the whole creature instinct with almost every quality of physical perfection that harmoniously can adorn manhood.

Noticing this change, I have made other discoveries concerning him. And commencing at the first with matters of mere habit and costume, I have noticed that the shield, which still as by force of custom he bears around with him, is not of iron, as I had at first supposed, but is of stiffened layers of bull's hide, bound together with metal rivets. There are strange characters embossed upon it, however, defying my interpretation ; and the crest of his helmet together with the projections of his breast-plate, bear unknown figures by way of ornamentation. Once I have seen him prostrated in devotional attitude before the rising sun. Who, indeed, — I then again for the hundreth time said, — can be this creature, strangely raised into life from his icy tomb? In regard to this, however, I have not been long in gaining some knowledge. I cannot, as yet, it is true, decipher the inscriptions upon shield or helmet, and for a time his language seemed merely a series of uncouth articulations; nor could I detect the slightest recognizable sound in the utterances, which, at certain moments, he instinctively poured forth. But I have been, in past years, a diligent student in languages, giving myself up to the philosophy of philology and fond of tracing up modern sounds into their Sanscrit and Shemitic roots; and thus it chanced that a few days ago I fancied that in a random utterance of this strange creature, I detected a familiar articulation. Upon this, I grew more intent, and with similar utterances of my own, encouraged him to speak. Little by little I managed to connect his articulation with ancient roots, the one running into the other and then back again so as to form an almost incomprehensible maze, yet fraught with certain suggestions of method. And this very morning it has happened that a single expression of his has let into my mind a flood of light. All the loose ends of uncertainty have now gathered themselves into place, making a woven web of consistency. And, with a thrill of joy I have discovered that, by using simple expressions, I am able to converse with him in his own language.

"Who are you?" of course, was my first inquiry

"I am one of Hannibal's men," he answered. "We are on our way across these mountains to attack the Romans."

"And how came you here?" I continued.

"That is what I scarcely know," he responded. "We left Carthage a few months ago, and went to Hispania. And when, by force of arms, we had occupied that country, we set out across the mountains to attack Rome. On the route I must have fallen into the snow, and been detained. But where, now, is the army? And where is Hannibal?"

"The army is gone,—all dead and gone,—and Hannibal as well," I answered. "You think that your mischance happened a few days past, do you not? Know, on the contrary, that it is more than twenty centuries ago."

"And what, then, is a century?"

"That is to say, over twenty hundred years ago," I explained.

"Do you think me a fool, to tell me such a story as that?" he exclaimed, with indignation. And for the moment, he would listen to no word further from me, but resolutely and speechlessly turned his back. And I could see that, with the revival of new thoughts, his glance passed inquiringly and longingly across the crest of that Alpine range, as though he might yet, in some far off point, behold a section of the long vanished cohorts winding its way across some open space.

Meanwhile, I have one duty to perform, and that is, to call the attention of the scientific world to the examination of my prize. I have the gift of language sufficiently to converse with him, but I have not the archaeological ability to make our conversation properly available. There are those alive who know how to examine him, through me, for the determination of important questions of antiquity; and I feel that I must lose no time in giving them the opportunity.

Will it be believed? So incredulous is the world, that all my efforts have been of no avail. I had thought to confer upon the world of science, art and history a benefit, in making it acquainted with my strange guest. But though I have written to scientific and antiquarian devotees in every direction, my letters have elicited no response. Each person has seemed to believe, either that I am practicing upon his credulity or that I am bereft of my senses. Indeed, in a German paper, yesterday, I read a republication of one of my letters, with sarcastic comments upon my sanity. There has not been one answer to all my appeals; and instead of the crowds of archæological inquirers whom I had expected to see pressing forward to my home, there remains almost unbroken solitude,—still, only the Carthagenian soldier, Ursula and myself.

Therefore, I now give up my efforts, and leave the world to that forgetfulness it deserves. Meanwhile, of all the three, Ursula, at least, has not been idle. Her womanly sympathy has been aroused, and she has desired to have the heathen soldier instructed in the mysteries of our faith. In vain I have proposed to instruct him rather in those usages and appliances of modern times, which, for his own comfort, it is most befitting that he should know. To every such demand upon my part she has had some ready answer with which, for the moment, to overcome me. Therefore have I yielded to her, and day after day have sat before the two, interpreting her instructions to him.

And all this has turned out as I anticipated. To her arguments upon the mysteries of our religion, he has exhibited utter inability of comprehension, while his attention has sorely wandered. To her narration of gospel history, he has manifested incredulity rather than want of interest. In no respect has he exhibited any serious regard to her words, indeed, except where she has spoken about the feast and ceremonies belonging to the church. Possibly he has found something in them akin to the usages of his own religion, thus awakening his memories of home. Doubtless, also, youth and vigor, accustomed to a life of gayety and pleasure, could not well fail to find some excitation of spirit in the recapitulations of observances relating to occasional admitted abandonments of discipline. Carthage, doubtless, had its feast days ; and it is easy for him to confound with these, the more serious and well tempered festivities of the modern church.

And amidst all this, there has come to me a new reflection, instinct with terrible anxiety. To-day I have happened to note, more narrowly than I have ever done before, what a very handsome young soldier this man of Hannibal chances to be,—how well-formed are his features and how gracefully poised, his head,—how finely shaped are his limbs, and how becomingly his armor sets them off,—how

he stands in height a head and shoulders over me.
And gazing stealthily towards my wife, I note how,
from time to time, she turns her head in his direction ; drawn thitherward in unconscious, unsuspecting admiration of that wonderful physical beauty.
I know that her heart is faithful to me ; and yet
I begin to think that the time might easily come, in
the which her admiration could unwittingly change
to love and I lose all. I have lived for months in
this desert solitude, so repugnant to me, only that I
may let her see no other man than myself, and
thereby be released from any chance of suffering
through ungenerous comparison. Must all my pre-
cautions now be set at naught by the presence of this
warlike young heathen Adonis ? Truly I must get
rid of him as soon as possible.

It is accomplished; and to my mingled gratification and surprise, more easily than I had anticipated.
"Why do you linger here ?" I said to him this
morning. "Have you no wish to go back to the
land of your birth,—to your own native Carthage ?
Though you may not see it in all respects as you left
it, will it not be something to see it at all and in
any condition whatsoever ? "
"You say well," he answered, starting up, as with
the impulse of an entire new thought. "I will go
thither at once. Only put me in the way of it."
Thereupon I have marked out his route for him
and told to what ports he must hie, and how thence

he could cross over to the opposite shore of Africa. And fearing, lest through the singularity of his costume, he may be detained ere he is well on his way, I have persuaded him to lay aside his armor, and clothe himself in the fashion of the day. To this effect, I have put him into a cast off suit of my own, judiciously altered by Ursula; and so have bidden him good-by and set him off upon his journey. And now, at last, surely I am ridden of him. For I can never even dream that he will be able to thread the mazes of unknown lands expertly enough to find his way back again; even if, as is very unlikely, he escapes being knocked upon the head, by reason of some unwitting trespass upon the rights of others.

Trouble upon trouble! He has been gone only two months; and this day, upon returning from a stroll, to my amazement I beheld him sitting contemplative at my cabin door. In disgust of modern usage, he had resumed his antique dress and armor, and now looked more gloriously beautiful than ever.

"Ha! Can it be?" I exclaimed, and in no hospitable tone.

"Listen," he said. "I went to Carthage, or what once was such. I crossed to Africa in some sort of a ship, worked by a power to which three banks of galley slaves with oars would be as nothing. I stood at last, not within Carthage, but only where it had been. There were merely a few sewer arches and a broken column or two. Why did you not tell me in advance that this was to be all? Where are my family, my altars, and my gods? Where is the army, and where is great Hannibal himself? I begin to believe that I may, indeed, have slept beneath the snow-drifts a little longer than I had supposed. Only a stone or two of the magnificent city now left! and they tell me that the Roman dogs whom we so often slew in heaps, have made all that ruin!"

"True, it is the Roman dogs that have done it," I responded, eagerly following out the new train of thought. "Why, then, do you not take your revenge in seeing how mercilessly they have been punished in return? Go now, therefore, to Rome itself, and observe how terribly the barbarians have overrun and devastated it."

"Yes, I will do that," he exclaimed, his eyes kindling at the revengeful suggestion. "That sight will give comfort to my heart! I will go at once and feast upon Rome's misery! There shall not be an hour's delay!"

Therefore, once more he has stripped himself of his armor and assumed the less noticeable costume with which I had furnished him. Once more I have bidden him God speed, with the secret hope that he may be so speeded as never to return.

"And yet," I mutter to myself with secret feeling of foreboding, "if such is to be the sequel, why is it that the bells of the convent chapel are tolling a saddened chime, as though there were misfortune still lurking in the air? If my persecutor is really

never destined to return, would not the bells leap
up and down in very cadence?"

Saying all this, it is not exactly with belief in Ursula's superstition about the bells.   But still, as she
there sits, oppressed with the melancholy chiming,
her hands pressed over her eyes, in spite of my better
judgment, I cannot help somewhat sympathizing in
her mood, and thinking that after all, perhaps, there
may be some method in the madness.   Did not the
bells ring out a requiem upon that unlucky day when
first I discovered this terrible disturber of my peace
lying in semblance of a senseless log?   Throughout
the coming months have the bells ever sounded one
pleasant note for us, and all the while has not ill-
fortune constantly gathered nearer?   Is this to last
forever, and will the bells never again pour forth
one merry peal to cheer us?

Now to God be all ——.   Yet let me not too prematurely hurry to the end; lest in my haste, forgetting anything now, my recollection may hereafter
go astray.

Last night was Christmas eve.   We had prepared
our cabin for the festive occasion after the manner
of my German home.   I had brought greens from
the nearest forest, and Ursula and myself had
twined them into wreaths, with which we hung our
walls, while in the center of the room, after the
manner of a chandelier, swung a great clump of
larch.   As the evening drew on, Ursula had re-

tired to rest, promising herself that she would arise at earliest dawn and greet the sunrise of Christmas day at the convent-chapel altar. Thereby I was left for the while alone ; and sat before the great fire of blazing, crackling logs, nodding over a favorite classic, and wishing that I, too, had the resolution to retire.

All at once I heard a heavy footstep crunching upon the trodden snow outside,—then it ceased and there came a sudden fumbling with the latch. A moment more, and the door flew open and I saw the Carthagenian standing outside. Without a word he strode within, and seizing a chair brought it down with a violent crash at the other side of the fire-place, and sullenly seated himself.

" Again returned!" I cried, still more discourteously than I had spoken at his previous reappearance. " What ill wind—— "

" It is that you have deceived me," he retorted. " Did you not assure me that I would have my revenge in seeing Rome in ruins ?"

" And is it not so ?"

" Here a ruin and there a ruin ;—but what is that compared with the utter devastation of my own city ? Do I not, in spite of it, find a city to which the whole world presses forward with abject reverence ? Do I not find families there existing, which, with more or less certainty, profess to be the descendants of the very race that made desolation of my own ? Do I not there see, almost uninjured, the tomb of the very man who led his hosts against us ? Are not the annals still remaining, which show the full story of our misfortune and disgrace? Am I to be satisfied, therefore, with the crumbling of a circus or the rending apart of a temple or two? What revenge is there in all that, indeed? Yes, you have deceived me!"

"I offered you the best revenge I could," was my retort. "What better could I do?"

"And is it so, that such is the best thing the world can give me?" he responded. "Then do I want nothing more from the world. I will abstain from it altogether. In future, this quiet spot shall be enough for me."

"What mean you?" I cried, struck with a horrible foreboding. "You intend——"

"I intend here to rest. Why should I go further into a world that brings to me merely scenes of misery and discomfort? Now I know that my race and city,—that the army and great Hannibal himself—are all gone, even as you first told me. Here, then, will I remain, content to ask no other place."

There was then silence for a few moments. He gazed moodily into the fire,—I sat pretending to look upon my book, but found the letters swimming before me, as I reviewed the terrible fact that this man was about to fasten himself upon my whole life like a hideous incubus. Suddenly he started, raised his head and drawing off from his finger a large richly chased gold ring, placed it upon the open page before me.

"Listen!" he cried. "She—" and he nodded significantly towards the other room, "has tried to teach me to believe in your gods. I believe in them not,—my own are sufficient for me. But yet, there are certain customs of your faith which are not all bad. To-night, I am told, is the night when in memory of the birth of one of your gods, men are wont to make gifts to each other. It is a good custom. So, there! Take that ring, therefore, for your own. I got it with a Hispanian princess. I took the princess, also, but I gave her away to my friend. The ring only did I keep, and now it is yours."

"And what—" I said.

"What shall you give me in return?" he cried. "What else, indeed, should you give me other than herself?" And again he pointed significantly towards the door of the other room. "I cannot live altogether alone, and she pleases me. Long enough already have you had her; and I know that she will soon learn to love my youth and manhood the best."

"And do you think that I will consent to——"

"Dog!" he cried, ferociously starting up. "Dog of Roman descent, it may be! Dare you object? Do you think we of Carthage ravaged Hispania and crossed these mountains to be thwarted in whatever we desire? Are we not the conquerors? Oppose me, and I will crush your poor limbs together at a single blow!"

I listened to him with horror. My blood curdled within me. There was no doubt that, if it came to force, he could do as he threatened and crush me like an egg-shell. Nor could I protect my rights by appealing to his reason or to the laws. The latter were too far off from me, in my isolation,—the former was not susceptible of guidance, in his present distorted state of mental vision. For I could see that he mingled the past with the present in such blinded shape as not to realize that the right as well as the might was not with him. He forgot, or rather could not comprehend, how many centuries had elapsed since the army had crossed the Alps in conquering array. Though all were now dust,—mere memories of a long-buried past,—to him there was remaining all the glory of a dominant race,—gilding his armor and making his recollections glow with pictures as of yesterday. In his sight I was no other than one of a subjected people, rightfully given up to pillage;—and to him would Ursula appertain as spoil wrested from a slavish race.

"Let us talk this over," I gasped forth at length, perceiving the necessity of temporizing with him. "You say well that this Christmas time is the period for exchanging gifts. But the exchange should be more equal than what you propose. Stay! we will talk the matter over at our leisure with a bottle of Falernian. You must before this have heard our Roman drink well-spoken of. And now, what more have you to offer for her?"

Gladly I saw that he was not disposed to be ungenerously exacting; and, for the sake of peace between us, would come to fair terms, even at some fancied sacrifice to himself. Therefore we seated ourselves at different sides of the table, and commenced what was with me a deceptive negotiation. Under pretense of the Falernian, I brought out a bottle of wine,—strong and insidious,—such as he

4*

could never have drank of before ; and filling up his glass, I bade him propose his terms. He drank, and I could see the liquid mount with irresistible effect, into his eyes. He would give for Ursula his brace-let,—nay, he no longer had that, having gambled it away during the Hispanian campaign,—but he would give his helmet and his shield,—if those were not enough, he knew where, before leaving Hispania, he had buried a cup full of coin, and he would take me to the spot,—he would give up for her, if necessary, his gods themselves. And so, profusely babbling forth his vain offers, at last his stupefied head sank slowly upon the table, and thence he gently slid upon the floor, and there at full length, slept.

Then,—restraining the momentary impulse to brain him as he lay, and thus, with one felonious blow, rid myself forever of the torment of his per-secutions,—I merely threw a long cloth over him to hide him from my sight, and opening the door that led into our chamber, called out to Ursula.

" Arouse yourself, Ursula," I said. " Dress in all haste and let us depart from here. There is work before us and it must not be delayed."

" And whither—— "

" Ask me not now. At some other time I will tell you. For the present, give little rein to your thoughts, and hasten."

In silence and in full trust that at the proper time I would reveal my meaning and so ease her wonder-ment, Ursula arose, and unhesitatingly prepared to obey me. A few moments, and all being ready, we departed. I led her quickly through the outer room,

—so quick that by the darkened light she could not see the form of the slumbering Carthagenian beneath the extended cloth. And so we hurried forth, and I turned the key in the lock, believing that I was leaving the cabin forever. What mattered it, after all, as long as thereby I might find some other nook of peace upon the further side of the mountain, to which the barbarian could not track us? Whatever of worldly goods I here lost, could I not elsewhere replace? Only let me now make timely flight before the foe had a chance to awaken.

So long had I been sitting up into the small hours of the night, before the Cathagenian had entered, and so protracted had been our subsequent negotiation, that it was now near three o'clock in the morning. The air was cool and crisp, yet not too cold. The snow was firm under foot, and altogether there was no bar to speedy progress. Within an hour or two silently threading the mountain passes, we succeeded in putting so great a distance between the barbarian and ourselves, that I feared not to tarry for a few moments' rest at a roadside hostelry. This rest we gradually prolonged until it was near morning before we set out again. Then once more we continued our route, gradually winding further up the mountain, while each moment with greater confidence I assured myself of safety. But as the stars paled out of the steel-gray sky and the dawn began to appear, I saw far down in the valley, and following upon our track, a single dark speck. I knew that it must be the Carthagenian, too soon awakened and become cognizant of our flight; and anon I perceived, by the wild exultant flourish of his shield, that he had detected our figures in bold relief against the white snow, and was animating himself to more vigorous pursuit. But I said nothing to Ursula about what I had seen, and merely pressed on, more rapidly, if possible, than before.

Soon as we ascended a slope of the mountain, I could see that our pursuer had already traversed half the remaining distance between us, and my heart grew sick with fear. The road we were traveling led to a village, gaining which, I might feel sure of protection; but this village was still many miles away, with no intervening cabins; and it was certain that before reaching safety, the evening would be upon us. There was only one hope of relief; and that consisted in the chance of losing ourselves from observation in some quiet by-path. This I now resolved upon attempting.

Between the rocks at my left hand was a narrow path which, leaving the main road, now passed from one mountain slope to the other, crossing, in its progress, the great Glacier. Down this we sped, until we stood upon the Glacier itself, half way to its source. Looking back, I could see that our pursuer had not been deceived by my divergence from the main road, but had himself turned aside, and was still vigorously following us. My heart stood almost paralyzed, for, now, alas! there was no further way of retreat. The only hope was to press on as before and trust to chance.

Differing from what it was below, the Glacier here was rough and broken, the surface at times

raised into unsightly hillocks of ice and snow, amidst
which the path wound deviously, here and there, at
only a few feet distance, hidden altogether from
sight. Slowly we picked our way ; and half across
we found that there had opened a crack or crevasse
in the surface of the ice, about seven or eight feet
broad and of unfathomable depth. At the other
side, the path abruptly terminated, and, owing to
some alteration in the mountain surface, appeared
to be altogether lost. Still I pressed on, however,
anxious for the moment only to reach the other
side of the crevasse. A loose log lay near, once
doubtless embedded in the ice. This log I now
placed across the gap,—cautiously we assisted each
other over to the other side,—and there resting,
there was nothing left for me to do but, as calmly
as possible, to await the inevitable issue.

Looking around I noticed that the dawn had already brightened almost into full daylight, though
as yet the sun had not risen. Here and there, however, some of the tallest peaks were already gilded
with its rays, and swiftly the glorious sheen of light
was descending along the mountain sides toward the
valley below. In the East the sky was one sea of
gold and purple clouds, showing that the sun itself
was now close at hand, rapidly climbing into sight
and at any moment might appear. Lighter and
lighter at each succeeding instant now perceptibly
grew the shaded valley. I could easily mark the
distant village where for us there would have been
safety. At one side and seemingly almost at our

feet stood the little hostelry where we had passed
part of the night,—beyond, our own deserted home.
The whole broad panorama was gorgeous with
natural beauty. Even I, though so accustomed to it
and withal so unappreciative, might have delighted
in it, but for one terrible blemish. This was the dark
spot which all the while, and as yet unperceived by
Ursula, was following us as relentlessly as a sleuth
hound along the path which we had just traversed;
—now seemingly at rest, now disappearing entirely
from sight behind one of the larger hummocks of
ice,—then again issuing into view and always nearer
than before !

Suddenly, Ursula, lifting her eyes to mine and
taking me by the hand, broke her long imposed
silence.

"Christmas morning at last," she said. "And
now I know why you have brought me hither. It
was kindly intended, though it has failed of its purpose, and therefore I thank you for it."

"And that purpose—"

"It was — you must not deny it — it was to do
this time that which I have so often asked of you —
to attend with me at the early mass in the convent-
chapel. But unaccustomed to the path, you have
missed the way. See ! yonder stands the chapel,
not so very far away, but that, in the gathering daylight we can mark nearly every window, every angle
of the roof, can even count the five little bells that
hang so motionless in the gable-turret. And look
again ! Some of the neighboring villagers are
already climbing the ascent to give the mass their

presence. Too late for us, though, now, I think. We should have taken the right-hand path."

"Too late, indeed!" I said, with inward groan, as I watched the pursuer still nearer than before.

"But that matters little, after all. For truly, the Vespers may make amends, and there is no better place than this, with only the grand presence of God's nature around us, in which to tell you all that I have so long treasured up to say. I have so ardently waited for this Christmas morning; and now that it has come, I hardly know how or where to begin."

"Speak out freely from your first thought, dear Ursula," I answered; and my heart sank lower than ever, as I wondered whether she was about to confess to me, as a secret that could not longer be withheld, her passion for the Carthagenian.

"It is this, then," she said. "Months ago — but where exactly it began, I cannot tell — I felt that, for your great love for me, you were giving up all the promise of your future life. I saw it in your abstracted moods when you would seem to pierce through the mountain sides and gaze again, in imagination, upon your own distant home; — I knew it from your mutterings in your sleep. Then I perceived that your heart was not in these scenes about us, — that you would have loved to return to your own city, and would have done so, but for one thing."

"And that one thing, dear Ursula?" I responded, dreading to learn how nearly she might have probed to the bottom of my suspicious thoughts.

" Why, what indeed could that one thing be, except that by reason of your love for me, you would not take me from these scenes which you thought I could best enjoy, having been brought up among them ! What, indeed, but that, for my sake, you resolved to school yourself to love these mountains and forget, as much as possible, your own much dearer home? But all the while, had I no love for you, that I should make no sacrifice in return? Therefore it was in my mind to tell you how cheerfully I will depart from here, and go with you whithersoever you would. And so I should have told you many months ago, but for the coming of this Carthagenian."

" Ah ! The Carthagenian, indeed ! "

" Then I delayed ; for I saw that in the occupation of fathoming the mystery of his appearance and history, you needed no other pursuit to make you happy. And then, too, there came upon me the selfish desire to please myself **a** little in bringing him, if possible, into the circle of our own dear Church. Therefore, to that intent, I toiled ; finding at first a pleasure in it, — then a weariness which only my sense of duty could help me to support, —then — "

" But why a weariness, Ursula ? " I could not resist exclaiming. " Would not the task be a pleasant one, always, with so fair a pupil ? "

" Fair, do you say ? Yes, now that you recall it, he was fair to some extent, though at the time I never thought about it. Strong and well formed, indeed, — yet for all that, it must be said, with little soul and intelligence in his face. Possibly, were I

like the maidens of this valley, not taught as I have
been by union with yourself to put my affections
upon those cultured graces that are higher than any
mere attractions of the physical frame, I might have
learned to admire that barbarian youth ;— but not
now — not now. None but yourself I think can ever
now hold my admiration, much less my love."

Hearing this, I drew a long breath and could have
even slain myself for the late cruel suspicions of my
heart. To atone for all must be the business of my
future life. And yet, what future life could be destined for me, with that hated pursuer every moment
drawing closer?

"And so at last," she continued, "my probation
came to an end as the Carthagenian left us, never
again, I hope, to return. And when he departed, I
would then have told you all, but that it was within
a month of this blessed Christmas, and so I thought
that I would wait. For thus I reasoned. I have
come to you poor and desolate. This is the season
for giving gifts ; but what material gift have I that
I can confer upon you? And then I said that it was
in my power, after all, to give you what you might
value far more than anything else, — your freedom
from this life that now so heavily weighs you down,
the resumption of those olden pursuits in which your
heart must be so much interested. Take then, dear
husband, upon this Christmas morning, and with
whatever rich treasures of my love I can pour out
in words, this gift of a newer and more suitable life
for yourself. I shall never repine at leaving the
mountains. Let us depart at once unto your own

native city. There, as well as here, I shall bask in the sunshine of your love ; and where your love is, there will always be my most happy feeling of home."

"Is it a dream?" I said, for the moment over-powered by emotion ; forgetting even the present peril we were in, and thinking only to gaze enraptured upon her face, so radiant with the divine luster of love and truth, and to wonder that I had been so blinded hitherto as not to read aright this faithful heart. And how blinded had I been, indeed, not to have recognized the certainty that, in the end, even my trials would result in good! For even at that instant of supreme joy and forgetfulness of peril, I saw how truly the presence of the Carthagenian himself had served its friendly purpose. Apart from him, indeed, Ursula would none the less have made to me, upon this Christmas morning, that priceless gift of self-sacrifice and love. And yet, apart from the memory of him, how could I, in accepting the gift, so completely have crushed out forever all the foolish jealousies of my heart? Still, but for him, there might have come, in the newer sphere of action, something of the olden dread of other admirations stealing her love away from me. But now that this glorious statuesque beauty thus freshly arisen as from another world had failed to kindle in her heart one response or even recognition of its power to charm, how could I ever doubt again?

"Is it a dream?" I therefore repeated. "Or am I indeed awake, and is this a sweet reality? Come to my arms, dearest Ursula ; and upon this blessed

Christmas morning, let me in turn confess to you—"

Yet ere I could speak further in acknowledgment of my fault, and tell the bitter story of my late distrust, I was recalled, as by a flash, to the perception of our present danger; for glancing up, I saw our dreaded pursuer now clambering over the rugged path not fifty feet away. Ursula, also, then saw him, and in helpless terror sank slowly from my arms.

"Yes—upon your knees now be it!" I cried, "and there pour forth such prayers for our deliverance as never yet you have learned to utter!"

And as I spoke, the enemy came still nearer, until he stood upon the further side of the chasm and faced me. I could see his features aglow with demoniac delight at having finally driven us to a stand. More than ever, too, did he now seem arrayed with glorious beauty of form, as light and athletic in shield and helmet, he there confronted me. Of that stately beauty, indeed, I could no longer hold one jealous feeling; but what hope of rescue could I have from that fierce determination towards wrong which glared so savagely in every feature? I saw Ursula bowed at my feet in prayer, her face turned with reverential instinct towards the convent chapel; but how could prayers or chapel aid us there? As for myself, with one vigorous motion of the foot, I hurled the log upon which we had crossed, deep down into the crevasse; but how could this obstruct one who, with overbearing leap across the chasm, could bear down my feeble frame before him, as if it were a reed?

"Dog of a mountaineer!" he said. "Will you surrender her to me? Or must I come thither and wring your base neck before seizing her for my own!"

"Barbarian whelp!" with violence, I retorted, mustering all of my remaining resolution in support of that last torrent of defiance. "If you think that she should be yours, then come across and take her."

He foamed at the mouth with rage at being thus addressed; and, for a moment, gazed around for some means of crossing the icy chasm. Finding none, he placed his shield and helmet upon the ice, retired a few paces, the better to make his leap, and then, like the wind bounded forward.

Just at that instant, the rising sun peeped above the mountain, and all the bells of the little chapel rang out their salutation to the new born Christmas. Was it merely some sudden current of air which carried the sound towards us? And was it a mere chance that all the bells now so loudly broke forth together? Or, on the other hand, has it been mysteriously so ordered for our protection? I cannot tell, indeed. I only know that though I had often heard the bells in their most lusty peal, I had never listened to them as now. Not one bell, merely — not even two or three; but the whole five bursting out with instant, hurried, tumultuous clash! Not coming to our hearing as from any distance; but in one loud, discordant clanging peal breaking in upon our senses, seemingly at our very ears with deafening resonance — almost overwhelming us with the sudden concussion of the metallic blast! Even in our instant of peril, it struck upon Ursula and myself as with vital, material force — bearing us back helpless with the torrent of sound! And it came upon our enemy like an avenging stroke at the very critical poise of his onward leap; so that confusedly his face turned wildly away, his limbs failed in their proper action, and in that supreme moment of his need, the full energy of his spring deserted him!

A moment more — and as I gathered my own disordered faculties together, I saw that my foe had fallen, with his whole body hanging within the crevasse, and supported only by his hands convulsively clinging to the edge. Vigorous as were his writhings, there was no hope of extrication. Each instant as there he hung, the partially softened ice began to break and splinter away beneath his fingers. One by one they relaxed. For a second I looked upon his face, marked not only with agonized despair, but also with baffled hate as he gazed upon me; and above all, I could also note, by the strained backward rolling of his eyes, that the discordant pealing of the bells, in that last moment of vain struggling for his life, was still overmastering and affrighting him. Then his stiffened hands relaxed their enfeebled hold, and falling, he passed forever from my sight. There was nothing left to tell me that it had not been all a dream, except the shield and helmet lying motionless at the further side.

"Down! Down once more into your icy tomb!" I cried, in an ecstasy of relief; while the bells, changing from their first unearthly clamor now broke

5*

into a softly modulated march of triumph. "Lie there, once more, for twenty centuries to come! It will not be I, who, at their end, will rescue you from your frozen sepulcher and once more warm your viper blood into ungrateful action!"

And now, once more and ever, all thanks to God, for that great and wondrous deliverance from peril upon this blessed day! And let the bells still ring their sympathetic peal of joy, for that upon this Christmas morn my heart has had its jealous clouds thus swept away and thereby gained that richest and most priceless gift of perfect peace and surety!

In Three Heads.

In Three Heads.

Chapter I

AGREEABLY to tell the story of the Hillebrandt dream is to repeat, as well, the story
of the Van Twiller Christmas party. For, though
the Byvanck letter gives faithful and accurate recital
of every incident directly appertaining to the dream
— detailing it with such old-time simplicity and
quaintness as cannot fail to commend it lovingly to
our regard — yet it must seem, at best, a cold and
cheerless narrative; needing, to give it proper life
and interest, the warming and enlivening qualities
that the description of accompanying festivity can
alone supply. And inasmuch as in this pleasant
season of the year, all hearts are turned so longingly
to whatever whispers thought or circumstance of joy
and gladness, it may not seem entirely out of place
that these bright tints of family traditional gaieties
should now be suffered to weave themselves, at will,
upon the sober ground-work of formal family record.
Thereby, perchance, the vary-colored threads of incident may pass in richer combination through fancy's

loom, and the whole fabric lie at last revealed in more harmonious aptness of design.

The invitations to the Van Twiller Christmas party were sent out in goodly season. About the middle of September, Gisbort Van Twiller being obliged, for the first time in ten years, to make a journey down the river, bade solemn farewell to all his family and friends, and embarked at Albany upon the little sloop Mohawk, commanded by Skipper Derrick Roos. Upon that occasion, Gisbort's maiden sister Mistress Lysbeth — the careful conductor of his household since the lamented decease of his wife Elsie — taking time by the forelock, stuffed his broad-flapped pockets full of ceremonious notes to many of the quality of New York, Brooklyn and Westchester, requesting their presence at the Van Twiller mansion upon the evening of the ensuing Christmas. One of these missives was to His Excellency Lieutenant-Governor DeLancey, then acting Governor of the Colony, others to members of his Privy Council and to officers of the army in garrison at Fort George, near the Bowling Green; and though it was scarcely to be expected that any of these persons could really lend their presence — inasmuch as a winter journey to Albany in that year of grace 1758 was not a thing lightly to be entered upon — yet, as Gisbort Van Twiller was a man of great note in the Colony by reason of his vast landed property, it was felt to be no more than proper that he should give to all existing civic and military dignitaries the compliment of an invitation. These formal notes were accordingly delivered by Gisbort

ten days after sailing, and were courteously acknowledged in as ceremonious manner by the next upward-
bound sloop.

In October, Mistress Lysbeth issued a new series
of invitations to personal friends and relations along
the river. There was a cousin Van Twiller, residing
at Claverack, who had married among the Steen-
wickes; and, of course, the abundant hospitality of
the period demanded that both families should be
called to the supper. There was a half-uncle Van
Twiller, at Coxsackie, in partnership with one of the
Osterhouts; and, therefore, of necessity, the Osterhouts must be expected. Then there were Steen-
wickes and Osterhouts who had intermarried, and
whose descendants, settling upon the manor of
Livingston, had allied themselves with the Hornebeaks; and, as the Hornebeaks thereby became
cousins, they must, on no account, be excluded. In
like manner, and for similar reasons, other families
were expected from Kats Kills and the region
round about Tappaen; and Captain Derrick Roos,
duly distributing the invitations as he floated down
the river, brought back the answers upon his return
trip.

In the early part of November Mistress Lysbeth
sent out her invitations to friends and kindred at
Kinderhook, Half Moon, Schaatkooke, Schenectady
and Rensselaer's Wyck; and in December, sum-
moning her state carriage and two horses, and
putting the negro driver, Cato, into his newest
livery, she sallied forth and formally distributed a
final package of notes among her acquaintances in

Albany itself. This finished that portion of the work. None had been forgotten, excepting three or four families upon the extreme borders of the Colony, who could only be reached by Indian runners, but who, being fourth cousins to the Van Twillers, naturally felt aggrieved at the omission, and cherished a burning hatred ever afterwards. Apart from this, however, everybody of any kinship or distinction in the Colony was invited, and felt satisfied. It was known, far and wide, that the Christmas party was likely to be a great success. The Van Twiller mansion, standing upon the principal street of the city, was large and so arranged as to be capable of entertaining an unusual number of guests. Its reputation for lavish hospitality was established; and it became whispered around that inasmuch as the party was intended to be such a grand affair, it would not begin much before seven, and would probably last until after ten. Therefore there was, naturally, much social excitement upon the subject. Few declined who could manage to come. The towns along the river turned out an unexpected number of acceptances; and though Lieutenant-Governor DeLancey and his Privy Council, all, as had been expected, sent regrets, these were worded with expressions of sad longing that bore the stamp of sincerity. There was now nothing left to Mistress Lysbeth but to count the heads and prepare the banquet.

There was only one bitter drop, indeed, in the cup of Mistress Lysbeth's satisfaction. It arose from the circumstance that the Hillebrandts and their kin all sent regrets. Most of these lived in Albany itself, and one of the most wealthy families of them close beside the Van Twiller mansion; and, hence, the slight was most keenly felt. But it could scarcely have been expected to happen otherwise, inasmuch as there had been much disapprobation expressed about the matter of young Heybert Hillebrandt. It was openly asserted that though old Gisbort Van Twiller had looked forbiddingly upon Heybert, as any man with such a pretty daughter as Geretie had a right to do, he had not exercised that discretionary power until Heybert had become poor; all friendly countenance having been withdrawn only from the moment when it was discovered that the Hillebrandt title-papers had been lost, and that thereby the squatters could not be driven off. In this assertion the Hillebrandts were more than half right, for Gisbort was, unquestionably, a prudent and calculating father. But there was no doubt that they were scarcely justified in imputing a crabbed and crafty disposition to Mistress Lysbeth, attributing her coincidence in her brother's views more to regard for her social position than for the happiness of her niece; inasmuch as Aunt Lysbeth was not without her many good points, and, in looking out for Geretie's advancement, was doubtless actuated by kindly motives. Nor was it exactly fair to stigmatise Gisbort so harshly for having gone to the Hillebrandt sale and there purchased the old family cabinet. It was said that, after what had passed, he should have stayed away; but, on the other hand, it is difficult to say why, having a taste for handsome furniture, he, as well as any one else, should not have indulged himself. But be that as it might, the act had given great offense; and, not unlikely, was looked upon as the most crying sin in his career, far outweighing his supposed instrumentality in sending Heybert off to die among the Indians, or his late marked favoritism of young Rollof Van Schoven's pretension to Geretie's hand. Therefore, as in duty bound, the Hillebrandts all sent regrets, resolving never to enter the house where the mahogany cabinet stared them in the face. And having intermarried with the Hogebooms, the Hogebooms also decided not to come. And the Hogebooms being first cousins to the Jansens, the Jansens of course regretted. And the Jansens being about to intermarry with the Van Tienhovens, the Van Tienhovens staid away, and, naturally, persuaded their cousins, the Wyncoopes, to do the same. In fact, one and all took especial umbrage about the mahogany cabinet; whereby it became necessary that their absence should attest their indignation, and a great gulf thereby be left unfilled at the Van Twiller Christmas party.

But, with all this, there was a certain amount of counterbalancing comfort. Young Rollof Van Schoven, the new aspirant for the pretty Geretie, was very wealthy, and, consequently, by his influence, led all his kinsmen with him. His oldest sister had married into the Swartwouts, and they were not more than two degrees removed from the Winegaerts. The Winegaerts were first cousins to the Schenckes, and they, in turn, were connected,

through a half-brother, to the Van Fredingborcks.
All these families lived in distant towns, two days'
journey off in summer, and seemingly inaccessible at
Christmas time. But with due and proper regard to
the interest of the Van Schovens, they roused themselves for a joint effort, there being an indistinct
half defined, but not the less powerful impression
among them, that at the Christmas party the engagement of their young kinsman to Geretie Van Twiller
would be announced, and that it was their duty to
be on hand at any trouble, to give the affair their
countenance and approval. Consequently, from
quarters whence only regrets had been anticipated,
day after day sloop captains and Indian messengers
brought in acceptances, upon receipt of each of
which, Aunt Lysbeth's face became suffused with
liveliest satisfaction, rejoicing in heart that with the
coming of all these wide-spread branches, the absence
of the many disaffected families would be less noticeable. Moreover she pleasantly reflected that —

But what it was that Mistress Lysbeth further
thought, or how thereupon she acted, it is scarcely
worth while now to tell. For the Byvanck letter,
though passingly alluding to the matter of the
invitations, refrains from all mention of Mistress
Lysbeth's further views or preparations, apparently
not deeming them essential in carrying out the
story of the dream.

CHAPTER II.

THE Van Twiller mansion stood in the principal street of Albany city, a little above the Dutch Church. It was a stately, double house, having two broad projections upon the street, each ending in a sharp step-shaped gable, crowned with ornamental iron tracery. The date of its erection, 1713, was noted in long iron numerals upon the front; and upon a side gable was perched a curiously fashioned weather-cock, the pride of the city, inasmuch as it was regilded every year.

Leading back from the wooden stoop was a wide hall, dividing the house into two equal parts. One of these was occupied by the state parlor, which was never opened excepting for such choice occasions as a funeral, christening, or the like. Upon the other side was the family sitting-room, of similar size. It had three deep windows and twice as many doors, leading severally into the hall or closets, or other rooms; and all these doors were so much alike that a stranger to the premises, entering heedlessly, might find it not easy to get out again. The room was furnished with stiff, heavy chairs and tables, generally standing close around the wall, and in the middle was a small carpet, reaching only within two or three feet of the edge. At one end was a broad fireplace, calculated for the consumption of great

logs rather than of ordinary sticks, with won-
drously stout ornamented andirons upon which to
rest them, a tall brass fender in front, and the
usual bordering of scripture-illustrating colored tiles.
Over the fireplace hung a somewhat worm-eaten
and time-stained portrait, not at all improved by
successive crude attempts at restoration, and supposed to have once represented Governor Wouter
Van Twiller, the ancestor of the Colonial branch of
the family.

Upon the evening before the Christmas party, the
little family had gathered together in this common
sitting-room. No candles had been brought in as
yet, but in the deep, wide fireplace a large pile of
logs was blazing behind the tall brass fender, sending forth a pleasant glow of brightness over half the
room. In front of the mantle-piece stood Gisbort
Van Twiller with his back to the fire, daintily toasting the calves of his legs, which being encased in
close woolen tights, offered little opposition to the
heat. He was in somewhat nervous condition of
mind, apparently oppressed with the burden of his
thoughts, judging from the manner in which he
shifted uneasily from one foot to another, scratched
gently a gray patch of hair peeping out from under
his carelessly adjusted and still grayer wig, then
plunged his hands as deeply into his wide-flapped
pockets as the broad cuffs of his coat sleeves would
allow, and gazed down, meditatively, upon his
shining silver shoe buckles. In fact, Gisbort, being
not as easily satisfied as his sister about the approaching party, was reflecting that the success of

`a single evening was not to be weighed against the realization of a plan for the happiness of a lifetime; and as it was his desire that Geretie should put an end to all discomforting tribulations of her heart by accepting young Rollof Van Schoven for her future husband, he had furthermore come to the opinion of all the Van Schovens, that the Christmas gathering should not be brought to an end without being signalized by the pleasing announcement of the projected alliance. To this purpose he had taken every opportunity, of late, to contribute his personal advice and persuasions; and upon this evening, believing that a suitable occasion was again at hand, began once more to press the matter.

"A fine young lad, indeed, Geretie, and I wonder you can be so blind as not to see it."

He spoke in a deep, gruff, impatient tone; but Geretie was not at all deceived by that. She knew that it was not his natural voice, but that he had adopted it, with some difficulty, for purposes of argument, inasmuch as he would not, knowingly, have spoken crossly to her for the world. Therefore she was not frightened into any response. In addition to which, the matter had been so often forced upon her, that she had at last discovered absolute silence to be her wisest policy. In that way her father sooner ran out in his expostulations, and returned to that tone of kindness which, being most natural to him, could not long at any one time be laid aside. Moreover, upon this particular evening, she was very greatly wearied, having been all day laboring at those more delicate preparations for an entertainment which can never be left to menials, but must be attended to by the head of the house. So, with her eyes half closed by fatigue, and her senses blunted for any kind of contention, she sat, listless and immovable, upon a large sofa, drawn up at an angle to the fire. Beside her, and in the same state of quiet repose, sat her Aunt Lysbeth, an ardent partisan of the projected marriage, indeed, but now as indisposed as Geretie for any argument upon the subject. Therefore it happened that her father had all the talk to himself and endeavored to improve the opportunity.

"Not to speak of five hundred acres of the best flat land in all the Colony — almost a square mile of the largest pine timber — a stone mill upon the Mohawk and a mortgage for 3,000 pounds upon the Provorist farm across the river, and soon to be foreclosed. What better can you look for, Geretie?"

Still, Geretie remained silent. What use in advancing over and over again, the same old answers she had made so often before?

"And next heir to his old Aunt Barbara," continued her father, assuming gruffer accents than ever, as he felt his ability for continued sternness gradually breaking down. "You may think, Geretie, that because she lives in that mean little house across the way, being her heir cannot amount to much, but you are mistaken. She lives there merely because she has become used to it, and does not wish to change. She could buy me out any day. She owns the Podushook property; and they say she has pecks of old Spanish doubloons and chests of family plate stored away in that musty second-story of hers. And it may be, Geretie, that you also think matters of property should not be allowed a hearing in such an affair as this; but that is because you are so young and foolish. Some day you will know better, perhaps when it is too late to know anything about it at all. A discreet young damsel will always look to these considerations. Your mother did, Geretie. Why, bless my soul! she would never have married me at all if I had not been rich. Not that she did not like me well enough, it may be; but, after all, I was not much to look at, even in the best of times, and therefore, of course, my money always was the most worthy part of me. But she was a sensible girl, and you see how she was rewarded for her caution by a very happy life."

Still not a word from Geretie. She sat gazing steadily at the picture tiles about the fire-place, wondering, possibly, why Jonah was made so little smaller than the whale that was about to swallow him. Meanwhile her father, awaiting force of new inspiration, stooped down and lighted his great carved pipe — an heirloom which he never allowed himself to smoke, excepting when the labors of the day were over — then, passing before her, slowly worked round to the back of the sofa. At that point was a chair, seated upon which Gisbort could face toward the window, and look out while he talked. That, thereby, he was turned away from the other two made little difference, inasmuch as he sat so near that the backs of all their heads almost touched.

"And so, Geretie, you see plainly where your duty as well as your real happiness lies," he continued, blowing out a preparatory cloud of smoke, and, in his growing consciousness of weakness, assuming the deep, gruff tones of a channel pilot. "And, as I have said before, there can be no objection to Rollof Van Schoven for himself, either."

"No, father; only that he is not Heybert Hillebrandt," she responded, worked at last into desperation prompting reply, being resolved to admit nothing in favor of the new lover, wherein comparison might be intended.

"No, not Heybert, of course. How in the world could he be another person, being himself all the while? Besides which you know very well, Geretie, that Heybert Hillebrandt has not been heard of for nearly a year, and must be dead by this time."

"No, father, not dead, or else — or else he would somehow have let me know."

"Let you know? And he a dead man?" exclaimed the old gentleman, rather startled at the illogical assertion. "That is nonsense, you must be aware. But come, Geretie, dry your eyes; I shall not say any more about it now, at any rate."

With that, his voice relapsed into all its accustomed tone of kindness. He had kept up his assumption of paternal severity as long as he could at any one time, and, for a while, the matter must come to an end. And, indeed, he had held out very well, considering that he had not had the benefit of his sister, Mistress Lysbeth's, support. Hitherto she had always come to his assistance, and it was scarcely the fair thing in her to sit there dozing on the sofa, not helping him with a single word. Therefore, nothing was more plainly to be seen than that, for the moment, the time for importunity and reproof was over. Perhaps he was secretly glad of it, not being cruelly disposed; not the kind who could shut up a daughter in a dark closet, with only bread and water, until she might yield to his wishes. His sole desire was for her happiness, only that his idea was different from hers as to how that happiness might best be promoted. With him there could be no prosperous marriage for a girl, unless pound was weighed against pound, and shilling against shilling; and it was with that conviction that now he pressed Rollof Van Schoven's suit, not wishing to act harshly, and feeling that he was doing all that could be done, if occasionally he threw in a few words of advice and wisdom. It was the continual dropping that he believed might wear away a stone, though he felt vastly dissatisfied that the stone presented such a granite-like texture. Now, however, he had thrown down one more drop; and, with the smoke of his pipe comfortably curling around his old nose and predisposing his nature to quiet, could well afford, for the time, to suspend the vexed controversy. Accordingly he placed his feet cosily upon another chair, and, lazily drawing in the blue smoke, surveyed the scene outside.

First he gazed, meditatively, upon the little single gable house of old Mistress Barbara Van Schoven, directly across the way. There was a light in the second story, and behind the shade the figure of a moving body. Mistress Barbara, of course; and Gisbort's lively fancy depicted her in the act of poring over her many chests of old silver and her bags of Spanish doubloons, all of which Geretie could so easily obtain if she would only so make up her mind. Then, turning from this subject of contemplation, he made observation of the weather. It was snowing hard, but that should make no difference in the Christmas party. Rather would it promote its success; for there had been much want of snow, lately, and it was well understood that Christmas always lacked half its enjoyment when there happened not to be good sleighing. A goodly depth of snow would make no difference in the coming of the city guests, and many of those who were expected from the country were known to have already arrived. Of others, the snow would facilitate the arrival, provided the wind did not arise to blow up drifts, and provided, also, that the fall was not too heavy. And there was no wind, at present. The flakes fell softly and gently, each in its proper place. Free from disturbance, the snow lay as evenly disposed upon steep roof and picket fence as upon the level ground; no irregularity visible in the horizontal lines of pure whiteness that adorned the step-like gables of each neighbor's house. Then, as to the continuance of the snow — lo! while Gisbort gazed, there came a broken rift in the dark mass of clouds overhead, through which the full moon shot a penetrating gleam, and it became evident that the storm was over By the next evening the snow would be

trampled down evenly on street and road, making
the sleighing all that could be desired. A pleasant
smile of satisfaction stole over Gisbort's grim features; his lips relaxed around the mouth-piece of
his pipe; the smoke died softly away; his head
fell just a trifle further back, and he passed into
refreshing slumber.

Upon the large sofa behind him, Aunt Lysbeth
had already succumbed to the fatigues of the day,
and now slept daintily, with her head poised upon
Geretie's shoulder. Geretie herself was still wide
awake, constrained thereto by her troubled state of
thought, and sat gazing listlessly before her. Past
the big log fire, which leaped and crackled upward
to the broad chimney, casting out flickering forks
of light, making the noses of Jonah and of Noah
upon the picture tiles seem very ruddy at times;
past the tall carved clock which mendaciously indicated a new moon when it was shining full outside;
or gazing into the great hall beyond. A broad
wainscoted hall, almost as wide as any of the
rooms, and hence furnished almost like one of the
parlors. At one side, a broad stairway, with carved
mahogany bannisters, ran zigzagging to the upper
story; at the other side stood the old carved Hillebrandt cabinet, a heavy, clumsily built piece of
furniture with grotesquely sculptured panels and
large brass hanging handles to all the drawers, and
quaint scutcheons to the doors, and a twenty-ribbed
projection at the top, seemingly sufficient for the
cornice of a goodly sized house. And opposite the
cabinet was the door into the principal parlor, now,

as usual, tightly closed, and not to be thrown open to the public gaze before the morrow evening.

Across from the parlor door and beside the cabinet was another door leading to a range of closets, and thence into the kitchen. The doors at either end of this passage were now open, and Geretie could look through to the end,—not altogether distinctly, indeed, for the evening gloom was upon everything; but in the kitchen were two tallow candles sputtering in their sockets, and by their thus unnaturally increased brightness, Geretie could distinguish much that otherwise would have been hidden. The long table at the side of the kitchen, now heaped up with mince and pumpkin pies as it had never been heaped up before; the piles of ole-kocks arranged like cannon balls upon bases of ten or twelve square, built up thence to a single one at top, and giving the table the appearance of a distant arsenal yard; the hundreds of New Year cakes, stamped with the figure of King George, holding a crown and sceptre, and all packed away in close layers like shingles; the kegs of oysters brought up from New York, at great expense, in the boot of the weekly stage, and now arranged beneath the table; the hams hanging from the ceiling, and the legs of venison and dozens of wild ducks and partridges disposed around the walls on hooks — all these and many other preparations for the coming supper were made manifest to Geretie's listless gaze by the forced brilliancy of those two sputtering candles. At one side of the kitchen, and fast asleep in utter exhaustion from the labors of the day, sat the old negro cook, Chloe, with a long pewter ladle still clasped in her relaxed hand — the unsurrendered emblem of authority — her big round face disposed so exactly in front of a great white platter, standing on end against the dresser, that its blue border seemed like a saintly aureola around her head. At either side, and crouched upon the floor, and not the least bit in the world asleep or sleepy, were her two coal-black grand-children, Tak and Rak, engaged in a pleasing game of their own invention. In front of each was a small pile of chestnuts, and the two urchins were tossing to and fro what at first sight seemed to be a black ball. It was not a ball but a hard apple — better to them than any ball, in fact, inasmuch as it would serve all the purposes of one, and moreover was, in its nature, so suggestive of gastronomic joy. Each of these little imps, upon throwing the apple, endeavored to make it bound upon their venerable grandmother's head; whereat, not in the least awaking, she would start up mechanically and rap one or other of her tormentors with her pewter spoon, then fall back again into her olden attitude. And whichever of the two happened to be attacked with the spoon was considered to have lost, and paid a portion of his chestnuts to the other.

For a few moments Geretie watched this pleasant sport. Then the sputtering candle-wicks falling left all in darkness, and put an end to the game. With that Geretie's thoughts were naturally driven in upon herself; and she looked back at the past rather than upon the present, and recalled, for the thousandth time, the last interview with Heybert Hillebrandt. It was after the ruin of his fortune seemed to have been completed, and her father had discouraged his suit, and Heybert had made up his mind that there was nothing better to be done than to seek his fortune at some other place; for he could not remain in that scene of his olden prosperity and basely delve with spade, while somewhere else there might still be lurking in his favor a happy chance. Even if he donned a hunter's dress, some unexpected favor of fortune might ensue. Therefore he had parted from her secretly and lovingly, and she had vowed to be true to him forevermore. He had placed upon her finger a ring, which she dared not wear openly or even show, but kept locked up in her private desk; though every night, when she had shut herself within her room, she put the ring upon her finger and so went to sleep, very often, in consequence, dreaming of Heybert half the night. And she had given him a ring which he had openly put upon his finger, and vowed that he would take it off only upon one occasion. This would be when he should have succeeded in whatever he might have undertaken; and then he would send the ring back to her, through some trusty friend, as a token that he was coming himself, at last, to claim it and her fair hand as well. But alas! two years had already passed, and the ring had not yet been returned. During the first year she had heard of Heybert as living a trapper's life among the Hurons, at times almost in savage destitution. After that, all track of him seemed to have been lost. It had been said that he must be dead; could it be really so? But she refused to believe it. With the old illogical faith, it seemed to her that if Heybert had ceased to be, somehow the cruel news would be borne in upon her.

Gradually with the darkness and the monotony of that olden ceaseless round of thought, and perhaps, also, of the slow, measured breathings of her father just behind and her aunt reclining toward her, she fell into a gentle doze herself, and thence into sound sleep. And, sleeping, she dreamed, though not about Heybert Hillebrandt. It might have been expected, indeed, that she would do so. Nothing more natural in theory, than that if one glides off into slumber with a prevailing thought coursing through his brain, the same thought will follow him in dreams, or, at the least, will color such dreams as he may otherwise have. But there is nothing more unusual in fact. Fancy plays strange pranks with our comprehensive powers; and, in the process from wakefulness to sleeping, not merely the person and scene will often suffer unanticipated changes, but the tone of mind as well.

Consequently, though by just right it seemed as though Geretic, falling asleep with Heybert's last words of love in her memory, and his name upon her lips, should have had visions only of him — seeing him as so often hitherto, either as when he had parted from her, or, as he had been pictured, ragged and worn among the Indians — the scene changed suddenly in all its elements. Instead of groves or camp fires there was a tenantless room, in which, for the moment, she stood alone. For a moment only, indeed, and then there entered, not Heybert, smooth-cheeked and flushed with the wished for success, but a strange, wrinkled, awe-producing old man whom she had never hitherto seen: a tall old man with heavy beard and full shaggy eyebrows, grayer even than the gray locks that hung in somewhat untidy straggling array over his broad white turned down tassel-fastened collar. Clad in a suit of coarse homespun, with something of a military cut about the folded-over sleeves, well adapted, indeed, to the shining steel breast-plate covering his chest, and the clumsy basket-hilted sword that was buckled to his side. This strange old man entering produced, at first, a feeling of terror, so different was he from any one whom she had ever seen before — so peculiarly fixed and unbending was his grim expression. But as he slowly paced the room toward her, though the stolidity and grimness of his features did not alter, it seemed as if there was a not unfriendly look in the quiet gaze he fixed upon her, an expression of personal approval, even, vastly reassuring her. So advancing within a foot of her he stopped, fastened his eyes upon her with the same steady but kindly gaze — seeming to warm into something almost paternal in its gathering softness — then thrust his arm deep within his breast, behind the steel breast-plate.

And this is where earliest we come across the dream; gathering from the Byvanck letter — which, herein, is especially minute in its description of time and place and circumstance — how, for a single moment, the dream came down and fluttered in the bewildered brain of pretty Geretie.

7*

Chapter III.

FOR a moment only. What the old man might have further done, Geretic could not tell; for, at that instant, there came a knock at the front door, and with a start she awoke. The same rap awakened, also, her father and Aunt Lysbeth. Each gave a little start backward, and it naturally happened that, in so doing, the heads of all three thumped together. No damage was done thereby, except that as Gisbort's wig had fallen a little awry during his slumber, leaving a bald spot on his head exposed to the air and Aunt Lysbeth's high metal comb now chanced to strike him exactly upon that place, there resulted to him a somewhat severe contusion. But wisely making no remark, he carefully replaced the wig, and the three awakened sleepers gazed for a moment abstractedly at each other, the mutual thumping of heads having effectually aroused them upon the instant.

"It must be Rollof Van Schoven who knocked," remarked Gisbort, breaking the silence and speaking with a kind of guilty consciousness that he could not altogether disguise. "I told him — that is, he said it was possible he might drop in this evening. It is getting very dark; why does not some one bring candles? And why is not the door opened? It is singular that, with so many servants in the house, no one is found to answer the door. All asleep, I suppose; though why any one should want to sleep in the day time — Lysbeth, do you get lights, and I will open the door myself, so as not to keep Rollof waiting."

Mistress Lysbeth hurried to the kitchen to procure a light — a candlestick in each hand — and Gisbort groped his way into the hall. He was only partially at ease, indeed, having a guilty feeling that he had too heedlessly betrayed his participation in the projected visit, and thereby might be brought under filial discipline. True, he had done nothing more than tell Rollof that he could come across upon that evening if so it pleased him, and Rollof had merely said that he would not fail. But much can be implied in very few words; and Gisbort felt that somehow, without half intending it, an understanding of parental consent had lurked behind the invitation, and that Geretie, deciphering the same, would not be slow to manifest resentment. Then he wondered whether Rollof might not be feeling still more discomposed; for, in the opinion of Gisbort Van Twiller, it was not an easy thing to make a formal visit with the intent of offering matrimonial alliance. At least it had not been easy for him, thirty years before, when he had made assault upon the heart of his Elsie; and even then he had been able to bide his time until the way seemed laid open to him at a Pinxter festival. But here was Rollof, coming in cold blood as it were, in fulfillment of a kind of tacit understanding — engaged for the task, however unpropitious might be the circumstances.

At the very thought of it, the perspiration broke out upon Gisbort's face as though he were the victim; and, as he opened the door, he half expected to let in a timid, crouching broken-down figure begging for respite.

He was a little relieved, as well as surprised, to see that Rollof appeared not at all embarrassed. Dressed with such scrupulous care as must, of itself, almost have declared the intent of his coming — in fact, it was Rollof making his toilet, and not the old lady counting her doubloons, whom Gisbort had seen behind the curtain — he stood erect and composed, and even with a tranquil smile upon his lips. Little reason, indeed, could the host but know it, why Rollof should not be at his ease, having his heart so thoroughly fortified with the power of one newly formed purpose.

Following his host into the sitting-room, and reaching it just as Mistress Lysbeth came in from another door, bearing before her two tall lighted candles in still taller candlesticks, Rollof gave hasty glance forward, and saw Geretie arisen from the sofa and making ceremonious courtesy. In her face was no sign or gleam of welcome, however; only a cold, fixed, impassive smile. For, as her father had suspected, Geretie had noticed the accidental admission that Rollof had been invited thither, and thereupon she had at once shut up all her kindly sympathy; in her fancy carrying her thoughts much further than she ought, and wrongly imagining that her hand had been especial subject of mention between the two, and the important interview planned with deliberate forethought. Therefore she felt that less now, than ever before, would she tolerate it; and sitting down once more, with her face steadily turned toward the blaze of the fire, she relapsed into the silence and immobility of a marble statue.

Rollof sat opposite, and gazing stealthily into her rigid countenance, felt that, had he been now disposed to tempt his fate, he could easily there read his doom, needing not words in explanation of it. A fixed and somewhat melancholy smile came over his own face; and, turning, he gazed around at Gisbort and Mistress Lysbeth. They had taken their places at either side of him, and there sat motionless; each so absorbed in separate train of thought as to forget offering even the customary commonplace greetings of the evening. With Gisbort was the satisfactory conviction that Geretie herself would not now fail to mark the courage and self-possession of Rollof, and so, at last, be favorably impressed by him; with Mistress Lysbeth, on the contrary, was full perception of Geretie's forbidding manner and Rollof's strange, fixed smile, together awakening in her a distracting instinct of something having gone wrong. Such dreadful silence — broken only by a few distinct sounds that did not fill the void, but merely made more noticeable the need of relief elsewhere. The shout of passing boy in the street outside; the snapping of the blazing logs; the measured ticking of the tall clock — neither of these weighed anything against the terrible stillness. So for a moment; and then Rollof himself made bold to break the silence. And it seemed fortunate, indeed, that he had something worthy to be told and need not deal in commonplaces. An hour before, he had met a scout from the upper regions of the Colony, and the man had given him much information that it might be pleasing for others to hear. Therefore, Rollof, crossing his dainty silk stockings, and hanging his natty little cocked hat over his knee, plunged at once into his subject.

It had so far been a mild winter at the north, — so the scout had told him, — and, consequently, there had been little difficulty in gathering supplies for the garrisons of the outposts. There had been a few skirmishes with small marauding parties of French and Indians, but with little important result. Upon the border, an outlying fortification had been attacked by a large Indian force, but it had been beaten back, with a loss of many killed, and no damage of consequence to the defense. In other directions, also, the Indians had been troublesome, occasionally co-operating with the French in the established war, and again indulging in acts of cruelty and rapine for their own amusement. A family of whites had been slaughtered on the borders of Lake Champlain; and among the Hurons, a white prisoner had been taken, and tortured for two days. Here Geretie, losing for the moment her impassive immobility, looked up with a pale face; and Rollof, still with that sad smile, hastened to add that the victim was an old, worn-out trapper, and by that timely correction gained from her one flickering glance of gratitude. And in every direction — praise God, for the great mercy — the war against the French was going on well, and with increasing advantage to the English arms. It was even said — but at that hour the report had not been verified — that Cape Breton had already surrendered to the joint attack of General Amherst and Admiral Boscawen. If this were true, it was a great triumph; and with its moral as well as physical effect, might, ere long, lead to the capture of Quebec itself. It was to be hoped that the tidings would soon be verified; and if so, it would make this Christmas a most joyful one to the Colonies of His Britannic Majesty.

Reaching this grand climax of his news, Rollof looked around to mark how his hearers received it; but, to his surprise, observed, that while he had been speaking, his host, who should certainly have been sufficiently interested to wait until the end, had quietly slipped out of the room. And while Rollof wondered at this, Mistress Lysbeth also, affecting to hear a call from old Chloe, arose and made an awkward retreat. The object of this could not now be misunderstood. He had purposely been left alone with Geretie, in order that he might take the opportunity to make his intended avowal. Looking across at Geretie, he could see by the increased fixedness and determination of her expression, that she, also, had well comprehended the enforced situation, and was nerving herself to meet it with all a mortified woman's resentment. That look upon her face was not needed, indeed, to assure him that she was no consenting party to the proceeding; but, nevertheless, had his intentions been different from what they were, it would have sunk crushingly into his heart, already so heavily laden with warnings of ill success. Possibly he would even have retired without another word, rather than advance to such well-assured discomfiture. But now, on the contrary, he remained; for a moment longer sitting silent, the yell of street boy sounding in his ear like a battle cry, and the monotonous tick of the clock like the thump of sledge-hammer. Then rising with hurried determination, he strode once up and down the room, and pausing, stood before her.

"I hardly know how to say it, Geretie," he began. "I had meant, upon my coming hither, to offer you my hand. Now — well now, I have no longer a thought of it."

Geretie looked up wonderingly at him. Certainly this was singular language. She had made up her mind, of course, that she would listen to no love tales from him; and yet to be thus quietly given to understand —

"Strange talk from me, Geretie, is it not?" he continued. "It is not that I would prefer to have it so, indeed; not but that I would have asked for your love if I thought there was any hope of gaining it. It is simply that something which has come to me to-day has assured me how hopeless it is to think of that. And so —"

As Geretie listened, and, with intuitive perception, gained comprehension of what he was so painfully endeavoring to explain, a bright, cheery smile broke forth in her face — the cheeriness of relief from long continued apprehension.

"But this is not what my father and Aunt Lysbeth expected you to say to me, is it, Rollof?" she interrupted with a rippling laugh.

"No, Geretie. Nor what my Aunt Barbara expected. Nor what the Swartwouts, and the Winegaerts, and the Fredingborcks expected; who all, somehow, seem to think they have something to say about it. Nor myself, who am more interested than any of them, I believe; and who would gladly have had matters otherwise if I could. But you see, Geretie, it has become easy for me to learn that what I so much desired can never be. And, therefore, I have asked myself what was best to do? Should I struggle in vain, and make my coming always an annoyance to you, and stand in your presence a baffled, disconsolate lover? Or should I pluck up a brave heart, resign my hopes, and try in some other way to remain your friend?"

"Pluck up the brave heart, Rollof," she answered, the pleasantest smile she had known for weeks now beaming upon her face. It was so comforting to her soul to know that the ordeal she had so long dreaded had thus sensibly passed over, and that she had gained a friend instead of lost an admirer. "And now sit down beside me, Rollof, and tell me further what all this means."

So he sat down upon the sofa with his back to the window, through which, at that very moment, his Aunt Barbara was ineffectually endeavoring to peer across from the seclusion of her parlor opposite.

She had noted the direction of his going out, and was now anxiously looking for further developments. To her, also, had come the comfortable conviction that this was the important evening; and it was hard for her to convince herself that, with clear eye-sight so very necessary, she could not see distinctly, through her spectacles and two small-paned windows and across a wide street. In vain she sighed and alternately wiped her spectacles and window panes; she felt, at last, that, for any definite information, she must patiently await Rollof's return. Gisbort here — Aunt Barbara there — other Van Schovens and their collaterals, everywhere — all eagerly anticipating tidings of the projected alliance; and here was Rollof, in utter disregard of their wishes, and as though he were the only party concerned, quietly baffling their expectations. For he told Geretie how that, for a long time, he had realized the vanity of his hopes, and many times already had been inclined to abandon the struggle; and how that, taking sober counsel with himself, he had at last resolved to act the manly part, giving her the acceptable Christmas offering of freedom from future persecution on his behalf, and asking in return the most precious gift of her sisterly friendship. Little by little, as he proceeded, Rollof felt his utterance, as well as manner of explanation, more easy — perhaps having actually been less interested in the affair than he had previously imagined — and, in the end, Geretie and he became quite composed, and even inclined to look upon the matter with something of philosophic spirit.

"But you said, Rollof, that your determination about — about the hopelessness of all this, you know, came partly from something you have heard to-day. Was it about Heybert? It may not seem quite right for me to talk about him; and yet there can be no use concealing from you, at least, an interest that everybody else seems to understand. Yes, there is really something about him in your mind," she continued, with sudden impulse of a quickened instinct; "something that perhaps you would like to tell me, and yet feel that you should withhold! What is it, Rollof? And why, if you must not speak, have you said so much already? Tell me everything now; that only is the part of a true friend."

"It is not much, Geretie," he answered, after a moment's pause, not wishing to excite false hope; yet feeling that since, with woman's quickness, she had divined so much, it might do no harm to brighten her life a little with anticipation of good that might possibly happen. "Not much, indeed, only that to-day, from the scout, I heard something; though, after all, I had better not now tell you what it was, for it may turn out untrue. If it is true, it is good news — so much I can venture to say; but, if false, then it will be as you have hinted, that I had better have told you nothing at all, and have left you in ignorance from the very first. Trust me, Geretie, for now acting as seems most wise. If you would know something of what I mean, I will tell you to remember that courage and perseverance some times find a position in which to reap their reward, and therefore — But wait, again I say; for, after all, it may be false report.”

“I will wait as you direct!” Geretie exclaimed, “for I know that when the proper time arrives, you will tell me all. But even now I will not believe that any part of it is not true. I have waited too long already, that fate should not prove kind to me at last. You need tell me nothing more, Rollof, for I can feel it all. It means that Heybert is indeed coming back to me! That all I have endured and suffered is to pass away forever — to be no more remembered, except it may be as we recall a frightful dream!”

The time-eaten portrait of old Governor Van Twiller shook a little to and fro as she spoke; but that was only the wind, nor could it matter how the dead might think or act. It was the living Van Twillers who were concerned; and, if Gisbort could have listened to the late conversation, how would he have shaken with disgust and anger of Rollof, at having thrown away an opportunity so carefully prepared for him. But Gisbort was far out of hearing, standing upon his front stoop ankle deep in snow. He had gone thither inconsiderately, in his transparent pretense of household business elsewhere; the door had blown to behind him, and he was now afraid to demand readmission lest his knock might be mistaken for that of new visitors, and thereby endanger the continuance of the all-important interview. He would wait outside, therefore, and endure the cold and snow until Rollof might appear to receive his congratulations and consent, and, if need be, his blessing. But Mistress Lysbeth, with better self-possession, had employed her time skirmishing to and fro between hall and kitchen; now rousing up Chloe to impossible tasks, then looking into closets for articles that she knew to be elsewhere, again returning to the hall and taking furtive peeps into the sitting-room. Now, seeing that Rollof and Geretie were sitting close together upon the sofa, smiling pleasantly upon each other, she could not fail to feel assured that her late discouragement had proved ill founded, and that true love had gained, at last, its successful termination. This happy conviction now irradiated all her features, destroyed her customary equipoise, and made her garrulous with exuberance of delight.

"Why talk about dreams? And what frightful dream have you ever had, Geretie?" she said, coming in with a little warning cough, and indistinctly catching the last few words. "Never trouble yourself about such vain things as dreams, Geretie, for they mean nothing. Do I not know, myself? The pleasantest dreams one can have — about flowers and fairies, it may be — will often come before a death; and many a time I have dreamed frightful things, and had them followed by good news. — Even as now, indeed," she continued, wagging her head archly, and with much significance of meaning, "for who would have thought that good things were about to happen, when, so little while ago, I dreamed about a horrid rough old man?"

"An old man, Aunt Lysbeth?"

"Yes; not an hour ago, when your father so

rudely waked me up by knocking his head against mine,—sending my comb, I verily believe, almost half an inch into my brain. A queer old man it was that came to me, frightening me almost to death with his terrible eyebrows and his great tangled beard. It almost seems as though I saw him yet. He had an iron breast-plate in front of him, and wore a clumsy old sword with hilt as large as one's two fists. I remember thinking, at the time, that it was a strange costume to wear in the presence of a lady; though, doubtless," —

"Tell me, aunt," cried Geretie, becoming suddenly interested, "did this old man walk into the room, and come close to you, and put his hand into his bosom behind the breast-plate, and " —

"No, he did nothing of the kind, Geretie. He did not come into the room — whatever room it was — for I found him there already; and so I suppose he came there first. And he had his hand behind his breast-plate when I first saw him. But, as I looked, he pulled it out, and there was something like a roll of parchment in his hand, and " —

"And what then, Aunt Lysbeth?"

"Why then your father thumped me, and I woke up; but, for the moment after, I was quite frightened, thinking that I saw the cross old man still standing before me. — And therefore, Geretie," she continued, again wagging her head with arch meaning, "do not trouble yourself about your dreams, even if they are frightful; seeing that, as in my case, they may all the same be followed by something just as pleasant the other way."

And so it was that, in due sequence, the dream came also to Mistress Lysbeth. The knowledge of which fact, however, might never have transpired, but for this visit of Rollof Van Schoven; inasmuch as — according to the Byvanck letter — Mistress Lysbeth was always so wrapped up in matters of household economy and care, that it was more than likely that, at the very next hour, she would have forgotten all about the dream.

BUT Geretie, however startled at the time, gave the matter little thought, when, somewhat later, she retired for the night. What though two persons had dreamed about one and the same queer, cross old man? Was not this a matter of mere chance coincidence that could not fail to happen often, did we but know it? Nay, the very departure from absolute similarity in the dreams was a mark of imperfection; while, surely, nothing whatsoever seemed likely to come of it. Therefore, dismissing the matter from her mind, she put on her ring, and surrendered herself to the influence of brighter visions — dreaming, as so often before, of Heybert. How that, as had been so pleasantly hinted to her, his trials all were over, and how that he must already be coming back. Mingling him, in her fancies, with much that was unreal and grotesque indeed; as when the painted tiles about the fireplace obtruding themselves, she dreamed that he was coming back in the guise of the prodigal son, bringing his own fatted calf with him to insure his welcome; and that, thereupon, Shadrach, Meshach and Abed-nego came forth to meet him, singing joyful congratulatory anthems. But, throughout all, there was the one real perception that Heybert must be coming back.

The song of the three fire-tried youths still sounded
in her ears when she awoke. But little by little it
resolved itself into anything else than ancient can-
ticle, and intoned by any other than Babylonian
voices; for, as her perceptions grew more collected,
she recognized the well-attuned notes of a choir of
little negroes, singing a Christmas anthem from
door to door. Thus cheerily reminded of the day,
Geretie sprang from her bed and hurried to the door,
outside of which hung her stocking; for she was
not yet so far advanced in years as to have grown
out of her childish pleasure in exploring the Christmas stocking, and developing its delightful mysteries. Then springing back into bed with the
laden treasure, excitedly she drew forth one and
another closely folded paper, laying them in line
upon the coverlet before her. The pin-cushion, so
long being made by old Chloe, and so often hidden
hastily beneath a saucepan when Geretie had chanced
to enter the kitchen; the gold chain and locket from
Aunt Lysbeth; the ten commandments carved by
Rak and Tak upon two conch shells, and the fox-
skin purse from Cato; the promised gold watch from
her father — all these at last lay spread out before
her. Nothing so small as to be despised, so faithful
.. and warm-hearted was its giver, — everything welcomed with almost equal delight, for the true affection that had prompted its bestowal. With her
hands thrown upon the pillow behind her, and supporting her head, Geretie lay back for a moment or
two, and tried adequately to realize how happy she
ought to be, surrounded by this wealth of sweet

regard. And how supremely blissful would she now be, if she could only hear from Heybert! Was Heybert where he, too, could hang out his Christmas stocking? Was he where he could boast any stocking to put out at all? She smiled to herself as she pictured him among the Hurons, hanging outside his wigwam a beaded moccasin as the best substitute for a stocking, to find in it the next morning, perchance, a scalp-bracelet or bear's-tooth necklace; enjoying her fancy the more heartily as she felt assured that it had no basis of cruel fact. For had not Rollof talked about preferment having come to Heybert, and predicted his return? This was the cheery idea that now underlined her whole tone of thought.

Newer sounds now arising from the street below, Geretie arose, gently drew her curtain and looked out. A bright sun was shining; the promise of the previous evening having been fulfilled in a clear, sparkling day. As her father had surmised, the snow had fallen gently and unobtrusively, making little chance of obstruction through drifts. It lay on roadway and fence and gable with uniform depth, so evenly fallen that it seemed as though fairy hands must have followed each flake in its quiet descent, and fastened it securely in place. How otherwise, indeed, could it be that the thick covering lay so motionless upon the steep roofs of the little church below, and upon the sharp gables of Aunt Barbara's house opposite? How otherwise could the flakes cling so firmly upon the insecure resting-place of the iron numerals upon the front, marking out the date in such clear bright lines?

In the middle of the street stood a row of market sledges from the country with beef and poultry. The owners haggled over their sales as usual; and yet it seemed as though their discussions were more good natured than at any other time, so genial was the influence of the day. Down the street from the fort two officers, tucked up in bear skins, drove along in their open sleigh; and, as they passed the Van Twiller mansion, a little negro took courage and threw a snowball at them. Thereupon it might be supposed that these insulted sons of Mars would descend, draw their glittering blades, run the offender through the body, wipe their reeking weapons upon the bear skin robes, and drive off with pleasant sense of vengeance satisfied. Instead, thereof, they arrested the sleigh for only a moment; and one of them reaching over gathered up a hard snowball, with which, taking correct aim, he hit the aggressor so plumply in the center of the stomach as to knock him over. Then they rode on again laughing, the very bells upon the horses seeming to turn their silver tinkle into a "Merry Christmas;" and the little negro rising unharmed and appearing rather gratified at the encounter, laughed in turn even still more hilariously. So did the pleasant inspiration of the Christmas morning brighten up every heart with charity.

At the door of the opposite house suddenly appeared a curiously enveloped figure, with not less curious head-dress. It was old Aunt Barbara. Before her stood a servant with empty basket; and now Aunt Barbara carefully piled the basket with pies and cakes, and in each corner a chicken — all destined for poor pensioners — and at last sent off the servant with minute and often repeated directions. Just then the choir of little negroes came down the street on their return, and, seeing her, formed in front of the house and sang their carol. Upon this Aunt Barbara retired into the house; and an unreflecting stranger might have supposed that she had peevishly gone away to avoid the singers. But not so; for, in a moment, she returned and distributed among them plenteous reward of cakes, which they proceeded at once to demolish, postponing, with the usual improvidence of their race, all further minstrelsy until new cravings of the stomach might call them to resume their labors. So, everywhere, beaming smiles and hearty good wishes were interchanged — even the spirit of trade having kindly charities mingled with it in correction of its customary acerbities — old age becoming, for the moment, young again, and dignity condescending to lively frolic. And all the while, the little bell upon the English church, away up the hill, rang out a joyful salutation to the day, with as merry spirit and consequential self-sufficiency as though it were a whole chime of bells.

Then Geretie, leaving the window and making her toilet, gently opened the door, with intent to slip softly down stairs on tip-toe, and steal a march upon her father and aunt, with the first greeting for the day. Not so easy, indeed, for she also had been waylaid with like intent. Beside her door crouched old Chloe, and on the first step stood Cato, and clinging to the bannisters were Rak and Tak. All these, as she appeared, screamed forth in one chorus a merry Christmas to her; holding up, in joyous acknowledgment of them, the little gifts she had put into their stockings. At the sound of this uproar, of course her father and Aunt Lysbeth darted out from below and caught her, unaware, upon the very last step — her father pinching her lovingly upon the cheek, and her aunt, with mistaken aim, kissing her in the middle of her chin.

Which being done, her father remembered how that he had just been told by Aunt Lysbeth about the undesirable working of matters the previous evening. How or why it had so happened he did not know; it was sufficient that hope for the Van Schoven alliance seemed at an end, and that he had caught a cold while waiting, to no purpose, outside in the snow. It seemed his duty to scold a little; and with that intent he proceeded to make himself as red in the face as possible, roughening his throat a little for a harsh, grating roar. But Geretie, perceiving his intent, kissed him so accurately upon the very center of his mouth, that she broke up all these preparations.

"Not to-day, father," she said. "Not upon Christmas morning, when all should be so happy and well pleased with each other, you know. And when, moreover, we have so much to do, that we have no time to be cross."

"No, Geretie, not to-day, of course," he responded,

breaking into a hearty smile. "Not when we have so much to do, indeed."

Which meant that, for him, there was nothing to do except to smoke his big carved pipe from immediately after breakfast to early dark, occasionally gossipping with a passing neighbor. But for Geretie, there was everything to be attended to, so that it seemed wonderful how one person could get through so much. There were visits to be made in different directions; visits of ceremony upon relatives, who would, on no account, think of Christmas passing by without her coming; and visits of friendly charity upon old dames who always looked forward to her approach as synonymous with the mince pies and krullers that she brought. There was a short service to be attended in the little Dutch church at the bottom of the hill, and there was the English church at the other end of the street, to be looked into; since it was always considered one of the most important observances of the season to note how tastefully the chancel and pillars were wreathed with pine and hemlock. All these formed only a portion of Geretie's duties for the day.

For, coming home, there was the state-parlor to be opened and dusted out as only its mistress could dust it. There was the little square carpet in the center to be taken away to make space for the dancing. There was almost all the lower floor of the house to be waxed under Geretie's eye. There were sconces for candles to be placed along the walls, and the parlor chandelier to be fitted with wax lights and decorated with Christmas greens.

There was old china to be ferreted out from the dark closet depths and arranged for use. There were quaint pieces of silver, blackened from want of use, and seemingly almost forgotten, to be taken out of their green baize coverings and polished up. And there was the great bowlful of punch to be concocted after her grandfather's receipt, and then carefully locked up, lest the cook and coachman might be tempted to try its strength, and, trying it too often, overcome their own.

Lastly, and late in the afternoon, there was to be a retirement of Aunt Lysbeth and Geretie to their respective apartments; to be speedily followed thither by sundry women well skilled in secrets of the toilet. Of this, the result became apparent a little before seven; for, at that time, the door of one room opening, let out Aunt Lysbeth, gorgeous with stiff brocade and gold-threaded turban, and with ample gold chains looped around her neck. Then from the other room speedily appeared Geretie, in dress of less cumbrous material, but with her heavy masses of auburn hair wonderfully built up over a high cushion, so as to show the whole pretty face up to the very roots of the hair, making also more evident the lustrous pearls forming her ear-rings. Her father was already down stairs and awaiting them; somewhat uncomfortable, perhaps, in his new wig and his tights, which he suspected had been made a trifle too tight. To console himself, he was trying to whistle the little negro boys' Christmas anthem, thinking that it was God save the King. But at sight of the new comers he forgot wig and tights and Christmas song; and hobbling forward, paid to his sister the expected compliments upon her appearance, while he embraced Geretie with abundant effusion of parental love.

"But take care, father, or you will pull down my hair," was Geretie's response, as she released herself. "And more than all, you will bruise your pretty Christmas present, which, as you see, I am wearing at my belt."

"A trumpery little watch — not half what a Christmas present should be," he muttered ruefully. "Do you know, Geretie, I had meant another kind of Christmas present for you — a rich young husband?"

"That is a present one should always select for herself, father."

"No doubt you think so, Geretie," he responded, feebly attempting a growl. "And therefore it is that so foolishly you have given up everything — the mill upon the Mohawk, and all! Not to speak of what I have learned this morning — that his old Aunt Barbara has begun to fail and cannot last six months! A young man about whom half the marriageable girls in the city are dreaming, while you persist in dreaming only about a penniless adventurer, roving around among the Indians, if he has not already been knocked upon the head by some of them. And what is more, Geretie, talking so much about him, as you do, that even I begin to dream of him; or rather, which is not quite as disreputable, of his old great grandfather."

“And how, father, did you know his great grand-father?”

“Did I say I knew him, you vixen? How, indeed, could I know a man who was one of Governor Stuyvesant’s councilors and lived nearly a century ago? But for all dreaming purposes, I suppose it is the same thing to know old Cornelis Hillebrandt’s portrait. It hangs in the parlor of Andries Hillebrandt, Geretie, who is the present head of the family, and if Heybert never comes back, will inherit the nothing he leaves behind him. Quite an interesting old portrait, indeed, seeing that old Cornelis is shown up in steel breast-plate and basket-hilted sword, as befits a brave warrior who in the old country served two campaigns with Prince Maurice, and generally looks grim and warlike too” —

“And you dreamed about him, did you say?” cried Geretie, starting. “And when was that?”

“Last night, I believe. No, not last night, after all; but yesterday evening, as we all sat nodding together, just before the lights were brought in.”

“And did he seem to come into the room where you were, father? And did he put his hand into his breast and pull out a parchment roll?”

“He did nothing of the sort, Geretie. He was in the room when I came in, if I ever came in at all. All I know is that I found myself standing in front of him, and might have been born there, for anything I can tell to the contrary. And if he had put his hands into his breast after a parchment, he must have done so before I came; for when I saw him, he was flourishing the roll in the air, and he said” —

"What did he say father?" Geretie almost breathlessly inquired.

"Now, that is what I do not remember," Gisbort answered. "It could not have been anything very particular, or, I suppose, I should have laid it more to heart. And then, again, you know, I am not very much in the mood to hold communication with the Hillebrandts, either alive or dead. Anyhow, before I could fix the matter, whatever it was, in my recollection, your Aunt Lysbeth awoke me ; very inconsiderately knocking her comb half through my bare skull, and leaving a dent in which I can almost lay my finger."

Geretie pondered the matter; a little confused at first, but light gradually breaking in upon her, as she began to put facts together and form something of a collected theory out of the whole affair. Might it not have been that old Cornelis Hillebrandt had visited her in a dream, to tell something important about her lover; that the dream had come to her ill-timed and at the moment of her awakening; and that, in the sudden knocking together of heads, it had been driven in detached portions from one to the other, her father holding that last fragment which, with the first and second, should have come to herself alone?

"Father," she cried, seizing him by the arm, "you must remember and tell me all that the Councilor Cornelis Hillebrandt told you. I am sure that it must have been something about Heybert. Think — think all you can about it, father, and let me know. It was not your dream at all, or even Aunt Lysbeth's, but mine; and you must not keep any portion of it. The dream was all my own, and Aunt Lysbeth knocking her head against mine, stole away a part of what belonged to me. Then you thumped Aunt Lysbeth and took away another and the best part of the dream from her. And, therefore, do you not see, father, that " —

"Why, what does the girl mean?" cried Gisbort, in natural astonishment. "Your dream, indeed! Have you so taken possession of the whole Hillebrandt family, that while you dream about Heybert you will not allow me a moment with his grim old great grandfather? There, run away Geretie, and think no more about such foolishness."

Whereby it will be seen that Gisbort, discovering himself to be the acknowledged complement of the charmed circle of the dream, was disposed to treat the matter with somewhat careless spirit; though, — as the Byvanck letter intimates, — it was not improbable that, secretly, he was a little discomposed about the meaning and effect of the dream's singular partition and sequence of delivery.

Chapter V.

BEFORE Geretie could make any response, the knocker of the outer door, announcing the first arrival, compelled her to hurry across the room, and take her allotted position for reception. Old Cato, the coachman, now on duty as door-keeper, startled by that first rap from a comfortable nook in the kitchen, shuffled hastily toward the front, putting on a new liveried coat as he went; and with that early arrival, almost at one instant, the great tide of the invited began to flow in steady stream. A lively scene out doors, where, from every point of the compass, the guests converged to the Van Twiller mansion as though by preconcerted signal. Young damsels, tripping along blithely, with thoughts all fixed upon the festivity before them; finely gotten-up old gentlemen pacing solemnly onward, in the importance of new laced and ruffled suits; maternal dames in brocade, picking their way through the middle of the street, lest chance falls of snow from the roofs might discompose their laboriously erected headdresses; officers in red coats and braided gold clink-clanking, down from the fort; not least of all to be mentioned, old Barbara Van Schoven, tottering over from her house, wrapped up as closely as though she were starting out for the Canadas, and reaching the further side of the street in state of great exhaus-

tion — so they came in gathering crowds. Most all
were on foot, for the city was not so widely extended
that many guests must ride. But now and then
would draw up some large covered sleigh, with two
or four horses, according as the dignity of the owners or the distance they had traveled demanded;
and from the dark recesses of these vehicles emerged
wealthy citizens from the neighborhood or Patroons
from across and down the river, from Rensselaer,
Livingston, and even from as far as Courtland
manor; or scarcely less powerful landholders
from along the Mohawk and down the Hudson;
almost every broad possession, as far south as Phil-
lip's Patent, sending its representatives. To lighten
these guests in their descent was the especial duty
of Rak and Tak, now newly clothed in liveries of
black, turned up in the cuffs and collars with red,
and who each bore a flaming torch, to the intense
admiration of other little negroes gathered around;
which torches being held up at each side of the
great sleighs, often made goodly chance exhibition
of rich laces and velvets, gold shoe-buckles, and
other, festive adornments upon those descending,
and called forth cheers from all the crowd.

In doors, a scene still more animated and resplend-
ent, as now the rooms began to fill, and every moment
the throng increased, until at last both parlors and
the broad hall seemed closely occupied. A brilliant
array of stiff-figured brocades and embroidered satin
vests — of sweeping trains and colored silk tights —
of high-heeled rosetted slippers and silver buckled
shoes — of artistically fashioned head-dresses and

carefully powdered wigs. Here and there the military uniform of officers from the fort or the official costume of Councilor of State, giving pleasant variety to the scene. An animated throng, which soon resolved itself into its proper groups and positions; a few old gentlemen immovably stationing themselves before the fire and beneath the picture of old Governor Van Twiller, there interchanging snuff and talking about the war with the French; old ladies sitting in corners and silently criticising each other's laces and jewels — heir-looms, brought out long ago from London or Amsterdam, as the case might be; the most decorously disposed damsels arranging themselves along the sides, and there awaiting invitations to the coming dance ; but the greater portion of the guests filling up the spaces between and loitering in slow moving tide from room to room, until it seemed as though all the expected guests must be already there. Which was the fact, — excepting, indeed, that two and the most desirable elements of the company yet lingered; and as Mistress Lysbeth passed around, bestowing here and there her greetings, she watched the door in anxious expectation of those still absent ones.

Having not long to wait, however, since very soon they came; — the minister of the English church, upon the hill, and the dominie of the Dutch church, at the cross-streets below, entering arm in arm, as befitted men whose Churches were in such pleasant and friendly unity. As sacerdotal guests, they were, of course, not bound down to any worldly follies of costume, — eschewing velvets and maintaining rather their accustomed broadcloth, and having their well-shapen legs attired in tights of plain black worsted, rather than of lustrous colored silks. And yet, for all that, there was something of scrupulous care to be detected in the accurate powdering of their white wigs, and in the dainty starching of the thin strips of plain lace peeping from their coat-fronts. Making their most dutiful compliments to the smiling hostesses, the pastors proceeded onward with cheerful sobriety of mien, distributing plenteous greetings to the many surrounding members of their several flocks; which being done, they accepted chairs of honor from which, themselves not dancing, they might watch the course of those who did, in the pleasant meandering through lively reel and stately minuet. Now, surely, the company must be all complete.

Not yet; for suddenly a large stage-sleigh, drawn by six horses for easier conflict with the up-country snow-drifts, stopped in front of the Van Twiller mansion, and a head and shoulders in military cocked hat and cloak being projected, inquiry was made as to the nearest crossing at the river. With him were eight other officers of the British army — the speaker explained — all participants in the late capture of Cape Breton, and now on their way with the glorious news to New York. Hearing this, Gisbort Van Twiller hurried out bare-headed and supplicated them to alight, and for that evening, at least, partake of his poor hospitality; alleging that he would never forgive himself if he suffered so many brave soldiers of His Majesty, King George, to pass his house, unrefreshed. To which entreaties after a little persuasion, the officers acceded; and when they entered and threw off their cloaks, they appeared attired in such spotless yellow leather tights, such, becoming and well-fitting red coats, and such carefully powdered locks, as made it more than lightly suspected that they had refitted themselves at the fort above in anticipation of a welcome, and that the inquiry as to the nearest river point was a mere pardonable subterfuge. However this might be, none the less was their reception hearty, and the favor shown them for their late gallantry most abundant. And at once did common consent unite to reward them with the prettiest partners for the coming dance; to which none showed themselves disinclined, excepting two or three, who, alleging recent incapacitating wounds, remained apart as mere spectators. And now, at last, the party must really be complete.

Not yet, indeed; for scarcely had those brave officers been welcomed, than from the head of the street, and simply coming on foot, appeared His Excellency, the acting Governor De Lancey. He had been unexpectedly summoned, during the past month, to the northern portion of the colony, on public business; which, having been completed, it was no difficult task so to arrange his homeward route as, after all, to enter the Van Twiller mansion, upon that Christmas evening. With his lavender tights and richly-chased silver shoe-buckles, his embroidered velvet coat and fine lace cuffs, and bosom plaits, his long buff vest and shapely peruke, the Lieutenant-Governor was a stately and pleasant sight to see.

Upon either side of him walked a member of his council, the companions of his journey, similarly arrayed, though with somewhat less degree of elegance, by way of showing all proper deference to rank; and behind, as his military body guard, were two full-uniformed officers of the British regiment in garrison near the Bowling Green. Attended by these four satellites, the Lieutenant-Governor made stately progress through the apartments; giving pleasant greetings here and there to well-remembered friends, neglecting no opportunity of complimenting matronly dignity or blushing beauty, and even bestowing most gracious and deferential smiles upon his haughty political rival of Livingston manor. And now, beyond a doubt, was the party all made up at last.

Little need, it may be, to tell at greater length than by mere suggestion, how, at the first, the ball was opened with single ceremonious minuet, wherein the Lieutenant-Governor gallantly leading out Mistress Lysbeth Van Twiller for his partner, headed the dance, while other dignitaries, with other dames of high degree, filled out the set. How slow and stately was the dance, performed to becomingly heavy music, with only here and there a quickened step, and mostly carried through with dignified balancing to the right and left, and with low and gracious bowing every minute to each other person's partner, the whole concluding with bows still lower and more stately than any that had gone before. And how, after this opening dance was ended, even those who had most attentively enjoyed it, drew deep sighs of relief, and searched out partners for themselves; whereupon, not one, but several sets were formed in parlors and hall, and the music fell into livelier strains, and form and ceremony were somewhat cast aside, and mirth and joviality began to take their place.

Or how, when, at last, the moment for supper arrived, the guests all crowded into the largest room, and there did full justice to the ample display. How, more especially, the men, both old and young, did honor to the great punch bowl, which, within the hour, was many times emptied and refilled. How, for all that, our ancestor's heads being made of strong and resisting material, there was no marked excess, each one coming away as soberly as he had approached; though it was cautiously whispered around that two or three of the old gentlemen, who had tapped their snuff-boxes beneath the portrait of Governor Van Twiller, went home with the queues of their periwigs a little askew. And how, that a lighter wine was furnished for the dames and damsels, who partook thereof with much affected reluctance and timid smile and blushes; but being at last persuaded, grew brighter in the eyes, and afterward danced all the better therefor.

These things need not be told, being so easily imagined. It is sufficient, indeed, to narrate the incident that made pretty Geretie's eyes grow bright and a roseate blush of happy anticipation suffuse her face. She had not danced every time, preferring to leave that pastime mostly to her guests, herself gliding from one to the other in pleasant greeting. Now, during a pause in the figure, and while for the

moment standing alone near one of the heavily cur-
tained windows, her hand resting lightly against her
side, she felt a little three-cornered piece of paper
gently slipped between her fingers. To cast it away,
as an uncalled for attempt to hold secret correspondence with her, was of course her duty; but at
the first moment, there was the instinct of crushing
the paper in her hand, to learn its nature. And
doing so, she felt that there was a ring inside.

With that, her heart gave a joyful bound. It
needed not that she should open the paper to learn
whose ring it held. There was only one ring that
could ever come to her in this manner — her own
little torquoise ring, which she had given to Heybert
Hillebrandt, and which was to be returned to her
only as a token that all had gone well, and that he
was coming back, at last, to claim her. No wonder
that the flush of assured hope mantled her face,
and that her eyes shone brightly with the intensity
of newly found happiness! Gently, and with almost
imperceptible sliding of her hand, she dropped the
precious paper into her pocket, — turning, as soon as
she could do so safely, to see who was the giver. But
there was now no guest standing very near her — no
one, except her father, who, catching her bright
glance, could not refrain from commenting upon it.

"No prettier damsel in all the room than my own
Geretie," he whispered, with bluff heartiness of satisfaction. "If you would alway look as happy" —

"Father," she whispered in return, sidling up
closer to him, "I am happy, because there is something that has made me so. No matter what it is,

now. But I think that you can make me still more happy, if you will only recollect what old Cornelis Hillebrandt said to you. For it is not your dream; it is mine. He came to tell me what has become of Heybert; he would never have told you, because you do not like Heybert, and would not care to know. And his face never would have relaxed from its sternness and looked kindly into your face as it did into mine. Men do not look at each other in that way, indeed. It was my dream; and you and Aunt Lysbeth have got it away from me by a mistake. If all our three heads at that moment had not — Now think hard, father, and let me know."

Old Gisbort, as she spoke, turned his face from her, reflectively, or rather with the air of one who tries to reflect, and, under the circumstances, finds it difficult to do so. There was so much noise around; — who, indeed, could think of anything? He looked first down at his shoe-buckles, finding no inspiration there. Then into the middle of the room where were two sets of dancers, through into the sitting-room where were other two sets, out into the hall where was still another set. All seemingly in vain; for how could any one reflect with that pattering of feet keeping time in every direction, that lively tune ringing in his ears? Such a very lively tune, indeed, kept back by the black fiddlers exclusively for this after-supper hour! Those who danced seemed to do so with more life than ever before; those who were not in the sets could not refrain from beating time with their feet, or with responsive nod of head. Gisbort himself began to rock his wig this side and that in unison with the measure, and was evidently forgetting all about Geretie's question, when she took him by the arm, and brought him back to the subject.

"The dream, father — the dream. What did old Cornelis Hillebrandt say? It has been so heavy on my mind all day; but I would not trouble you then, for you wanted that I should not be idle. But now " —

"Yes — yes, Geretie, the dream," he responded. "I will really try to think. He said — it was something — what was it indeed?"

Strange, perhaps, that her father should have submitted to her questioning with such easy acquiescence in its propriety — strange, perhaps, that he did not laugh at her, and treat her demand as the outcropping of mere exuberant fancy. In the morning he would certainly have done so. But it happened that within the past hour he had drank freely of his punch, — constrained thereto, by his duty as host, it being incumbent upon him, personally, to pledge many civil and military dignitaries, from the Lieutenant-Governor downward. He was not at all disordered thereby, the hard brain of that period never yielding to the hospitable labor of a mere hour or two. But still he was thrown into a pleasant glow of self-content, and into that impressive mood of mind wherein many things seem very natural that at other times might be considered strange. He could not have carried his fancy so far as to have imagined the presence of ghosts or spirits; but it was not so difficult to accept, as truth, the promulgation of a novel philosophical theory. It therefore happened that, with the earnestness of Geretie's pleadings, it seemed no more than rational that one person should, by mistake or mismanagement, have come into possession of another person's dream.

"Yes, I will try to recollect, Geretie; — as well, that is, as that capering tune will let me," he said.

Once more he endeavored to contract his brow with thought; then again gazed across the scene of nodding wigs and plumes and dancing feet, into the hall.   There, too, all heads were moving in symphony with that cheery measure. Even the negroes in the kitchen had been attracted thereby, and slowly, but not the less surely, had edged their way inch by inch through the line of intervening pantries, until they stood in the hall itself. Slaves of the household and slaves of other houses — some in the decent dignity of their masters' cast-off suits, and some in their own fresh liveries — some there as invited guests of the kitchen, and some there officially, as pages, or footmen, awaiting their masters' departure; little by little they had stolen into the hall, and open-mouthed with admiration and excitement, stood looking on in long, unobtrusive row, close against the wall on either side of the mahogany cabinet. As Gisbort now gazed thitherward, a light began to break into his eyes — the light of recollection — and then he turned once more to Geretie.

"It was something about the cabinet, Geretie — it was — yes, I know it now.   Old Cornelis Hillebrandt said —and he smiled pleasantly at me, Geretie, as he might have at you, in spite of all your ideas to the contrary — he said — and he held out a long roll of parchment and shook it, as it were, in my face — he said —'*search the mahogany cabinet.*' But what I am to search for, or how or when, I do not know. It seems, indeed, that we all own this Hillebrandt dream, Geretie; and, therefore, it should be sent for something very important. But if, after all, this is the whole of it, why then the sooner we take no further notice of it and forget it altogether, the better."

So Gisbort pleasantly spoke, with a knowing wink; emboldened, — as the Byvanck letter seems to hint, — into passing ridicule of the Hillebrandt dream, by the subtle power of the punch.

Chapter VI.

EVEN as Gisbort thus spoke, there came from the hall a slight cry of alarm, mingled with the sharp sound of splintering wood, the mahogany cabinet was seen to bend forward with a rocking motion, then recovers itself, while a portion of its heavy cornice fell to the floor. There was a momentary stir among the guests, and Geretie and her father hurried to the scene of the disturbance.

Nothing alarming, indeed. It was speedily ascertained that the mischief all came from the little negro boys Rak and Tak. They had been in the line of self-invited guests from the kitchen; and finding it impossible, by reason of their immature stature, to see all that they desired, had climbed upon the shoulders of two tall footmen, steadying themselves in that uneasy position by clinging to the front cornice of the mahogany cabinet. There for a while standing content, until their supporters becoming restive beneath their weight had suggested a descent. Thence it was no more than natural that Rak and Tak, looking around for respite and seeing how smooth was the top of the cabinet, should have decided upon climbing thereon. But the heavy cornice, upon which for the moment they hung wriggling in their attempted ascent, though stoutly framed had not been calculated to sustain the weight of two clumsy, half-grown negroes; and therefore breaking off with a crash had let them down upon the floor, itself tumbling after them. No bodily damage was found to have been done. The authors of the mischief picking themselves up, slunk off between the legs of the other servants into the kitchen, there doubtless to meet the ire and the uplifted spoon of old Chloe. The guests prepared to resume the interrupted dance; no evidence of the disturbance remained except the mutilated front of the cabinet. Where once there had been a cornice, there was now exposed a long narrow opening, not before known to have existed — in fact, a secret recess.

"See, father," cried Geretie, grasping him by the arm, and, pale with sudden excitement, pointing upward to the opening. "Surely it must be there that you were told to search."

At first sight, indeed, there seemed nothing to tempt a search; but following the direction indicated, her father raised himself upon a chair and thrust in his arm. Far back in the cabinet, his hand encountered a roll of parchment, dusty, torn and time-stained. Carefully he spread it out between Geretie and himself. And lo! a word being deciphered here and there revealed the long missing Hillebrandt Patent, signed by their High Mightinesses of Holland, and with their great, heavy seal attached; furthermore signed and sealed by His Excellency Governor Stuyvesant; and in order that no formality might be neglected, having in one corner a rude picturing of bow and arrows, the emblematic signature of some

Indian chief who had previously owned the patented tract of land.

The Hillebrandt Patent, indeed! The long sought evidence wherewith the heir might now recover all his rights! As Gisbort once more rolled up the parchment, there stepped before him a young, slight-built officer of the British army — one of those two or three who had not danced, and quietly took the patent into his own hands.

"Mine at last, is it not?" he said. "I could not but believe that in the end fate would favor me."

The light-brown beard and his studied seclusion in a distant corner of the room had hitherto prevented Heybert's recognition; not to speak of the alteration made by the military uniform, so honestly won by brave deeds against the French, upon the Canadian frontier. But, in spite of all such disguises, the voice could not be mistaken; and with a cry, Geretie threw herself forward and clung to him. A foolishly impulsive girl, of course; and who, more properly, should have stood apart in maidenlike reserve, until she might be asked for, with all solemn dignity of form. Indiscreet, indeed, to make a scene before that wondering crowd. But it passed off very well, somehow; nor was she obliged to endure the ignominy of repulse, inasmuch as Heybert placed his arm about her, and drew her still closer to his side.

"You see how it is," he said to her father, with a quiet smile. "You cannot but feel that after all it must be so."

"Yes, Heybert, I suppose that it must be so," Gisbort rejoined. And this is all that passed. But every one soon knew what had been said; and so, in a moment, the word went round that Heybert Hillebrandt had returned, and that Geretie had at last become his promised bride. And though there were those who said that old Gisbort Van Twiller would not have consented, except for the fortunate discovery of the missing patent, they did him wrong; since in his heart he had already relented, seeing that the affair with Rollof Van Schoven had by no means prosperously advanced, and that Geretie would doubtless have proved obstinate in her choice to the very end.

Therefore the matter stood thus decided in those few words; and after some temporary buzz of comment, the dancing was resumed as though it had never been interrupted. And now, Gisbort, taking pleasant consultation with himself, and, doubtless, gaining courage through one or two additional glasses of punch, came to one of those resolves, that if failing, gain all the odium of foolhardiness; but that, if succeeding, are looked upon as the product of pure inspiration. Nothing did he say to Mistress Lysbeth, who, doubtless, acting according to the dictates of social ceremony, would, from the very first, oppose his plan; but craftily retiring into a distant corner, he beckoned up young Johan Van Twiller, his nephew.

"Run, Johan," he whispered, " run at once to the Hillebrandts and all the rest of them. Tell them that Heybert has returned and is to marry Geretie; that the old quarrel should be made up at last; and that they must, every one of them, come without delay, to the Christmas party. Tell them, too — if they say anything about it — that when Heybert and Geretie are married, I will give them the mahogany cabinet for one of their wedding presents. Now start off at once; and, as you know what is good for you, never stop to say a word about it to Aunt Lysbeth."

With a nod of shrewd comprehension, young Johan hurried off and soon delivered his message in different quarters of the city. There was much excitement thereat, and hurried putting on of old brocades and satins, and stitching together of laces and piling up of head-dresses; for all those guests who had remained away from the great entertainment had done so with regret powerfully tugging against the necessary display of resentment, and each one now hailed with pleasure the opportunity to come in at last, with dignity unimpaired. Never in all Albany, or elsewhere, indeed, either before or since, had so many fair dames and damsels departed, with such success, from their custom of giving up many hours to the toilet, and made themselves ready in so few minutes.

At one time, indeed, there was a chance that their coming might work disastrously, after all. For when, in the Van Twiller mansion, it became known that Heybert was to be permitted to marry Geretie, the Van Schoven family and all their adherents naturally took offense, conceiving that a slight had been committed upon their young kinsman, and, therefore, that family self-respect demanded the ceremonious departure of each and all of them.

Whereby such stern resolves began to be formed, that it became more than likely that the stream of reconciled Hillebrandts, Hogebooms, Jansens, Tienhovens and Wyncoopes coming in would encounter at the very door a tide of angry Van Schovens, Swartwouts, Winegaerts and Van Fredingborcks going out. But young Rollof Van Schoven, seeing that a storm was brewing, took his kindred one by one aside; and told them that he had renounced all claim to Geretie, not merely now but the day before, inasmuch as he had then met a scout who had led him to suspect that Heybert, instead of being destitute among the Hurons, was serving, with glory, in the British army, and would soon return. Whereat they being all, in secret, loth to depart from such a pleasant party unless obliged to by their principles, wisely argued that if Rollof was not dissatisfied, neither should they be; and so remaining, joined heartily in the grateful work of reconciliation.

And now once more the sets were formed, and the three black fiddlers played another tune still merrier than any that had gone before, though that might seem scarcely possible; so that it was said that the Lieutenant-Governor became inspired to engage in another minuet, and essayed to lead out old Mistress Barbara Van Schoven. This, indeed, was scarcely credited; though many of those who disbelieved the story, afterward gave unwavering credence to the tradition, that the portrait of Governor Van Twiller had nodded its head all through the dance in pleased sympathy. And, again, was the punch bowl filled; for, of course, Gisbort and his friends must drink many reconciliatory glasses with the newly arrived Hillebrandts and Hogebooms and all the others.   And so the Christmas party was kept up, with fun and frolic, even until the clock struck twelve — a departure from time-honored custom — which caused much comment; whereat the English minister and the Dutch dominie, upon the next Sunday, felt constrained to interpolate their sermons upon the "Character of Jereboam" and the "Massacre of the Innocents," with some suitable remarks about the growing tendency to social dissipation.   This reproof was properly received by all the young, and, doubtless, did them much good; but was not as well favored by the wardens and elders, inasmuch as it necessarily caused an alteration in discourses that might better have been left as they had always been used to hear them.

So, after all, on that Christmas day, the pretty Geretie obtained her present of a husband, and chosen by herself, as she had proclaimed to be her right; while at the same time Heybert Hillebrandt regained his ancestral manor.   Not much of a manor, indeed.   Only some three or four miles broad upon the river and ten or twelve miles deep, and with not more than eighteen or twenty first-class mill sites.   But, for all that, a property well suited for the support of two young people of moderate tastes and ambition; while the future soon revealed the story of its proper management.   For, before many years, the Hillebrandt house was built, not far from the Van Twiller mansion; not as large, indeed, inasmuch as already property upon that street was becoming costly, and even the most wealthy could no longer afford houses of over seventy-five feet front. But to make amends, it rejoiced in the hitherto unknown extravagance of a stone stoop, and had a gilded weathercock upon the gable as handsome as the Van Twiller weathercock. And within the house was a large sitting-room, in all respects like the Van Twiller sitting-room, except that over the fireplace, instead of the portrait of Governor Van Twiller, hung that of old Cornelis Hillebrandt. It might have been thought, indeed, that Geretie Hillebrandt would set little value upon the portrait of one who, coming in a dream to visit her and tell about the missing title-patent, so stupidly blundered in his ill-timed approach, that the dream, instead of pertaining to her alone, was broken up, and lay scattered in three heads, and almost irrecoverably lost. But, possibly, she regarded rather the good intent of the act than its careless carrying out. It is certain, indeed, that she looked favorably upon the old councilor; for, in the letter which afterwards, in accurate and circumstantial narration of the dream, she wrote to her dear friend, Mistress Anneke Byvanck, of Kinderhook — the time-stained letter of which we have heretofore so often spoken — she alludes most lovingly to the picture of old Cornelis Hillebrandt, and evidently regards it as the chief and crowning glory of her mansion.

The Ghosts at Grantley.

The Ghosts at Grantley.

CHAPTER I.

THE London stage-coach dropped me at the gate-lodge of Grantley Grange, and according to my usual custom I started up to the Hall on foot. It was such a pleasant Christmas morning as perhaps is not often seen, and might well have tempted to a longer walk than that short mile up the carefully trimmed avenue. There had been a slight fall of snow, a mere sprinkle indeed; but it was sufficient to clothe the brown turf with a dainty tint of pearl, and to make the dry leaves rattle crisp beneath the feet, and to project the great oaks in seemingly more ancient grandeur against the brightened back-ground, and generally to give an unusually cheery and exhilerating aspect to the whole scenery of the park.

When I had nearly reached the Hall, the church clock struck noon, and immediately all the bells began to ring out a merry Christmas peal. Up and down, hither and thither, now a snatch of tune and again a meaningless clashing of all the bells at once — single notes and double and triple concords, and, in fact, every thing that well-disposed bells ever

can or will do — so it ran on right cheerily. Now
it was that I anticipated my Uncle Ruthven would
hasten out to meet and welcome me. For I knew
that he was fond of listening to the chimes; and
when the changes were being sounded upon them he
would not unfrequently sit at the open window, the
better to enjoy them. And of course, as I could now
plainly see the Hall through the leafless trees, he from
his open window could as readily watch my approach.
Somewhat to my momentary chagrin, however, he
did not come forth or even meet me at the door, and
I was suffered to enter unannounced. And passing
through the main hall, I wandered into the library.

There I found my Uncle Ruthven standing in the
middle of the floor, his head thrown back, his eyes
fixed intently upon the opposite wall, one arm raised
in front to the level of his face, the other hand thrown
behind him, an expression of resolute determination
impressed upon every feature, his whole appearance and position resembling that of the antique
Quoit Thrower. Evidently he had been engaged in
similar action; for, in a moment, he stepped to the
other side of the room, picked up a short, fat book
which had been thrown thither, and replaced it upon
the table.

"Anatomy of Melancholy," he remarked, turning
to me with a little chuckling laugh. "The first
person who for a long while has got the book all
through him — eh, Geoffrey? Though, of course, we
all relish a little of it, now and then. Hit him directly
upon the breast, and it went through him as through
a summer mist, dropping out behind between his

shoulder blades. Of course he has vanished, taking the hint of not being longer wanted here.”

“Who, Uncle Ruthven?” I asked.

“Why, the ghost, of course,” was the answer.

I was a little startled at this. It is true that I had sometimes thought that the library at Grantley Grange might be just the place for ghosts. It was wainscoted heavily with carved oak darkened in tint with the seasoning of four centuries. Above, the walls were covered with hangings of Spanish leather, stamped in quaint pattern. The fire-place was deep set and broad — so deep and broad, indeed, that the great logs smoldering within appeared no larger than ordinary sticks. The windows were projected into oriels with heavy mullions and let in the light, encumbered with a thousand stray shadows. The tables and chairs and high book-cases seemed almost immovable with their sculptured massiveness, and as though designed for a race of giants. Queer lamps hung from the ceiling and grotesque candle-sconces projected themselves from the walls, each with heavy metal shades that would shut in more light than they sent forth. Over the mantel and beside the doors were paintings blackened with age; a Salvator Rosa, turned by the grime of time into a mere confusion of different shadows, with only here and there a touch of faded light for contrast, and, on either hand, eight or ten old portraits in ruffs and crimson coats and armor, cracked and worm-eaten and sometimes almost undistinguishable in face, but serving in costume to show the different careers into which, in times past, the fates or inclinations of the originals had carried them. A gloomy old library, indeed, full of crevices that would not stay closed, and cobwebs that could not be got at, and drafts that came from no one knew where, and flickering shades that seemed to obey no philosophic law, but stole here and there across wall and ceiling as their fancy led them. So that not unnaturally it appeared at times as though the place could never have been made for man's enjoyment, but rather as a hall for witches' Sabbath or ghostly revels; and as I watched the subdued and hesitating flickering of an errant sunbeam across the tarnished gilt pattern of the Spanish leather, it was not difficult for queer fancies and imaginings to take hold of me. But, after all, they were mere idle conceits, and at the most I had not for an instant anticipated the actual presentment of unearthly visitants.

"The ghost, did you say?" I therefore repeated, in some amazement.

"Yes, the ghost. Has been here every Christmas for many a year. Always comes just as the chimes strike up at noon, as regularly as though they had waked him. If you had ever before this happened to spend a Christmas with us, you might have met him yourself. Assumes that he belongs to the house, and that therefore he has his vested rights in it. Frightened me a little at the first, but have become used to him now and do not care. Am rather disposed, indeed, to lord it over him with high hand; and he is such a patient ghost that it hardly seems to make much difference with him. Am sorry always, in fact, if I speak crossly to him.

But, then, you know my temper, Geoffrey, and how
little I can brook presumption. How, then, would
you feel if a ghost were to come, implying that he
was the master of the house and that you were
merely a visitor? Gets just so far, indeed, and then
vanishes without telling any thing important."

I looked wonderingly at Uncle Ruthven thus
calmly discoursing about the supernatural.

"But do you ever let him get further than that?"
I suggested, my eyes wandering to the book upon
the table.

"Perhaps not, Geoffrey — perhaps not. I suppose that if I were more patient he would talk a
little better to the purpose. But then I am very
quick tempered, and it is so exasperating, every
Christmas to go through the very same thing. I
always throw a book at him and am sorry for it
afterward. It is certainly not the hospitable thing
upon my part. But then to be so constantly beset,
year after year, and not to know how many more
there may be of them. For there is at least one other
ghost somewhere about the house, Geoffrey. I have
never seen him, but Bidgers the butler has, and he
says it is as like this fellow as two peas. And if I
am too polite to them, who knows but that they
may be encouraged to come in swarms and make
the house very uncomfortable? But let us leave
all that for the present. You will be wanting to
see your room, I suppose. The South Oriel, just
past the second landing. Bidgers will carry up
your portmanteau. Am sorry, by the way, that
Lilian has not yet returned from the continent.
She could, of course, make your stay much more

pleasant for you than I can. But will do my best, Geoffrey. Luncheon at one, as usual."

Escorted by Bidgers, I proceeded up stairs to the South Oriel. It was a large apartment upon the south side of the house, with a broad octagonal window projection. If possible, the furniture was heavier and more antiquated than that of the library. There were quaint old tapestry hangings to the bedstead, so queer and faded that it seemed almost as though they might have been embroidered during the Crusades. The wardrobe was a marvel of size and solidity, and gave the impression that in troublous times, obnoxious owners of the estate might have safely been concealed in a false recess. Other articles of furniture were in similar style, and all together gave quite a gloomy aspect to an apartment that naturally, if left to itself, might have been well disposed to be cheerful. The effect was not diminished by a dingy picture over the mantelshelf, representing a funeral urn and drooping willow worked in hair, with an exceedingly numerous and mournfully dressed family coming two by two down a winding path to weep in concert around the tomb. While I gazed solemnly at this work of art, a ragged yew tree kept striving at every breath of wind to thrust one of its gnarled old branches in at the window; and putting all things together, the cheerfulness went out of me entirely, and the idea of ghosts came in quite as naturally as in the library. I tried to shake it off, remembering my late experience and not wishing to have my mind burdened with any further queer fancies of the kind; and after a moment or two, indeed, seemed to be succeeding very tolerably and became able to hum an operatic drinking song with comparative ease and correctness. Just then, however, happening to turn my head, I saw a strange figure standing near the foot of the bed and gazing at me with fixed but not unpleasing or unfriendly expression.

The figure of a pleasant young fellow; not, to all appearance, over twenty-two years of age, and exhibiting a life-like rotundity and opacity that would have prevented any suspicion in my mind of the supernatural, if I had not had my uncle's word for it, or if I had discovered any way in which the stranger could have entered the room without my seeing him. A handsome young fellow, courtly in manner and dress, with coat of purple velvet, slashed and embroidered the whole length of the sleeves, a dainty little rapier swinging at his side and a plumed cap held in his hand. Hair falling in long curls over his broad lace collar, and the beard twisted into a point, while the small mustachios also twined into points turned up against the cheeks. A mild, responsive kind of face, with courteous smiles and replete with indications of gentle disposition.

"I am exceedingly happy to meet you," he remarked, playing with the gold-lace upon his sword hilt. "The more so that since I have been ill, so few persons come to visit me at all. I do not know that I have seen anybody of late, excepting the butler; and even he appears to be a new butler, most unaccountably put into possession by some other and pretended authority. I must inquire into it when I am completely restored."

"You say that you have been ill?"

"Yes; a faintness and much uneasy want of rest at night, principally arising from this lump in my chest; and that, in turn, coming from the attack upon me by my brother Harold. Would be glad to introduce him to you if it were not for that. But I put it to you now: after what has happened could I show him any such attention, or, indeed, associate with him at all? If cousin Beatrice were here, now —"

At this moment there came a rap at the door; and the ghost, shrinking a little toward one side, began to pale before me, and I saw that he was slowly fading away, beginning at the legs, and so the line of invisibility extending upward until gradually the whole figure had entirely vanished. Again I saw in its entirety the carved foot-board which he had hitherto partially obscured; there was nothing left, indeed, to remind me of the strange visitant. And opening the door I saw only Bidgers, the butler.

"Luncheon is ready, Master Geoffrey," he said. "No fish to-day, for the West stage is not in, but the mushrooms is particularly fine. Heard you talking to the ghost as I came along — the upstairs ghost, not Sir Ruthven's down-stairs ghost. Sir Ruthven has only seen the down-stairs one, but I've seen both. Saw this one last Christmas, about this time. He would not speak to me, however, it being that I am only the butler. They're very much alike, Master Geoffrey. There's a very nice haunch of venison for dinner to-day, let me recommend; and the kidneys is not to be despised, either."

Chapter II.

After that, and during the remainder of my visit, nothing else happened especially worthy of mention. The Christmas festivities passed off as they generally do; and the next morning I returned to London, where my recollection of the ghosts soon began to die away. At first, indeed, as is natural, I could think of nothing else. But inasmuch as my Uncle Ruthven had taken the matter so coolly, I began to be impressed by a careful and more deliberate consideration of his manner, and to wonder whether I might not have imagined many of the most singular circumstances attending the incident; until, at last, I concluded that there could have been no ghost at all, but that I must have dreamed the whole story.

In addition, my time became so fully occupied that I had few occasions in which I might engage in desultory wandering of idle curiosity or speculation; for during the first eight months I was diligently employed reading for my admission to the Bar. After that, I was actively forgetting most of what I had learned, giving myself up as escort to my cousin Lilian. She had returned from her travels upon the continent, and with her father was stopping awhile in London before continuing on to the Grange. It was my pleasing duty to remain at Lilian's side most

of the time, Sir Ruthven being glad to avoid the toil
of active companionship. I was very much in love
with Lilian, but would not for the world have prematurely told her of it — it would have made her so
tyrannical. At last, of course, we quarreled. It
was the day before Sir Ruthven and Lilian returned
home; and she informed me that she was going on
the 10.45 stage-coach, and that she would be seriously displeased if I attempted to see her off. This
looked well for me upon the whole, I thought,
and I started for the coach at once. As ill luck
would have it, I missed it, a circumstance which
really helped my cause; since Lilian, being thereby persuaded that I understood it to be a lasting quarrel, felt suitably piqued into anxiety and
regret.

A little before Christmas, Sir Ruthven wrote me
to run down to the Grange as usual. With his
letter came a perfumed note from Lilian, stating that
if she could, she would gladly be away at Christmas
with her Aunt Eleanor; but since she could not, but
was obliged to remain home, she would consider it a
great insult if I presumed to visit the Grange before
she could get away in some other direction. I was
wonderfully encouraged at this, feeling that all was
going on well; and packing my trunk at once, I
went down by the earliest stage on Christmas
morning.

Again the chimes happened to be ringing just as
I alighted; and, as before, no one coming forth to
meet me, I pressed on to the library, there to make
my respects to Uncle Ruthven, feeling well assured

that I should find him in his accustomed seat beside the fire-place. He was in the room, indeed, but not sitting down. He was standing beside the chair and bowing with great affectation of cordiality to some one in the further corner of the room. Looking in that direction, I beheld a young fellow in court suit of two centuries ago, with hand upon his heart, bowing back to my uncle with still greater excess of old-fashioned courtesy and cordiality; and I did not for an instant doubt that I was looking upon the down-stairs ghost. Almost the duplicate of the other one, indeed. Evidently about the same age, with equally agreeable, sunny, ingratiating expression. Like the other, he had thick curls falling over the collar, beard cultivated to a point, slashed velvet coat, laces, gold tassels, and a slim, daintily decorated rapier. The most notable differences consisted in his complexion and hair being a shade darker, and his coat being of a lively crimson. It was a pleasant thing to see these two persons salaaming cordially and ceremoniously to each other; my uncle bowing until he struck the table behind him, and the ghost bending over in responsive courtesy until the point of the scabbard of his sword tipping up, made a new scratch upon the worm-eaten picture of Salvator Rosa.

"You see, Geoffrey," my uncle whispered between his repeated genuflexions, "he has come again to the very minute. The very same time as last year, just as though the chimes waked him up. I remember that you then thought that perhaps I was accustomed to cut him short rather too suddenly. We will be more cautious now, and will not end until we get his whole story out of him." Then to the ghost: "I am rejoiced to see you once more, kind sir."

"It gives me equal and exceeding pleasure," responded the ghost. "And I know that my brother Arthur would be similarly gratified could he only know about your arrival. But, then, how is he to know? After his conduct toward me — the obloquy he has thrown around me, in fact — it certainly would be beneath my dignity to approach him, even for the sake of imparting information. I can, there-fore, merely myself welcome you."

"Now, just listen to that!" muttered Uncle Ruthven, beginning to flush up angrily. "I have done my best; but is it possible to continue polite-ness with a person who insists upon treating me as his guest? I treat him with all the cordiality I can muster, and the only result of it is that he turns around and seems to patronize me."

It chanced that, moved by the first warmth of my uncle's courtesy, the ghost had advanced a little, as though to meet us, and thereby he now stood between us and the window. This change of posi-tion seemed to produce a marvelous alteration in his appearance. The face so fair and genial and prepos-sessing became at once a queer confusion of lines, every feature being obscured by what looked like converging cuts and wrinkles, making the whole expression of the countenance unintelligible. It was only for an instant, however. The next moment, the ghost moving away from the window, his face became as before — clear, distinct, filled with amiable and courteous refinement and intelligence. It was not until afterward that the mystery explained itself. Now, indeed, the singular appearance had lasted for such a brief moment that it seemed scarcely worth while to seek an explanation. The only thing, in fact, that particularly struck me was a red line extending around the throat, as though the result of a forced compression. This was observable even after the ghost had passed from directly before the window, and until he had moved completely out of reach of the entire spread of sunlight.

"If Cousin Beatrice were here," remarked the ghost in continuation, "she would undoubtedly be very happy to take part in entertaining you. But where is she now? It is some days since I have seen her. Do you think it possible that Brother Arthur, in addition to the ignominy to which he has subjected me by his unjust suspicions, can have influenced her mind against me? If so, as long as I live, I will never—"

"Listen again to that! As long as he lives! How can anybody stand such drivel?" cried Uncle Ruthven. "I suppose, Geoffrey, you will now see that it is as well to put an end to this first as last?"

With that, as upon the previous Christmas, my uncle seized a large book and vindictively let fly at the stranger. If until that time I had had any doubts as to his unsubstantial nature, they were now relieved. Corporeal and opaque as he had seemed, it was none the less true that the volume, striking him in the stomach, passed completely through him as through a stratum of air, falling upon the floor behind, while the figure remained unblemished and uninjured; with this exception, however, that naturally he seemed scarcely pleased with the roughness of the reception, and a shadow of discontent flickered across his face. Then appearing to comprehend that possibly he might be unwelcome, he slowly faded away.

"Middleton's Cicero, this time," remarked my uncle, wiping his face and gazing toward the weapon he had just so successfully used. "And the fellow has digested that as well as the volume last year. At this rate he will get my whole library into him before long. I cannot help it, Geoffrey. You saw that I tried my best to be polite. But when a ghost acts as though he owned the house, and moreover talks as though he were alive, mortal man could not withstand the temptation to cut him down. Well, well, get ready for lunch, Geoffrey. The South Oriel, as last year."

Of course, being sent up to the same room and the old programme seeming to begin being played, I expected once again to meet the purple-coated ghost. And as is natural, I went up with some little trepidation. For it is one thing to have a ghost appear to you, good natured and smiling from the first; and another thing deliberately to throw one's self in the way of a ghost who might not happen at the moment to be in a very pleasant humor, and might exert some supernatural power to make himself extremely disagreeable. All the time I was dressing, I looked uneasily over my shoulder, in search of apparitions. But inasmuch as we seldom find what we most surely expect to see, I was left entirely undisturbed, and finally began my descent to the dining room with feelings greatly relieved and composed.

Passing the drawing-room, I heard the subdued rustle of silk, and entering, found Cousin Lilian all arrayed for luncheon and smoothing herself out before the fire. Of course after what had passed in London, she swept me a stately courtesy, addressing me by my surname as though I were a stranger whom she had casually met the previous day; and of course I bowed in her presence with ceremonious reverence befitting the first presentation of Raleigh to Queen Elizabeth. Then Lilian, slightly lifting her eyebrows in spirit of wonderment at my intrusion, remarked that she believed Sir Ruthven was in the library. I replied that I had already seen Sir Ruthven and had found him busily engaged with a ghost; and that as this seemed to be their reception day and others might be expected by him, I would not intrude upon him for a while, but with her permission would prefer to remain where I was.

These preambles having been thus satisfactorily entered into, of course we began making up by throwing at each other little spiteful remarks of an epigrammatic nature; now and then spontaneous, but for the most part carefully manufactured weeks before and treasured up for the occasion. Snapping these off from side to side like torpedoes, and mutually rebounding them harmlessly from our casemated natures, we gradually composed our feelings and began getting along very well on the path to reconciliation. How long it might have taken under ordinary circumstances I cannot tell; but it happened all at once that Lilian was startled into an unexpectedly rapid advance. For of a sudden I felt her hand grasping my arm, and she called me by my first name in the old familiar manner; and turning, I saw her gaze fixed with a wondering but not altogether alarmed expression upon the opposite corner of the room.

"See, Geoffrey!" she whispered. "The up-stairs ghost! How comes he in here?"

Chapter III.

URNING, I saw the purple velvet ghost at last, bowing low to the floor, with a humble courtesy that disarmed wrath, though none the less did an explanation seem necessary.

"Really, my good sir," I therefore said, "this intrusion — "

"I must apologize for it, certainly," he remarked, again bowing low. "I was a little behindhand this morning in reaching the South Oriel. And passing through the hall, I saw a female figure inside this room. I entered, expecting to meet my Cousin Beatrice. I see that I am mistaken. Last night I slumbered more uneasily than usual — the lump in my chest causing me very great disturbance, and doubtless it has excited my nerves and made me easily deceived. It has all come from Brother Harold's outrage upon me, I suppose. Which being so, it only remains for me to take my leave, with apology for the intrusion."

"Stay yet a moment," I said. "This is my cousin Miss Lilian, who certainly will not fear you and will forgive your slight mistake. And — and I have so much to say to you."

In fact, I felt that this might be the last time I should see him; and that it would be no more than a charity to enlighten him as to his true condition.

It was a very sad thing to see a bright, amiable young ghost going around century after century as though he were still alive, and I decided that it would be a kind action to correct his error. Moreover, it happened that just at this moment, chance threw a convincing explanation within my reach. For as the ghost stepped a little to one side preparatory to taking his departure, it came about that he stood between me and the window, just as the other ghost had done; and in like manner, every feature seemed obscured with a network of contrary lines and wrinkles. But as he chanced to remain there a little longer than the other one had done, the mystery became almost at once revealed. I saw that the singular appearance was caused by the strong sunlight showing through him, whereby his whole head appeared as a transparent object. It was exhibited as a mass of dim, lurid light, not entirely endowed with all the bright translucent qualities of glass, but rather as when a sheet of thin porcelain is held up to the light, so that its semi-cloudy transparency is revealed, and with it, any dark spots or imperfections in the surface are brought to notice. In like manner, our visitor's head now seemed transformed with the brightness of the sunlight behind it, so that its former opacity was gone and there was a light, cloudy appearance as of a dissolving mist, marked in every direction with straight and curved lines of greater or less intensity. At first, the features, excepting as they appeared in profile, seemed entirely to have vanished beneath a confusion of other lines; but a moment's observation assured me of the contrary. They were all still there — the sparkling eye, the delicate mouth, the well-shapen ear. With a little attention, I could still trace the sweep of their several outlines. It was merely that those outlines were now somewhat confused by the addition of other lines appearing from within the skull. These also, I found that with a little study, I could still make out. There was a broad, irregularly-curved mark showing the outline of the lobes of the brain. I could follow the whole ball of the eye beneath its socket and the fainter lines which connect the eye with the brain behind. The drum and the small bones of the ear, and the twisted passages from the nose to the ear were all now clearly defined. The palate, too, and the sides of the throat, until hidden at last beneath the laced collar of that courtly coat. In fine, under the influence of that bright sunlight behind it, the young fellow's head became something like one of the modern medical wax preparations, exhibiting every portion of its frame in exact position; except that, far superior to any work of art, it did not require to be taken apart for study, but could be examined in detail, just as it stood.

"How long," I said, myself moving a little one side so that he might not appear between me and the window; by which judicious movement he became at once like any other person, his features returning to their usual distinctness of outline, unclouded by any rival lines and curves from behind; "how long have you been thus ill and disturbed at night by pain within your chest?"

"A week, or even more, I think," he said.

"Pardon me," I responded; "here is where you have made a trifling mistake in your chronology — you, and the other, as well. This little episode which you believe has occupied a few days or so, has lasted, in reality, upward of two centuries. You have been thrown into a certain condition of mind in which you are unable to take due note of time. Why this is so, I cannot attempt to explain. The melancholy fact remains that you have already been wandering some two hundred years, and for all we know, may be destined to wander to all eternity. In proof of this, I might refer you to your costume, which is of the fashion of Charles the Second; while, in fact, we are living in the thirty-eighth of Victoria."

I paused for a moment here, thinking that he might wish to ask some question. But as he maintained a perplexed silence, I continued:

" You are in further error in believing that the only consequence of some injury you have received has been mere restlessness at night. Instead of which, you died and of course were suitably buried. And consequently, you are not now a man, but merely a ghost. It may be unpleasant to be told this, but it is as well that you should know it first as last. And, after all, there can be no harm in being a well-conducted, creditable ghost. As such, you are allowed to appear each Christmas day for a few minutes, at the expiration of which, doubtless, you return to your grave. There, I presume, you slumber until the next Christmas day, for you seem to have no definite knowledge of your whereabouts. At the least you must be comfortable, which perhaps is more than can be said of many ghosts. Even Hamlet's father seems to have suffered torments; though there is presumptive evidence that he was a very good man, and totally unlike his brother. You are incredulous about what I am now telling you? In proof of it, let me stand you directly in front of the window, so that the sunlight will strike full upon your person. Then let me hold this looking-glass before you. Now studying your reflection carefully, you will see that you are transparent; which, I take it, is the surest proof any man can enjoy of his being a ghost. You can trace out the passages of your ears, the convolutions of your brain, the course of your jugular vein. This line, which you might easily mistake for a nerve or cord, is merely a crack in the looking-glass. Should you feel disposed, hereafter, for your amusement, to study your internal anatomy more thoroughly, I would advise a new and more perfect mirror. But can you any longer doubt your condition?"

"I can no longer doubt, indeed," groaned the ghost. "But what, alas, can I now do?"

"A thousand things," I responded. "I take it that, inasmuch as men must not live idle lives, in like manner ghosts, also, may have their duties to perform. Surely, it can scarcely be intended, in the economy of the unseen world, that they should pass lives — or, rather, existences — of careless idleness. I know that, were I a ghost, I would do my best to find some useful employment. I think that I would endeavor to obtain some occupation that might be

of benefit to the world I had left behind. Suppose,
for instance, that you endeavored to retain some,
even trifling, recollection of the nature of your
abode in the unseen world, how you are associated,
whither you are sent, and other facts of a kindred
character, and were to impart them to the human
race from time to time through myself. Do you not
think that you would be doing great good, as well
as entitling yourself to the gratitude of all living
men?"

The ghost mutely shook his head. Evidently he
did not care particularly about the gratitude of
living men.

"Or suppose," I continued, struck with a new,
and, in my estimation, better idea — for it happened
that I had lately been interesting myself deeply in
medical jurisprudence — "suppose that you were to
apply yourself to the benefit of the human race in an
anatomical or pathological capacity. There is on
record the case of a man who had a hole in the side
of his stomach through which processes of digestion
could be watched, to the great service of medical
science. Need I say that, for every purpose of
interest or utility, you surpass him infinitely? I
must assume, with tolerable certainty, that if your
head is transparent, so, also, is your whole body;
and that the workings of your inner system are
simply hidden from sight by your clothing.
Divested of that, you could easily unfold, in the
strong light of the sun, the entire operations of
your heart, your lungs and your stomach. Daily
could you have your seances, and new discoveries

could be noted down. There must be some thin, ghostly, almost impalpable fluid in your system answering the purpose of blood in the human frame, and of this physicians might succeed in watching the circulation and flow. There are vexed questions in medical science as to the real use of certain vessels and attachments — whether they are actually necessary in the human constitution, or whether they are mere rudimentary relics of a lower organization. These questions you might succeed in determining. In fact"—

I had reached thus far, becoming so transported with the increasing magnitude of my speculations that I no longer looked at the ghost, but with half-closed eyes gazed upward at the ceiling; when suddenly Lilian plucked me gently by the sleeve, and, with quiet movement of the eyes, called my attention more directly to our visitor. He was standing motionless beside the window; but I observed that the pleasant expression had faded from his face, an angry flush was mounting into every feature, grim, transporting rage was clouding every line. And, as I paused in natural hesitation, he turned roughly toward me.

"Have you done?" he cried, bursting out with an old-fashioned oath of the days of the royal Stuarts. "Have you come to the end of your base proposals? Have you reflected sufficiently what it is to dare to suggest to Sir Arthur Grantley, of the Court of Charles, that he should pass his time illustrating the labors and theories of leeches, quacks, and charlatans?"

Another old-fashioned oath, a half withdrawal of the slender rapier from its sheath, a driving it down again with impetuous, angry energy, and the ghost strode wildly out of the drawing-room, and was no more seen. But for two or three moments we could hear him growling forth his queer old court oaths as he rattled away along the outside passage.

Chapter IV.

LILIAN and I gazed at each other in speechless wonderment. The bell rung for luncheon, and we passed toward the dining room; still with thoughts too deep for words.

"Can it be," I said at length, as we entered the other room, "that this person, whom we had supposed to be merely some retainer of the family, was in reality its head? That he could have been an ancestor of yours, Lilian?"

"Papa will know," she answered. "We will ask him at luncheon." Then, when the old gentleman sat eating his nuts and raisins and sipping his wine — before which time he disliked to be disturbed about any thing excepting the occupation immediately in view — she began:

"Was there ever a Sir Arthur Grantley, papa?"

"Let me think," mumbled Uncle Ruthven. "Yes, there was a Sir Arthur about two centuries ago. And now the story begins to come to me. There were two brothers — twins; the oldest having the estate and title, and the youngest being a captain in the Royal Guard. One would have supposed that, being so nearly of an age and closely related, they would have kept the peace; but the contrary was the fact. They quarreled so that one of them murdered the other, and was suitably hanged for it."

" Is there record of the fact, Uncle Ruthven ?"

" Nowhere, unless it may be in the State Trials. I have never looked there. You will find no allusion to it in Burke or Debrett. Those useful and accommodating compilers, out of regard for the family honor, I suppose, merely state that Harold Grantley died, aged twenty-two: a piece of reticence which, after all, was scarcely worth while, considering that it happened so long ago. Time is a great cleanser of family escutcheons. It would be unpleasant to have a murder attached to the reputation of one's father or grandfather; but carry it two centuries back, and no one seems to care. If it were not so, there is scarcely a royal family on earth which would not be hanging its head. I do not read that Her Most Gracious Majesty Victoria ever makes herself miserable about any suspicions attaching to the memory of Queen Mary of Scotland. In fact, rather a disreputable ancestry, if distinguished, is better than none at all. It is scarcely to be supposed, for instance, that any of us would take it much to heart at finding Guy Fawkes seated upon one of the limbs of the family tree. At any rate, we have no reason to complain of this little murder in the Grantley line, seeing that it finished up the direct descent in that quarter and sent down the entail to us through a collateral branch."

With that, having exhausted his knowledge upon the subject, Uncle Ruthven went on sipping his wine and turned the subject upon the culture of turnips. But after luncheon Lilian and myself, feeling by no means contented, slipped up to the library again and took down one of the time-worn dusty volumes of the State Trials. The books had evidently not been moved out of place for years; but it was easy, having the reign, to find all that we wanted, and in a few minutes we opened at the case of *Rex* v. *Grantley.* The book was very heavy, and at the first we spread it upon the table. This proving inconveniently high we took to the sofa, where we let the volume rest on both our laps and read together. It was very pleasant, altogether. It was necessary for Lilian to lean over so that her curls brushed across my shoulder, and at times I could feel her breath warm upon my cheek. That she might have greater strength to hold her share of the book, I passed my arm sustainingly about her waist; a fact which she did not seem to realize, so intent was she upon the story of the murder. We have often read about young men and maidens looking upon the same book and in just such positions. In those narrations it is generally a book of poetry, or at least a novel that interests them. I question if very often a young lady sits with her lover absorbed in the story of a murder committed by one of her own family and reads it without any feeling except of curiosity about its mere incidents, and as coolly as though it were Jack Shepperd or Oliver Twist. But then, as Uncle Ruthven justly observed, it was so long ago.

It appeared, then, from the account in the State Trials, that Arthur and Harold Grantley were twin-brothers of the age of twenty-two. As Uncle Ruthven had stated. Arthur was the oldest and in possession of the title and estate, while Harold held commission in the Palace Guard. Naturally the two brothers were thrown much together, and were supposed to be greatly attached to each other. Of course, they sometimes had their little disagreements; but, until the period of the murder, it was never supposed that there was any especial ill feeling between them. The trouble ensued about noon one Christmas day. Harold had obtained leave to visit his brother at the Grange; and after an early dinner — for they were alone and much form and ceremony was dispensed with — they sat at the table, conversing, eating filberts and drinking their wine. Possibly they had been drinking too much; but not so much, in fact, as to exhibit its effects upon them to any great extent. The most that could be said was, that it might have tended to make them quarrelsome; but as it turned out, this after all was the whole mischief in the case, and much worse in its results than downright and less harmful intoxication. It chanced that Sir Arthur had taken the opportunity of exhibiting to his brother a certain valuable heirloom, known in the family as the great Lancaster diamond, having come into the line from a collateral Lancaster branch. It had lain concealed in a secret closet during the Cromwellian troubles, and had just been brought to light again. It is supposed that Sir Arthur, being attached to their cousin Beatrice and wishing marriage with her, had designed presenting her with the diamond; and that Harold, being equally in love with her and perhaps with no less prospect of success, had made objection; and that from this fact the quarrel had arisen. Be that as it may, their voices were heard in loud dispute; and suddenly Harold calling out for help, his brother was found lying upon his back lifeless and with every appearance about the throat of having been foully dealt with. Harold's account of the circumstance was to the effect that Sir Arthur all at once had thrown himself back in his chair and gasped and seemed to have been seized with a fit. On the other hand, it was argued that young men of his vigorous constitution did not readily die in fits — that the appearances of foul play by strangulation were too evident — that there had certainly been high words between them, a fact, indeed, which Harold was obliged to admit — that the known passion of both the young men for the same lady would have been sufficient of itself to produce fraternal hatred and strife — and furthermore, that Harold would have a supreme interest in his brother's death, by reason of the succession to the estate. And then again, the diamond had disappeared. If the death had been a natural one, the diamond would not have been disturbed; but inasmuch as it was the leading cause of the dissension, nothing was more natural than that the murderer should have made away with it, by throwing it out of the window, into the lake, most likely, so as to remove one great evidence of the crime. Altogether the feeling ran very high against the surviving brother, political prejudices that could scarcely now be explained intervened to increase the excitement, while certain favorites of the king, desiring promotion in the Guard by removal of one person of higher rank, prejudiced the royal mind against pity or pardon. In fine, after much agitation and a protracted trial, young Harold was found guilty and executed.

"And this explains," I said to Lilian, "many circumstances that hitherto have not been clear to me. The red line around the throat of the down-stairs ghost; the pain in the chest of the up-stairs ghost -- a difficulty most naturally resulting from outside pressure — all these things now tell the story very clearly, and agree most wonderfully with the State trials account. Only — which at first seems strange —the murdered now does not seem to remember that he was put to death, nor the murderer that he was executed for it."

"That is, indeed, singular," said Lilian. "But, then, ghosts are so silly!"

"At first sight, it may seem strange," I answered; "but not after a moment's reflection. Violence endured by us in life is very often with difficulty afterward brought to our memory. One has a fall or is stricken down by a club and made senseless; he recovers after awhile, and knows that in some way he has been injured, but does not remember the actual fall or blow. And why should it be different if the injury leads to death? Looking upon it in this light, and with this philosophy, we see the young baronet awakening in the grave with no conception of ever having been killed, but merely with some indistinct idea of previous attack or vituperation. And, in the same manner, we find the younger brother awakening in the belief that he is still alive, and remembering not his execution at

the hands of the law, but only the fact of having
been charged with some outrage against the other,
the nature of which he cannot comprehend, while
the circumstance of any charge being made at all
grievously offends and distresses him."

"All very plausible, indeed," responded Lilian.
"But suppose that, after all, he was innocent?"

"A thing very hard to believe, with so much contrary evidence," I said. "All that is a mere woman's
unreasoning supposition, with endeavor to wipe off
a blemish from the family escutcheon."

"Pho! for the family escutcheon," responded
Lilian, putting up her lips in pho-like form. And
as she spoke she looked so pretty that, having my
arm still about her waist, I began seriously to consider whether I had not better improve the opportunity and now make my offer. So much was
already understood between us, indeed; and every
one, even Lilian herself, knew very well that it was
destined some day to come about, as a suitable
family arrangement long foreseen and often talked
about; and, therefore, what better moment than the
present to unburden my heart?

"I think, Lilian," I said, "that it is about time
I spoke a word or two to you about our future."

"Well, Geoffrey," she replied.

I saw the flush gather in her face, that she
knew what must be coming, that she anticipated
tender avowal with loving expression. In this
last respect, at least, mindful of recent aggrava-
tions on her part, I determined that I would dis-
appoint her.

14

"No," I said, "it is not probable that Harold was innocent. And therefore you must see for yourself, Lilian, that your family have been a most disreputable lot. But for all that, having unfortunately a strong personal prejudice in your favor, I am inclined to believe that I shall not be doing myself too great injustice in offering you my alliance."

"You are very kind, certainly, Geoffrey," she responded. "I cannot but feel intensely gratified at the preference. I suppose that every family must at some time or other meet its misfortune of a public execution or some similar disgrace. I consider it particularly fortunate that with us it has already happened. In your line of the family it is yet to come; and if I may judge by circumstances, it will probably take place during the present generation. And merely that I may legally enjoy the privilege of standing at your side and comforting you during that closing ordeal, I take pleasure in accepting your offer."

And this is how Lilian and I became engaged.

Chapter V.

IT was understood that tne wedding would not take place immediately. Uncle Ruthven had some old-fashioned notions about matrimony, prominent among which was the idea that no young man should marry without having the means of support from his profession, so as to be independent of the fluctuations and liabilities to loss of private fortune. Upon this basis, it was determined that we should not wed until I had made a public and creditable appearance at the Bar.

This came about in the following October. I had been engaged as third counsel in the great case of *Charity-boy v. Churchwarden*, for assault. Churchwarden had boxed the ears of Charity-boy for playing marbles on a tombstone; but unfortunately had not succeeded in catching him to do so until they were over the boundary-line of the graveyard. Upon this defect, want of jurisdiction as to place was alleged, and action brought. The suit had been running nearly five years, and therefore could now reasonably be moved for trial. The rector, curate, half the vestry and three of the bell-ringers had been subpœnaed to give evidence and stood ready. It was necessary to have, in addition, the testimony of the toy-maker who had sold the marbles; and he, it happened, was on his death-bed at the north of

Scotland. A commission had been issued to take his testimony. The toy-maker lay delirious for the most part, having a lucid interval of about half an hour each day, during which he desired to make his will. He was constantly prevented from doing so, however, by the entrance of the commissioners demanding to take his testimony, which so confused him that he always went off wandering again. Pending the execution of the commission, of course an adjournment was desired.

Now it happened that, both the senior counsel being away, it devolved upon me to make the application for the adjournment, and with a little difficulty about the pitch of my voice, I succeeded in doing so. The judge said that if the other side were agreed, there could be no objection; and the other side having duly consented, the adjournment was ordered. Whereupon I wrote down to Sir Ruthven that I had made my first appearance. Sir Ruthven immediately wrote back, asking whether my speech would be reported in the Times. I replied that I did not suppose it would, as the papers were unusually interested in the Montenegro difficulty, to the exclusion of much other valuable news. Uncle Ruthven thereupon responded that he was satisfied, upon the whole, even if the Times was silent about me; and that now that I had resources for support independent of inherited estate, the wedding might come off immediately after Christmas. And he told me to run down the day before Christmas, so that we could have a pleasant little Christmas dinner by ourselves, before the invited visitors began to arrive.

Accordingly, I arrived at Grantley Grange upon the afternoon of the twenty-fourth, and was at once shown to my room by Bidgers, who not only lighted me up, but followed me in to assist in unpacking my wardrobe. And while doing so, naturally with the self-allowance of an old family servant he let his tongue run loose with the gossip and events of the day.

"A hamper just come in, Master Geoffrey, with a fine large salmon; but that is for to-morrow. You must praise it when you see it, for Sir Ruthven sets great store in having got it. There has been no ghosts seen since you was here last — perhaps they have all gone away for good. There is talk that the Earl of Kildare will be at the wedding next week; but any which way, he has sent a silver pitcher. Maybe, after all, the ghosts have all been locked up where they are. Miss Lilian's Aunt Eleanor has done better than the Earl of Kildare though. She cannot come, they say; but such diamond earrings as she has sent — almost as large as filberts, Mr. Geoffrey! As to the grapes to-day, I am fearful there's a little mold on some of them; but the oysters —"

"That will do — thank you, Bidgers," I said, tired of the running stream; and Bidgers, taking the hint, affected to blow a speck of dirt off the sleeve of my wedding coat, and gently glided out of the room. I was not so much tired, indeed, as that I felt I would like to be alone for thought. Something in Bidgers last remark had awakened an association of ideas in my mind; but of such intangible, confused character that I could not follow it up to any

definite purpose. Diamonds as large as filberts —
filberts and diamonds, so ran the words, through
and through my mind like the strain of a tune; but
out of it all I could not, with the utmost concentra-
tion of thought, gain any clue that I might follow
up to a satisfactory certainty.

At night the same — I fell asleep with the old
sequence of words running in my head, still like the
strain of a tune, as sometimes we will set to meter
the thumping of a railroad car. In the middle
of the night I awoke; and then there flashed upon
my mind a solution of the puzzle, but so wild and
improbable, so idiotic and fantastic did it seem, that
at once I discouraged it. Even then, when scarcely
half aroused, and at an hour when the waking fancies
run riot in premonition and alliance with hardly more
fanciful dreams, did I laugh at the crude conception
and try to beat it down, falling asleep again at last
with mind apparently entirely relieved of the foolish
notion. But when in the morning I awoke with the
sun broadly shining in upon me, there again was the
queer idea; and now, wonderful to relate, though I
lay with the collectedness of thought appertaining
to the open day, and with little chance of crude
fancies any longer overwhelming me, the idea,
though still as strange and ghost-like as before, no
longer bore that first impress of the ridiculous, but
was as something real and to be soberly and carefully
considered. At least the experiment suggested by it
might be tried, though secretly and cautiously, so as
not to provoke ridicule in case it came to nothing.

Dressing myself, I stole softly down stairs. It

was still very early, and there was no one stirring below, excepting a housemaid dusting the furniture. She merely looked up and then continued her task, my habit of morning walks being too well known to excite observation. I passed through the long window and came upon the bare winter-stained lawn. There was the gardener, muffling anew some plants in straw; but he too, merely touching his hat, said nothing. Then I followed a gravel path around the terrace to the rear of the house, and thence struck off to a little grove of pines a hundred yards or so away.

In the midst of these was the burial vault of the Grantley family. It was by no means a repulsive object, being merely a brick erection a few feet above the surface of the ground, and originally constructed with some pretense of architectural symmetry. Neither was it an object of superstitious or sentimental reverence. In fact, at the present time there were not more than twelve or fifteen of the family laid away in it. It had been built four centuries ago, and with accommodation for a hundred or so; but at the time of the rebellion a party of Cromwell's troops came sweeping down upon the house, and, being in want of material for bullets, turned all the dead Grantleys out of doors and took their leaden coffins to cast into ammunition. After that time the burials continued for only a few generations; since which, the yard around the village church had received the family dead. About ten years ago it had been found necessary to open the vault in order to get the date of some particular death for legal evidence. The long-closed door had stoutly resisted, and at length the lock was obliged to be broken. It was intended, of course, to restore the fastenings; but equally of course, and as happens so often with matters that can be done any day, the duty was postponed from time to time, and gradually came to be no longer remembered. The closed door then warped open a little of itself, and the gardeners leaned their tools against it, and after awhile pushed the door further back, and slipped their tools just inside out of the rain; and so, step by step, the almost empty vault became only used as a tool-house. Vines were trained to grow over it, ferns gathered around its base, and a stranger would have taken it for a somewhat dilapidated ice-house.

I pushed the door open yet a little further and peeped within. The sunbeams, still low and shut out by the screen of trees, could not now enter; but enough light stole in to show a pile of rakes and hoes just inside, and a little further along, a row of empty recesses, built for coffins, but long since made vacant. Entering, I could see that the recesses ran in double rows for some distance in front of me, being at the further end shrouded in darkness. I drew out my cigar lighter and by the aid of repeated tapers proceeded to explore. Then I could see that at the further end, a few of the recesses were filled with coffins. These were in various stages of decay. In all cases, the dark coverings of cloth had mouldered away and lay in fragments at the side or on the stone floor below. In some, the outer wooden shells were nearly whole; but in others, they had crumbled into dust and splinters. With a few of the recesses, the names and dates of the remains within were fastened at the lower edge upon brass plates; with others, the plates had entirely disappeared. There was one recess which contained a worm-eaten coffin of somewhat plain construction, but no name or date or even evidence that any such had ever been affixed. I could not resist the impression that here lay the unfortunate Harold Grantley; given, as matter of right, a place in this ancestral vault, but, through some charitable idea of letting his unhappy fate become forgotten, denied all record that could lead to future identification. Passing onward, with gathering assurance that my search would not prove unavailing, at each minute renewing my quickly expiring tapers, I carefully read every name, now and then rubbing the brass plates with my handkerchief before I could decypher the blurred old-fashioned letterings. Then, for a while, as the number of remaining niches one by one was lessened without rewarding my search, hope began to give way to disappointment. Only for a moment, however; for soon, to my abundant gratification, I read upon one of the plates the words and characters, "Arthur Grantley, Obt. Dec. 25, 1663, Aet 22."

Here then, lay he whom I sought, and I scrutinized attentively all that remained. A moth-eaten, rat-torn pall, a nest of coffins, and that was all. Uneasily for the instant I turned my head, dreading lest the blithe young apparition with its purple and laced coat and dangling sword should arise and demand wherefor I was about to disturb him; but all remained quiet about me. I was alone with my own thoughts and purposes, and could prosecute my designs unquestioned and unimpeded.

I had feared lest I might be obliged to seek for assistance, but it was not so. Every thing, in fact, seemed made ready and convenient for me. The outer box was worm-eaten, warped and decayed, so that it could be broken and brushed away in places with a mere stroke of the hand; the leaden coffin inside had corroded, and the solder of the seams parted, so that the joints had spread apart, and, with no great effort, I was able to bend open the end; the mahogany coffin inside of all had suffered similar decay with the outer box, and readily parted. In a moment the outer end of all three coffins lay open, and I could easily insert my hand.

For a moment I hesitated. What if, as sometimes happens, the remains had not suffered corruption, and my touch were to encounter a solid form! Repressing this fear, I passed my hand stealthily within, finding no obstruction. Only a little dust at the bottom, hardly deep enough for a finger to write a name upon. This was all that was left of the gay young courtier, twelfth baronet of Grantley. Slowly I let my hand wander up along the bottom of the coffin, groping among the dust, until two-thirds up to the top; then I struck against a small, hard lump. My heart gave a loud thump of excitement. What could it be? Was it the prize that I had hoped for, or was it merely some fragment of unpulverized bone? Half wild with tremulous expectation, I grasped the little lump of substance firmly between thumb and forefinger, and hurried with it to the door of the vault. Even as I approached the dim, lurid light just within the half-opened entrance, I began to feel my assurances grow more sure; and when I emerged into the bright glow of day beyond, and held my prize up against the golden rays of the risen sun, I could no longer doubt that I had gained possession of the long lost Lancaster diamond.

Chapter VI.

WHEN I returned to the house, I said nothing about what I had been doing. It seemed as though the time for explanation would not come until toward evening. How, in that broad garish light of morning, could I venture to reveal that secret of dreams and darkness and rifled tombs? How, indeed, would my story be believed, unless with the glow of nightfall thrown around it to attune the listeners to credence?

Moreover, what if, during the day, the ghost were to appear, condemn my invasion of his sepulchre, demand his diamond, and possibly, by threats of supernatural force and terrors, obtain it? Certainly the accustomed hour for the ghosts was close at hand, and at any moment they might visit us. Already Sir Ruthven sat in the library awaiting his especial apparition. My uncle was, for the time, in no particularly friendly mood toward ghosts; and he now loudly declared that, whatever might before have been his courtesy, his forbearance had at last ceased, and he would not tolerate their coming. Certainly not now, he said, seeing that the house was preparing for a season of festivity, and had other things than the next world to think about. Accordingly he sat, watching, in his great elbow chair, with the heaviest volume of the Encyclopædia

Brittanica at his side, in readiness to crush out the first sign of ghost before even a word of salutation could be uttered.

But to the wonder of all and greatly to Sir Ruthven's disgust as well — seeing that, having made up his mind for action, he did not like to feel that his time had been thrown away — no ghost appeared, upstairs or down. Punctually at twelve, indeed, the chimes rang out the merriest peal we had enjoyed for years — the changes were sounded by the hundred with unusual exactness and celerity; yet all the time my uncle sat unmolested, with his Encyclopædia lying idle beside him. At length the day wore itself out, the bell sounded for dinner, and we repaired to the dining room.

It was to be our last little dinner by ourselves; a very small Christmas party, indeed, but on the morrow the guests would begin to arrive and to break up our privacy, and then there could be no complaint about lack of excitement in the household. This last day Sir Ruthven had desired we should have for ourselves. But few as we were, no one had forgotten that it was the Christmas season and should be honored accordingly. Holly and mistletoe decked the room in every direction. A great yule-log lay cosily esconced in the chimney-back and good humoredly tried to blaze up as merrily as the smaller branches that crackled around it: though being so unwieldy, it was not very successful in the attempt. But those smaller branches, invading the yule-log's smoldering dignity with their blithe sport of gaiety, snapped and sputtered around it with uproarious

15

mirthfulness; sending none but the prettiest colored
smoke wreaths up the chimney, and casting out
bright tongues of flame that lighted up every corner
of the room and gave a ruddy glow to the time-
faded portraits, and even brought out patches of
cheerful sunlight upon an old cracked Rembrandt
that no one had ever been able to decypher.

The table was set for us three only; but, in honor
of the day, with as much ceremony as though there
were to be twenty present. A tall branch wax-light,
used only on occasions of great festivity, was
brought out from its green baize covering and planted
in the center. Treasures of antique silver, the very
existence of which Sir Ruthven had nearly forgotten, were exhumed from their places of long concealment, and now once more, as in past centuries,
pleasantly glimmered in the gentle gleam of wax-
light.   Flowers here and there unobtrusively exhaled
sweet odors from tiny vases.   There was to be a
boar's head brought out and placed on the table at
the proper time for each of us to look at and taste
and pretend to enjoy. The plum-pudding was turning
out a great success — the greatest for many years, as
Bidgers whispered to me. All the circumstances of
the scene around us were soft, harmonious and cheerful; certainly now was the time for me to tell my
story.

With some little affectation of ceremony, perhaps,
I drew forth the Lancaster diamond and placed it in
Lilian's hand.   I told her that I could make her no
more valuable Christmas gift than to restore this
rich family relic of the past. Lightly I touched

upon the process whereby I had found it; rather elaborating, instead, the train of thought that had led me to suspect where it had lain hidden. I explained how the finding of the diamond gave new illustration to the record in the State Trials, proving that the younger brother had not been guilty of any murder at all — that during the agitation of a quarrel the older brother must have accidentally swallowed the diamond, mistaking it for one of the filberts that lay beside it near his plate, and which were of similar size — how that this unfortunate error had been sufficient of itself to cause his death by suffocation — how that thereby the discoloration around the neck of the deceased, as well as the disappearance of the diamond were properly accounted for — how that, most probably, it also gave an explanation of the unpleasant lump in the chest of the crimson-coated ghost.

"It is doubtless so," a soft voice thereat interrupted. We all looked up; and, at the further side of the table, we beheld both the ghosts. More alike now than ever before, it seemed to me; only with that single difference of color of the coats. The same bright engaging faces, the same gentle manner; as now, all heart burnings seemingly healed, they stood with their arms bound lovingly about each other in fraternal embrace.

"We have heard it all," continued the crimson ghost, "and thereby we find an explanation of some things that we never thought of before. Both Brother Arthur and myself now know that we are dead ; and that it is fitting, therefore, that we should no longer haunt these scenes, to which indeed, we have no claim. I know that I have been hanged; a matter, however, which occasions me no concern, seeing that I deserved it not. I should at any rate have been dead long before this; and since my family can be satisfied of my innocence and I know that my Brother Arthur, in spite of a few harsh words, loves me still the same, I care not for others' opinions."

"And I," said the purple ghost, "cannot sufficiently thank you for the relief you have given me. Nightly have I lain in what I now perceive was my grave, unable to sleep by reason of the strange lump in my chest. This morning about eight, there came sudden relief; such sweet relief, indeed, that I overslept myself, and for the first time in many years have missed the chimes, and neglected at the appointed hour to make my usual Christmas visit. Even this bodily relief, perhaps, is not equal to what I feel at knowing that in reality I have suffered no wrong at the hands of Brother Harold. I think that if now we could only agree about the only subject which has ever estranged us — by which I refer to our mutual attachment to Cousin Beatrice we might —"

"I think I can easily make your mind easy about that matter," remarked Uncle Ruthven, coming forward. "If you will bear with me a minute, I will show you the life-like picture of your Cousin Beatrice in after days."

He lifted one of the branch candlesticks from the table, and directed its light upon a painting on the wall. The portrait of Cousin Beatrice in more advanced life. A cracked, blackened and moth-eaten picture; but in which, by singular chance, the face had remained intact. The face of a woman who had long survived the natural freshness and graces of youth, and had gained in place of them none of those more matured and ennobling qualities that dignify age. The patched and painted and powdered face of a woman given up to all lightness and frivolity; a face in which there was nothing sweet or pleasant or kindly; in which all the art of Sir Godfrey Kneller had not succeeded in mingling with accurate likeness one spark of generous nature or blotting out the appearance of sordid vanity that pervaded it throughout all.

"The portrait of your Cousin Beatrice in her fiftieth year," remarked my Uncle Ruthven. "She never married, and was noted at Court for her skill in cheating at cards."

The two young ghosts gazed for a moment intently at the picture. As they did so, it seemed as though their embrace grew more intimate and fraternal. At last they turned again, as satisfied.

"I do not think that we shall ever quarrel again about Cousin Beatrice, even if at times we forget that we are all dead," the older ghost then said, with a sweet smile. "And now that all differences are so pleasantly made up, it remains for us only to bid you farewell. And since Brother Harold can now rest in his grave untroubled by any idea of wrong from me, and I can sleep, no longer annoyed by the lump that pained my chest, it is probable that we shall never be aroused to visit you again."

"But stay a moment," cried Uncle Ruthven, fairly

touched at heart, and no longer remembering the Encyclopædia. "You will not go so soon? At least you will take dinner with us?"

As he spoke the ghosts had already begun to vanish, the line of invisibility starting at the feet, as before, and working upward until they were half gone. Then, for a moment, the line trembled irresolutely, and so began to descend until again they stood entirely revealed. It was as though a person going out at a door had indeterminately held the handle for an instant and then returned.

"Moreover," continued my uncle, "I have apologies to make for many a past act of rudeness toward one of you."

"It is forgotten already," said the crimson ghost, bowing. "What do you say Brother Arthur, can we wait a little longer?"

"A very few minutes, Brother Harold, if only to give myself time to make amends for an act of impoliteness on my part toward this other gentleman only last year."

So they seated themselves at the table and the dinner began. It was pleasant to watch the old-fashioned politeness with which they conducted themselves — the courtesy with which they bowed to Lilian at each word they addressed to her — the grace with which, wishing to cause no remark, they affected to eat and drink. Not able to do so, indeed, by reason of their incorporeal nature, but all the time lifting the full glasses and laden forks to their mouths and dropping them again untouched. It was delightful to listen to their conversation, marked here and there indeed, after the fashion of their time, with a light oath, but bright and sparkling throughout all, with vivacity and wit. At first, indeed; the time was somewhat occupied by Uncle Ruthven giving sketches of the late history of the family; but after that the ghosts were encouraged to talk, and pleasantly beguiled half an hour with hitherto unknown anecdotes of the Court of the Merry Monarch. As I listened my thoughts naturally strayed from the present back to the romantic past, and my imagination carried me, unresisting, into the olden days of the Stuarts. I was no longer in the prosaic nineteenth century, I was in the midst of a laughing, careless throng of king and courtiers, all busily making up for their enforced deprivations during the sombre period of the Commonwealth. Hamilton and Nelly Gwynn, De Grammont and Villiers and Frances Stewart, these and others of those long dead disreputables, whose actions may not have been comely but whose names live vividly in story, and to whose memories some glamor of romance still kindly attaches us, now crowded around and made the past a reality and the present a mere unstable myth. In the hallucination of the moment even the portrait of the poor old card-cheating Beatrice Grantley seemed to invest itself with something of her long-departed youthfulness; and as the mingled gleam of wax-lights and yule log flickered upon it, it was as though some hitherto unnoted beauties of expression came to the surface, and the whole countenance became once more aglow with that youthful loveliness which, doubtless, in the time of it, and during her occasional visits to the Court, must have enticed Charles himself awhile from his more stable attachments in order to enjoy passing flirtation with her.

" A joyous Court, indeed; and sadly now coming to my memory as I feel that I can never mingle with it more," said the purple ghost. " A Court to which I know that my fair young kinswoman would have done ample honor, could she have been there," he added, bowing to Lilian; " even more abundantly, indeed, than Cousin Beatrice. Growing old with more grace and dignity than did Beatrice, I am very sure. And that she may live to grow old in such gentle manner, let her take heed and not make my sad mistake."

As he spoke, he pointed significantly to the Lancaster diamond which chanced at that moment to be beside her plate, and, by a singular coincidence, among a little pile of filberts.

" Yet I am sure," he added, still with the courtly manner of his period, " that such sweet lips could never make mistake about any thing. Rather should the diamond, with its appropriate mate, be reserved to grace those beauteous ears."

" Its mate, do you say ?" I remarked; not sure, for the moment, but that the young ghost had swallowed two diamonds, and that I had not carried my researches far enough.

" Yes, its mate," he said. " Surely you must know ? Not so, indeed ? Well, there were two of these great diamonds, the Lancaster and the York. They had come into possession of one family through union of adherents of those two rival parties, and thence into our own line, through subsequent alliance of that family with the Grantleys. In Cromwell's time, the diamonds were hidden in separate places to preserve them from confiscation, the knowledge of those places being handed down only by word of mouth, for greater security. At the Restoration, I alone knew the secret. At the time of my death I had already brought the Lancaster diamond to light, as you are well aware. The York still remains hidden. Permit us now, my brother and myself, to offer it to you as our joint Christmas present. You will find it in a little metal box close beside — "

At that very moment it chanced that a small bantam rooster outside the window set up a crow. It was a miserable little banty, scarcely half fledged. It had a drooping wing, and a twisted toe; and for these defects and others, perhaps, which we had not noticed, was constantly driven away from the general society of the poultry-yard. Even the hens were accustomed to pick at it. Its crow was weak, and piping, like a school-boy's first attempt at whistling. Nor was this the hour of midnight or early dawn, but merely seven in the evening. There seemed no reason why any ghost with self-respect should be moved by such a feeble crow from such a despicable source, and at such an early hour. And yet there may be a certain, inflexible rule for well-constituted ghosts; and perhaps, in cock-crowing, the line cannot easily be drawn between different styles. Be that as it may, at the very first pretense of sound from the little banty, the ghost stopped speaking, gazed inquiringly at his brother and received an answering nod; and then without another word they slowly faded away.

"Ghosts are so ridiculous!" said Lilian. But I thought that as she gazed at the Lancaster diamond and reflected how well the two Christmas gifts would have looked if worn together, she seemed sadly disappointed that the little banty had not put off his crowing for a minute longer.

The Secret of Apollonius Septrio

THE SECRET OF APOLLONIUS SEPTRIO.

IT was Christmas eve, and I sat before the broad kitchen fire; and there, as I stirred up the rich yellow fluid in the iron pot, which swung over the coals in front of me, I mused upon the realities of the past and the possibilities of the future. The hour was late; and the hands of the clock pointing towards twelve, showed, that, in a moment or two, Christmas eve would be over, and Christmas day begun. From out my lattice window, and through the naked branches of the village elms, I could see the old stone church, with its queer little square belfry lit up, in readiness for the sexton to chime forth the midnight Christmas carol; while round the porch clustered a group of small urchins, waiting in breathless expectation to take their part in ringing out the peal. And in a moment more the sexton, with keys in one hand and lantern in the other, came struggling through the snow, on his way to the church. He was old and infirm, and could with difficulty plod along; and I wondered how he could ring in as a joyous thing that Christmas, which, in all probability, would be his last. But for all that, he seemed cheerful enough; and though in general he was a surly fellow, yet, as he now answered the welcoming shout of the urchin group, there was a very pleasant and lively tone to his cracked and husky old voice. And while I thought upon his shortened tenure of life, and the possibility that for me there might be laid up a long and useful career, the liquid before me suddenly boiled over the edge of the pot, and began to drop hissing upon the coals below.

When, in the six hundred and seventy-third year of his life, the celebrated Apollonius Septrio wrote out his method of prolonging human existence to an indefinite period, the agents of the Inquisition seized him, and, after a hasty trial, he was condemned as a sorcerer. "Thou pretendest to have lived over six hundred years, and to be able to live a thousand," said the Grand Inquisitor, when the sentence was pronounced; "we will now try whether thy words and doctrine are true. If they be true, thou needst not fear us, for we will be unable to kill thee. If, on the contrary, thy doctrine is not sufficient to save thee, then hast thou practiced abominations, and deservest to die." So Apollonius was led away to the stake and fagots, where he miserably perished.

But in spite of all that was said and done, Apollonius Septrio was no sorcerer. There was no taint of quackery or deceit in his process. Neither did it derive importance from cabalistic machinery, or spiritual invocations, or any of the thousand methods whereby unlettered visionaries have been wont to delude the public, and confuse their own minds in vain attempts to control the steady step of death.

Apollonius had merely drawn conclusions from certain well established laws of vitality, and thereby had enabled himself to employ nature to control his own organization; that was all. He had reasoned that the human body was subject to a constant waste, which, if allowed to continue without interruption, would result in its destruction, otherwise called death; that this waste might be retarded or accelerated by the observance of peculiar rules in the use of air, exercise, or food, whereby what is called death might be delayed or hastened; and he had hence reflected that it might be possible, by natural laws, to retard the customary rate of decay, and increase the vitality which a healthy body is constantly generating, so that the latter might neutralize the former, and thus death be kept away for ages. And acting upon such reasonable data, he had finally, after long-protracted experiments, attained success, and been enabled to enjoy a life of many centuries. But in his discovery there was, of course, no preventive against accident or violence; and thus, in the end, it happened that his body succumbed to the tortures of the Inquisition, and his narrow-minded enemies were enabled to pride themselves upon having exposed the error of his pretensions.

Of the twelve copies of his book, which Apollonius had laboriously written out with his own hand, seven were seized by the Inquisition, and destroyed with him; four were accidentally lost; and the remaining one lay hidden in the dusty recesses of an old Italian library, until exhumed by my unguided investigations. But I soon found out, that, to own the book, was not to possess the secret. At the very beginning, the cramped and faded writing, in an unknown tongue, seemed likely to baffle me; and three years of hard study elapsed before I was able to read the characters. And then a new difficulty arose, since whatever I read seemed to be the most unmeaning gibberish. For old Apollonius Septrio had been a jealous man; and in his unwillingness that men should easily attain that knowledge which had so long defied his own unaided researches, he had taken marvelous pains to cloud and embarrass the meaning of what he wrote, in order that none but persons of learning and perseverance equal to his own, might ever hope to arrive at the grand secret. There were abstract equations to be worked out; difficult analyses to be made; mystical keys to be fitted to still more mystical complications; and the whole so blended and woven together, that the loss of a single link of the marvelous chain would destroy all hope of ever attaining the wished-for result. And to add to the difficulty of the task, the rats of three successive centuries had attacked the little vellum volume, and had, here and there, nibbled away important elements in the calculations; so that additional analyses were often rendered necessary, for the purpose of supplying what even Apollonius Septrio had chosen to render clear to the comprehension.

As I pursued my investigations into the volume, there had been times when I shrank back affrighted at the magnitude of the task before me; and it

required all my energy to induce me to persevere in
what seemed a hopeless labor. At other times, however, I madly and defiantly dashed ahead, feeling a
savage desire to learn the secret, even though it
might prove worthless; if I might only thereby
boast to myself that I had not been foiled. And so,
little by little, the mysteries of the volume began
to be unfolded to my eyes, until, upon that Christmas eve, I stood in breathless suspense at the very
threshold of the end.

For the little iron pot, swinging over the fire,
contained the materials for the last analysis which
would be necessary; and if that succeeded, the
grand secret would be my own. Anxiously I watched
the bubbling of the liquid; and as at last it boiled
over the edge, I caught, with nervous hand, a single
vialful. Tremulously, I then held the vial towards
the light; tasted, and applied yet more severe tests;
and then, leaping from my seat, dashed around the
room in frantic joy. For the analysis was correct
and complete; sight, taste, and smell were satisfactory; and now it was but the labor of a moment to
run through the already developed chain of equations
and the work was done. It was but a simple receipt,
after all, that old Apollonius Septrio had discovered.
It consisted solely in the use of a common little
weed, which men every day trod under their feet,
but which, though thus carelessly treated, was more
valuable than mines of gold and jewels. For, in
its dust-covered leaves, it had a wonderful power of
bodily recuperation; and having its strength drawn
forth by occasional mastication, it would completely

16*

regenerate the wasting energies of the human frame, and thus insure to man as near an approach to immortality as could be rendered consistent with the frailties of an earthly nature.

The Christmas-bells rang forth loudly upon the clear night-air, as the great secret stood revealed before my eyes; but what cared I for Christmas, then? It was, after all, but an ordinary day to me, for I might yet see as many Christmas festivals as ordinary men see common days. For though there was nothing in that precious little weed capable of averting extraordinary dangers; though I was still as liable as other men to be struck down by an assassin's hand, or be crushed by a falling wall, or be torn piecemeal by a steam explosion; yet I knew that but a small proportion of men met their deaths by accident; that the great majority either died in old age, through the gradual exhaustion of the vital flame, or else succumbed to the power of wasting disease; that the virtues of the little weed would not only preserve the flame of life in a steady glow, but would also nerve the system against fever, plague, or any customary form of sickness; and that, consequently, there was no reason why I might not look forward to centuries of health and strength.

" And less jealous than old Apollonius, we will let the whole world share in our discovery," I said to the young wife whom I had married during the year just passed. " All men shall learn to live as long as we; and thus all men, in time, will become good. For those who are already good can increase their works and influence throughout centuries, while the bad will have longer time for repentance, and will learn, by more lengthened experience, how much better is the policy of the just."

But when I attempted to promulgate my discovery, I found that the world did not seem to appreciate its merits. In fact, the world is but a bull-headed fellow, after all. There are times when it is simple and easy to delude; and then any artful pretender can make a sport of it, and pillage it. But there are other times, when, fretted and soured with the consciousness of past deceptions, it will believe nothing, and trust to nobody; but with teeth set, and brow wrinkled, will scorn and trample upon any suggestions of value or benefit, however cheap and easy of application. It was in this latter mood, that, at the time of my discovery, I found the world. Only a little while before, crafty empirics had promised it all kinds of wealth, health and prosperity. It had been offered long life, easily manufactured gold; in fact, every thing which had ever been striven for, to make any reasonable world happy and contented. It had paid large prices for useless instruction; had lightened its coffers to purchase vain receipts; had discovered ruinous failure in every method which had been proposed to it; and, in the end, had always been soundly laughed at for its stupid credulity. So the world had relapsed again into an unbelieving state; and when I offered it the benefits of my discovery, it would have nothing to do with me. It mattered but little that I made my secret known, without demanding any recompense; the world said that all such generosity was a pretense, artfully contrived to cover a trick. Some few, indeed, listened to me for a while, but only for a while. There was a score or two of converts, who, for a month or so, tried my process; but when they found that no immediate result ensued, their zeal abated. They not only desired not to grow old, but also seemed to expect to be made young again; and when they found that their wrinkles did not fill out, and their bent backs become straightened, they grew angry, and, under the conjoined influence of their own indolence and the ridicule of others, pronounced my discovery to be an imposition. Others, again, discussed the subject; not as one of immediate practical interest, but rather in a vein of speculative philosophy. Metaphysicians derided it; pulpits fulminated against it as a wicked perversion of human talent, if true, being an infringement of the divine law which limited life to three-score years and ten; statisticians exclaimed against any thought of such a change of nature's laws, as would, in time, lead to too dense a population upon the world. In fine, all men had their kick at the discovery. All classes denied the merits or practicability of it; and at the same time, in speculative vein asserted, that, if any such secret could be made, it would be either wicked, unwise, or inconsiderate. And finally, a famous college of physicians took up the subject; plucked up a bushel of the little weeds, placed them in caldrons and retorts, analyzed, found nothing, made a verbose and inflated report full of high-sounding terms, and pretended to have crushed an error. The world read the report, tried to understand it, could not, but still believed the conclusions; and then, as some new object of interest arose, forgot the discovery altogether.

That is, all forgot it but a few; who, being my nearest relations, should have treated me with some consideration. But from the fact of their relationship, they were my heirs; and self-interest urged them to commit a grievous wrong upon me. The temptation was a fair one; the opportunity was favorable. I accidently discovered that they were plotting against me, with the intent to use my pretensions as a discoverer, to my disadvantage; to have me imprisoned in a mad-house, as one bereft of sense; and then to share among themselves my not inconsiderable property. For the loss of property I would have cared but little, but the deprivation of liberty would have been fatal to all my prospects. How, in a narrow cell, could I ever obtain that little weed which was to prolong my stay upon earth? So, in the right time, I gathered up such jewels and gold as I could most easily lay my hands upon, and fled away, leaving all my houses and lands to become the prey of those crafty people whom it was my misfortune to call kinsmen.

Two persons only followed me in my flight. One was my twin brother; the other was my wife. Why she had ever married me had been a wonder to many; sometimes, even, to myself. For I was forty years old, bent with toil and study, care-worn and wrinkled; and she was young and fair. Twenty summers had not shone upon her; and such was her loveliness of person and disposition, that those who had aspired to her affection might have been numbered by scores. Nevertheless, moved by some inexplicable sympathy of soul, she had rejected all the crowd of rich and titled and youthful suitors, and had clung unto me alone; and now, in my misfortune, she gave the strongest proof of attachment which woman can give, by leaving friends and relatives, home and home comforts, and flying with me into exile.

And hand in hand we three now wandered out into new scenes, where we were not known, and where the shafts of malevolence or violence could not reach us. We endured hardship and poverty, but we did not complain. Why, indeed, should temporary vicissitudes induce us to despair, when we could look forward to so much of hope? For with me, both my wife and twin brother had learned to acknowledge the powers and benefits of the great discovery; and, together, we all three daily ate of the little weed which could confer almost immortal natures upon us. And with centuries of life before us, there need never be such a thing as despair. Other persons, limited to three-score and ten years of life, might, after one reverse, sink back baffled with the knowledge that there would not be enough time left to them to enable them to repair their mis-fortunes; but we could look hopefully forward into the vista of coming centuries, with the full assurance, that, in the course of that long career, there would be abundant chances for the wheel of fortune to revolve and re-establish our broken and fallen position.

And thus, in security of heart, we wandered about the earth, taking but little thought of chance reverses, but ever cheerfully awaiting the inevitable return of more prosperous days. And we moreover determined to keep our great secret to ourselves. The world had once rejected it with scorn; we would no longer, through misguided benevolence, subject it to further insult. Let men die, then, as of old; it was nothing to us. We would live; and as we saw generation after generation rise into the world, and after a brief flutter of existence sink into the tomb, we would hug our secret to our own hearts, and exist and care only for each other.

And so centuries passed away; and as we had anticipated, revolving years brought successive changes of fortune. At first we moved out upon one of the furthermost prairies of the West, and there awaited our own good time. Fifty years passed over our heads, and then that prairie became the location of a great city, and we were looked up to as its wealthiest inhabitants. Fifty years more rolled away, and the knavery of others stripped us of every thing; and again we strolled forth to renew our fortunes. Then we chose a site among wooded hills, far away from men, and for a while lived contentedly upon the roots of the soil and the water from a spring which trickled down beside our cabin.

And soon rich mines were discovered near us, and again for fifty years we lived in affluence; and yet, again, lost all. But why continue the theme? It is enough to say that each century saw us rich and poor by turns; that, when rich, we enjoyed our wealth in a rational manner; and that, when poor, we hopefully looked forward to the certain return, in due time, of good fortune.

And thus we lived, true to ourselves and to each other, while all things about us gradually changed. Costume and language slowly and surely altered. What was deemed right and proper at one epoch, was discountenanced at another. Great discoveries were made and lost again. Mankind, by toil, turned sterile provinces into smiling gardens; and again would nature regain its rights, and reduce all to worthlessness. Canals were dug through inaccessible lands, and navigable rivers were dried up. Governments also changed; and from east to west, in succession, arose republics, kingdoms and despotisms; each, in the opinion of its founders, being certain to endure forever, and each, in its turn, becoming finally dismembered, or overturned through force, faction or corruption.

And with all these opportunities of lengthened life and unbroken health, did I fulfill my earliest dreams, and become a better and a purer man? Alas! there would be few, who, with the fear of death so far removed, would have cultivated the noble, heaven-born graces of the soul, from a mere abstract love of virtue. And I was not of those few. It is true that I did not become what the world would have called a sinful man. There was ever in my mind an innate perception of what is right and proper; and consequently, the lapse of all those centuries seemed to bring me no nearer than before to the crimes of low dissipation, theft or murder. But still, though the outward man appeared unchanged, the heart within was slowly hardening. To live so long and see so many generations go down to the tomb, like insects of the day, while I remained alive in all my original strength and vigor, could not but tend to lessen my sympathies for my fellow-men. What, indeed, were their swift-passing fears and hopes to me? Or how could I, a being of such superior attributes, descend to interest myself in the joys and misfortunes of their petty lives? So, year by year, and century by century, my heart slowly fortified itself more and more against all that might once have touched it; and though I was conscious of the change, and at times struggled desperately against it, my efforts were all in vain, and the terrible process still went on with steady and never-ceasing progression.

Fifteen hundred years slowly passed away. During this time, whatever changes took place happened so gradually, as, in the ordinary lifetime of man, to be almost imperceptible. But as we looked back and reviewed our experience, and thought upon all that we had seen and heard, it appeared as though the march of time had not been loitering; so many were the events which crowded our recollection. In that time, we saw all Europe become effete and barbarous; its kingdoms split into fragments; its people lost to education and enterprise; its once vaunted cities falling into decay. We saw the American Republic gradually become too thickly settled to insure perfect unity of action, and then sever into diverse kingdoms, in which were enacted, as had once been in Europe, all the dramatic progressions of intestine revolt, gigantic wars, and vast schemes of feudal aggrandizement. We saw palaces built, and conquerors arise and load their cities with trophies, while they enriched their plains with the blood of their subjects. And still were going on those same warring elements, and mustering of armies, and crowning of kings, and invading of defenseless provinces, in aid of what was yet, as of old, the world's favorite dogma — the preservation of the balance of power.

And far off in the great Pacific, new scenes, or rather old scenes upon a new platform, were enacting. For during all those fifteen hundred years, the little coral insect had been busily at work, joining shoal to shoal, headland to headland, island to island; filling up bays and choking up straits; until, where there had been only scattered dots of soil upon the broad ocean bosom, a glorious continent now began to spread out. And these people had settled, and invited to themselves the surplus population of other nations; and great States had grown up, and united themselves for common defense; and each rostrum echoed the words, "liberty and equal rights;" and journalists pointed in disdain to the monarchies of America, and thanked God for their own free government; and statesmen predicted the dawn of great and free institutions spreading over all the earth, and, at the same time, cast a cautious glance abroad lest foreign conspiracies might hopelessly mar the bright prospect. In fine, we saw enacting around us, that great drama which had so often been played before; and I might have smiled, were it not that there was something of sadness in such a picture of baffled human expectations, and the smile would be checked by unbidden tears.

And I and my wife and twin brother were living in this great Republic of the Pacific. We were not near any of its great cities, however; for again the wheel of fortune had turned, and our lot had become that of poverty. And, accordingly, after our old custom, we had removed to one of the extremes of the nation, where land was cheap, and living to be easily earned; and where we could wait for fifty or a hundred years, if necessary, until the progressive march of civilization and improvement might make us wealthy again. Before us, and beating against the sandy shore, rolled the Pacific; behind us was the dense forest. We had but few neighbors, and these were rough in manner; but we were company enough for each other, and cared not for the society of other men.

For the first time in many years, I was not happy. A certain inquietude weighed down my heart. For I saw that with the lapse of centuries, and the universal change of nature, mankind also had altered.

At least I began, for the first time, dimly to suspect the fact. It seemed to me that those whom I now met were larger, more powerful, and more vigorous men than the men of a thousand years before. I was reminded of olden theories — so old that they had been forgotten by all but myself — which asserted the existence of a constant progression in the human race, whereby, during the lapse of ages, mere inert forms of animal life had gradually developed into man, and, in accordance with which, man might some day become developed into something higher. And, as I looked around, it seemed to me that this development was slowly taking place; so slowly, indeed, as to be imperceptible to man himself, but obvious to me, who had for so long a time known the human race, and could compare myself with it as a fixed and undeviating standard.

Could it really be so? And as I reflected upon the subject, a party of men came down from the wood, approached the water's edge, and prepared to cast a net. I attentively considered them, and saw that in stature they greatly exceeded me, that in frame they were more powerful, and that in every movement they made there was a wondrous grace, and in every feature superior intelligence. And yet I saw that these men were no better than others who moved about us; that if any thing, they were inferior, by reason of their rude and toilsome manner of life; that among the rich and educated of their time they would be looked down upon as beings of a lower order. And withal, how greatly even they surpassed me in every thing which in the estimation of the common mind is requisite to make up the full perfection of man! For, during these many centuries, while this almost insensible progression had been taking place, I, alas! had never changed. When I had made my great discovery, I had reached the grand climacteric of life. In me there could thenceforth be no alteration for the better; and all that the little weed could do would be to maintain me in a stationary state, and prevent further vital decay. The reflection burst upon me like a thunder clap. I reeled with the stroke of the new and bitter knowledge.

Pretty soon, however, I attempted to reassure myself. I determined that I would not encourage such terrible ideas without further investigation. I had seen these men at a distance — I would go nearer to them. It might be that some magical mirage, some deceitful phantasy of the atmosphere had deluded me; and that a nearer inspection would operate as a grateful disenchantment. And so I slowly drew nearer to the fishermen.

And when I approached and stood beside them, I saw, with an increasing sinking of the heart, that I was among beings not one of whom did not stand a full head and shoulders higher than I. I had never been noted for height, to be sure, being only of medium stature at the best; but even then I remembered that in the days of past centuries, he who could overlook me by half a head had been considered a tall man. But how different was it now! Among those fishermen, who were certainly not aware of any distinct peculiarity in their figures, I was as a boy. And I could perceive that they looked disdainfully down upon me; not exactly with an open sneer, but with an air of mingled pity and indifference — just as, centuries before, I might have gazed upon a dwarf.

How, indeed, could they help it? They were not my superiors in size only; for the progress of human development, the truth of the theory of which I could no longer doubt, had given them precedence in every other physical attribute. I felt more and more sickened at heart as I contrasted my round-shouldered frame, stooping chest, and care-wrinkled face with their athletic proportions and soul-lit features.

A stone lay in the way of the net, and one of the fishermen carelessly raised it in his two hands, and flung it on one side. It seemed a heavy mass to move, and, by way of experiment, I attempted to carry it myself; but with all my exertions, I could only raise it a few inches from the ground. At this, a boy — or one at least whom they must have considered a boy — laughed, and unfeelingly pointed towards me. I was angry; but the young fellow could easily have thrashed me in a twinkling, and I was obliged to swallow my indignation. Ah, me! How blinded had I been for centuries, not to have before perceived that I was destined to become a pigmy among my fellow-creatures! Oh! that the little weed which had endowed my life with continuance had also given me the gift of progression, so that I might at least maintain my proper place among the animated works of creation! And seeing a bunch of the little dust-colored leaves growing at my feet, I frantically seized and thrust them into my mouth, with the silly idea that now, in my need, they might do what they had failed to do before, and by some miraculous power, as it were, enable me suddenly to retrieve my fallen dignity. But of course the paroxysm was an useless one, and merely served to cover me with ridicule. As the men saw me tearing the leaves between my teeth, in the same voracious style with which a beast of the field would pull the grass, they stared in wonderment, and finally broke forth into open laughter; and I, in confusion and shame, ran back to where I had left my wife and brother.

"They, at least, are left to me, and cannot ridicule me," I said to myself, "and whatever progression may happen to mankind in coming centuries, we can always find some nook of the world into which we can retire, and there, away from the gaze of all curious eyes, contribute to each other's happiness as we have always heretofore done."

And here, alas! where I had most hoped for and anticipated comfort, I experienced a dreadful blow. My twin brother, it is true, remained unaltered like myself; but as my wife smilingly came forth and approached me, it struck me that she was taller than she had been when I first knew her. At that time she was rather small of stature, and reached but a little above my shoulder; but now her height was almost equal to my own. And beautiful as she had before been, it seemed as though new beauties had gradually unfolded themselves until her whole countenance glowed with almost celestial charms. The horrible truth then flashed upon me! When my brother and I had first commenced tasting the immortality-giving weed, we had passed the age when man can improve his system, and were hence debarred from any other advantage than that of preserving such powers as at that time we possessed; but she, being then still young, still growing, and still endued with the attributes of further development, that power of future development had been preserved in her system, and had ever since been in full and constant operation!

I staggered against a tree, and then fell at its foot in all the wildness of despair. The sudden light upon my soul seemed to crush me into nothingness. Why, after so many centuries of blissful ignorance, during which I had so accustomed myself to her that no alteration in her form or features had struck upon my attention, and made me suspect the wretched truth — why was I now to be thus rudely enlightened, and made miserable? And how long, while I would thus remain an unimproving landmark of the past, would she continue to preserve those wonderful attributes of constant progression, and century by century find an ever-widening distance between us? Forever, I could not doubt. The law which my discovery had once called into activity, it was now beyond my power to restrain. Frantically, therefore, as I gazed forward into coming centuries, I exclaimed:

"You will not — you will not ever leave me?"

"Leave you?" she cried, with a sweet look of affection, in which I could see was mingled an expression of doubt and surprise. "Why talk of having me leave you? Have I not followed your fortunes for fifteen hundred years?"

But how can mere protestations of affection cheer a doubting heart? Though I knew that my wife cared only for me, I could not but tremble at the thought that perhaps she merely loved because her eyes were sealed to the truth, as mine had so recently been. What would she think, when she came to know the reality which some day would surely be forced upon her — when she should discover that around us moved and breathed other men to whom, in every manly quality, I bore no other proportion than that of the court-dwarf to the stalwart warriors who crowd the audience-chamber — when she should learn the truth about herself, and know that each century the void between us was widening, and that she was throwing away upon a poor puny abstraction of a man these treasures of beauty and affection which might bind in chains the soul of a conqueror? The time will come, I reflected, when the dreadful truth can no longer be concealed from her. She does not now perceive it; but neither did I until a chance moment awakened my attention to the fact, and led me to compare myself with other men about me. That moment of comparison and examination may any day come to her, and then, then how can I dare to stand before her ? She will despise me — will accuse me of long-continued deception — will spurn me from her — will leave me for others, who, in truth, will be more worthy of her than I ; and I will be obliged to creep alone about the earth, envying the superior powers and attributes of all whom I meet — a scorn and derision to all — and seeking in vain for comfort or companionship.

And I resolved that the unhappy day of trial should be postponed for years, for centuries, if intrigue and cunning could be of any avail. I would retire from even this thinly populated coast; for I feared that the sight of merely those few fishermen might awaken terrible comparisons in her breast, as it had in mine. I would take her away, even into the dark forest, where she could see no human beings besides my brother and myself. No man should come near to tempt her thoughts to odious distinction, but I would ever remain at her side, and wait upon her as a slave ; and she should never learn that I was in any respect more unlike the men around us than I had been fifteen hundred years before. And if she chanced to pine under such forced seclusion, and to desire any other society, I would leave her hidden in some dark cavern, and would search the world to collect together its most feeble and most puny offspring ; and I would bring them to her, and tell her that all things had retrograded, until at last I had become a giant among my fellows. She would believe me, as she had ever yet done ; and then in the mazes of the forest we would hold our mimic

court, and in the midst of those few selected outcasts,
I might still, by comparison, hope to retain her
affection.

So I told her that we must move away; that we
had become yet poorer than before; that we could
no longer afford to stay upon the borders of the
ocean; that we must betake ourselves to the inland
country, and there, in that less expensive region,
commence a new struggle for wealth. She listened
with surprise; for upon the previous day I had been
telling her of the little that we needed to exist upon,
since our small cabin and the spot of land about it
were our own, and the earth gave us its fruits and
the sea its fish without cost. All this I had told her
but a few hours before; and we had grown to love
our place, and the murmur of the waves, and the
rustle of the vines; and had anticipated leading
many years of quiet blissfulness in that little nook.
But she had learned to shape her will in all things
with mine; and so, without a word of remonstrance,
she gave a single farewell longing glance upon
cottage and hill and ocean beach, and prepared to
follow me into the forest.

So far all was well; and it only remained for me
to consult my brother upon the subject. I anticipated considerable objection from him, for I imagined
that he also had learned to love our present location.
But, to my surprise, he readily consented to depart
with us.

" Anywhere, everywhere, and at once!" he
exclaimed. "I shall be satisfied with any lot, so
long as we may leave this dreadful coast!"

"Why, how now?" I said in astonishment. "What has so suddenly disgusted you?"

"Is it not enough," he fiercely rejoined, "to find ourselves yearly growing more and more unlike the rest of our species? To know that the time may come when, in comparison with others, we may be but as apes, or even something worse?"

"Then you have noticed that change?" I sadly inquired. "And when?"

"Years ago," he said. "But at the time I made no remarks, since you still seemed to be unconscious of it. But now that you know it all, let us depart. Let us fly into the deepest shades of the thicket — to the bottom of a well, even — if by doing so we may never again see the hated faces of men!"

So we wandered away, and, after many days, found a location fit for our purpose. It was a cave by the side of a mountain-stream, and in every direction nature brought forth its supporting fruits without requiring the labor of man. There was no city, town, village, or hamlet near. For miles in every direction lay the dense forest, unbroken by the axe or plough, and untrodden by the foot of man. And there we placed our lot, and I innocently trusted that in such seclusion I could preserve my happiness; nor ever dreamed that in the midst of that peace and fancied security, trouble was coming upon me with rapid strides.

I had noticed that for some weeks my brother had

been becoming more and more fretful and moody; and one day, upon his return from a long and listless wandering, he approached me and said:

"Do you know that there are men near us? A village has sprung up but a few miles to our right. I saw it to-day, as I returned."

"A village!" I exclaimed in affright. "Then we must move still further into the forest."

"We must do no such thing!" he exclaimed, imperiously. "I have had enough of this. I thought that I could endure it patiently, but now find that I cannot. And I will not! I must now and then look upon the faces of my fellow-men, or this solitude will craze me. Yes—though it be with fear and jealousy—though all men may look down upon me with contempt—yet I cannot consent to live on and see no human face again."

"You can look upon my wife and myself," I said. "It is enough for her and me that we three are together. Why cannot you also be content?"

"Are we the same, then?" he hissed forth in sudden anger. "Have you not just stated that you have a wife? And will she not always cling to you, even if all the world should desert you? Have you not her love and sympathy to console you in your obscurity? Why then need you ever pine for the world? But, on the contrary, what am I? Who cares for me in my loneliness? And how can the mere friendship of two persons recompense me for the loss of all besides? Harkee, brother!" he added, seizing me by the shoulder with a strong grasp. "You are learned and wise. Get you to work and devise some means to break this spell of unprogressive life, so that we also may find ourselves subject to the operations of a constant development, and thus keep pace with our fellow-creatures."

"It cannot be," I mournfully answered. "If it could be done, would I not do it? Even Apollonius Septrio could not have done it, and he was wiser than I. But be content. At the very least I have given you life."

"And what is the worth of a life like this?" he fiercely exclaimed. "Take it back, if you will; I care not for it! It is but a load of misery to me now! By your vile invention you have but betrayed me to endless torment — that is all!"

And then more high words passed between us, until, in my exasperation, I took him by the throat. He shook me off, glared sullenly upon me for a moment, muttered some words about having his revenge — and so we parted.

The morrow was Christmas day. It was upon Christmas that I had discovered my great secret, and I had ever celebrated the anniversary as a holiday, to be devoted to social harmony, love and joy. Now, afflicted by my quarrel, I determined that this Christmas should not pass without a complete restoration of peace. At our festive board I would take my brother by the hand, we would talk freely and lovingly together, we would each forgive the harsh words of the other; and we would inaugurate a new era of tranquillity which would last unbroken for years, in spite of all unpleasing interruptions from the outer world. Accordingly, after a sleepless night spent in such reflections, I arose early, took my rifle, and sallied forth to make provision for the day.

About noon I returned, loaded with game, and pleasantly depicted in my mind the joyous smile with which my wife would run forth to relieve me of my spoils. But no note of welcome came to my attentive ears, as I approached; and, when I stood before our little cabin, I saw by the signs of struggle which met my eye, that a band of lawless rangers had roughly seized my wife and borne her away, leaving no trace by which I could follow them.

Transported with grief, I staggered, and a mist gathered before my eyes. Suddenly I heard my name called from above; and, collecting my sight, I looked up. Upon an overhanging crag stood my brother, waving his arms to me with ironical greeting, while every feature bore the flush of fiendish triumph.

"Aha!" he screamed. "She is gone now! I led them here to capture her! She is far away from here now, and where you can never find her! And we are even at last, are we not? You will now know what it is to be alone in the world. And will you ever again take me by the throat, do you think?"

Overcome with rage, I raised my rifle and fired at him. The ball struck the cliff below, and glanced harmlessly off to one side; and with another shriek of triumphant malice, he passed away from my sight, and I fell helpless to the ground. And as I lay there, the agonies of my mind were increased by the reflection that I had brought my deprivation upon myself, and that thus it was, in a measure, a well-deserved judgment upon me. For had I frankly told my wife that in the lapse of ages not only other men but she herself had changed, until I had become inferior to all around me, but that, in spite of all this, I was the same man that I had ever been, and had only suffered by comparison, and that I loved her as devotedly as before, I do not doubt that she would still have continued to pour out her heart's affections upon me, regardless of all external alteration; and that, in our little sea-side cabin, and under the sheltering wing of the country's laws, we could have continued united for many centuries to come. But instead of all this, I had allowed my heart to feel distrust, had deceived her about my plans and motives, and had removed her to a desert wild, forgetting that where man had no settled abode, lawlessness could not fail to prosper. And I felt that, hard as my lot might be, my conscience could not hold me acquitted of all guilt.

Nevertheless, I would not despair; and for years I sought my wife through every land and clime. And though ever unsuccessful, there was still a lurking hope in my mind that some day I might meet her again; that she might escape from her captors, and that once again we might renew our past lives of union and happiness. But gradually even that hope began to fade. I reflected that she might have been slain, at the first period of her captivity; or, despairingly, have slain herself; or have been dragged away to lands where the life-giving weed did not grow, and there, in common with others, have become exhausted with infirmities, and finally sunk into the grave; or, what seemed infinitely worse, that she might have become reconciled to her life with others, and have forgotten me. In any event, she seemed lost to me for ever, and, as the only means of happiness left to me, I strove to forget her; and if at any time, in dreams, I imagined that she might be thinking upon me with affection, and, in the hope of regaining me some day, be still sustaining her life of youth and beauty, by means of the great secret which I had taught her, I cannot say that the reflection gave me any real happiness. It seemed but a childish thing to look forward to a train of circumstances against which so many chances were arrayed; and I gradually accustomed myself to think upon it rather in a spirit of speculative philosophy, than in any vein of real well-founded hope.

And so, with blighted heart, I still continued to live on; almost mechanically renewing my life with the little weed which every where grew at my feet. And thus a thousand years passed away with its many changes. Were it necessary, I could tell strange stories about these thousand years; for whatever of great importance happened, it seemed to be my lot to witness. I was present when the locks which regulated the flow of water in the great Darien Canal burst away under the impetus of mingled tide and storm, and the floods of the two oceans swept together midway, with a force to which man could offer no resistance. I stood on the brow of a neighboring mountain, and beheld the roaring torrent, having once gained a passage, increase in force and velocity, and rush on, sweeping away cities, and ever widening its banks, until, in place of the quiet canal, there was a great winding strait of many miles in breadth, which feeble man could never again close up, and through which poured the diverted tide of the great Atlantic Gulf Stream. It was I, who, then first crossing over into Europe, discovered that, by reason of the different direction attained by that great warm current, those lands which had once enjoyed a mild and pleasant climate had succumbed to a new and harsh temperature; until, in what had once been merry England, deep snows for ever covered the ruins of palaces and cathedrals, and further south, the pleasant Rhone and Garonne became coated with eternal glaciers. And I was present, when, in the great Pacific Republic, the mighty and crafty General Ogoo assembled his armies about him, and planted his throne upon the ruins of free States.

But of all this it is useless to speak. With mere events I have but little to do, for my eyes were fixed upon those other changes which mankind itself was undergoing, and which, more than the mere founding of States and fall of empires, affected my welfare. For during these thousand years, I could not but notice that the process of human development into something higher and grander was still going on. As before, the great work was slow in progress, to be sure; so slow, indeed, that single generations could take no note of it. For who, of all men, would know that in two or three hundred years the human race had gained an inch in average stature, or a shade of progress in mental or bodily accomplishments? To the life of common man all this was imperceptible; but I, with my thousand new years, could look back upon the ages which had gone before, and with these recollections and my own unchanging self as an undeviating standard, could read, as plainly as though it were written in the sky, the terrible fact, that, though I had once been equal with my fellow-men, I had now already lost such equality; and by comparison with others, was assimilating more and more to the lower orders of creation. The thought was becoming more maddening every year. In the centuries gone by, I had left my happiness; already was I looked upon with scorn and pity, as a poor, misshapen, stunted creature; and looming up in the vista of the future, was — what?

And yet, though beneath this everliving consciousness of degradation, and fear of the trials which the advance of future centuries might bring forth, I had become timid and cynical, and felt my life a burden to me, I could not, indeed, make up my mind to die. Whatever might be my present misfortunes, I shrunk from courting the unknown mysteries of death. In life, I at least knew what my trials were;

but who can gaze beyond the grave, and tell what awaits him there?

So I continued to live on, and my only care now was to disregard what might be spoken of me behind my back, and avoid present and personal insult. To do this, I knew of but one way, and that was to become rich. For with all its changes, I saw that, in one respect, the world had not improved. Science and arts had flourished; men spoke with wondrous self-gratulation about their advance in charity, education and religion; but still humanity wrapped its affections in gold-leaf, and bowed down to Plutus with the same zest and subserviency which they had displayed ages before. I reflected, that, as a poor man, I would be hooted at in the streets by boys, who, though but boys, outranked me in height and strength; but that, as a rich man, I would receive honor, titles, and adulation from all, even though I might, in my personal attributes, sink to the level of the ape.

And so, having elaborated my plan, I commenced putting it into instant effect. Beginning with humble materials, I laid the foundation of my fortune. And from small beginnings, I was gradually enabled to increase my operations. In fifty years, through diligent perseverance and judicious investments, my name began to be heard more frequently in commercial circles. Then as interest rolled in, and was added to interest, my wealth continued to increase in constantly accelerating proportion; until finally, towards the end of a century of care and anxiety, I was looked upon and respected as one of the wealthiest citizens of the great commercial centre of the sea-port of Tooxo.

And then, in accordance with my long-settled policy, I began to make lavish display of my wealth, since I found that, however freely I used it, its accumulation would still go on. I purchased town and country-houses, where I lived in wonderful magnificence. My carriage, with liveried servants, rolled daily through the principal streets. Every night my windows shone with lights, and music sounded through my marble halls, where I entertained, in sumptuous style, the wealth and fashion of the city. And of course I had the world at my feet, and every day new honors were thrust upon me. Now it was my name which was needed to head a plan for some city institution, and thus give dignity to the enterprise. Then it was a post of authority, in the National University, I was requested to accept. And again, it was a title of nobility, which a grateful and admiring nation begged me to attach to my name. Everywhere the empire rang with the report of my wealth, and the story of my munificence. Everywhere men, to whose shoulders I could hardly reach, cringed before me. What, though at times, when I sat at the tables of the titled and powerful, I caught the stealthy sneer of some tall menial? What, though in the public streets, derogatory remarks would occasionally assail my ear? These were only the accidents to which all men were more or less liable. To my face there was nothing but compliments, smiles and adulation. My aim was nearly attained.

Great, however, as was my wealth, there were others who, in that respect, equaled me; though through prudence or closeness of disposition, they did not display the same liberality and magnificence in their manner of life, and thus commanded less attention. But to complete my triumph, and satisfy my own mind that I was clearly entitled to all the adulation which I received, I felt it necessary to advance one step further, and become, without question, the wealthiest man in the empire. And so I remained still at work in my counting-house; and sent out my atmospheric ships to distant climes; and rolled up my shares in atmospheric roads; and built new rows of magnificent warehouses. One by one my rivals in wealth finished their short lives, and their estates were divided among their heirs. Step by step my fortune became more colossal. And at length, after twenty years, I one day inventoried my vast possessions, and ascertained that, beyond all chance of dispute, there was no one in the whole empire who could pretend to vie with me in the amount of his wealth. And then I resolved to close up my business, and retire to a life of luxury and independent idleness. The next day was to be a grand festival-day in the city; for on that day, Ogoo the Seventeenth, was to ascend the throne of his race, and be crowned Emperor of the nation. I resolved that the same day should also inaugurate my release from business cares, and my new life of magnificent leisure.

Upon that next day the sun arose without a cloud. At an early hour, the city was all astir with life and animation. The national balloon floated over every staff. Troops defiled in vast regiments through every street. National music everywhere sounded upon the air. In the parks were shows and exhibitions of every kind. The corners of the streets were packed with crowds of people, all on the move to enjoy the great national holiday to their utmost. And I arose, and also prepared to take the full benefit of my first great holiday for years.

First I opened the daily volume of news, which, according to custom, had been thrown into my door. There was but little in it to attract me, however. The first two hundred pages were filled with an editorial life of the man who was that day to be crowned Emperor. Then followed an article of thirty pages, in which it was attempted to prove that his name was a corruption of Oboo; which, in turn, had been corrupted from Obro, or Bro — which was a further change from Brow; and that thus he was probably a lineal descendant of the great clan of Brown, which, twenty-five hundred years before, had almost overrun the earth, and which, by reason of its strength, had finally vanquished another great clan which went by the name of Kelly. Then followed details of the proposed arrangements for the day; then a notice of an exhibition of antiquities, from the site of the once famous city of New-York; then an account of sundry political riots, a favorite pastime in which the world still occasionally indulged; and after that came three or four hundred pages of the usual advertisements of the day. Finding nothing very attractive in all this, I threw the volume aside; and as the stir and tumult in the streets were becoming every moment greater and louder, I strolled forth.

Wending my way up and down, I finally reached the Museum of the National University, and entered. A little group was collected in one corner, and I approached and mingled in it. I found that the attraction consisted in two broken stone capitals of columns. At one side stood the Professor of Mental Gymnastics, who, by reason of his eight feet of stature, was considered a tolerably well-proportioned man. At the other side was the Professor of Ancient Languages, whose diminutive six feet and a half of height provoked many a sneer from the uneducated, but who, among men of cultivated intellect, had become quite a favorite, owing to his new translation of "Shakspeare," with notes, and his discovery that the ancient British poet, Hood, had been starved to death by King Peel, in revenge for the ridicule which he had cast upon a great national causeway, in an article entitled, "A Bridge of Some Size." The two men were now discussing the pieces of ruin before them.

"These stones," said the Professor of Ancient Languages, "I have ascertained to have come from one of the public buildings in the old city of New-York. It was a building denominated the Exchange, which is equivalent to the word ' to barter,' in our language; from which we might naturally infer that the place was a kind of market, where articles were sold for money. But that is not the truth, as I will show you. I find that the only articles there bartered were what they called 'stocks;' and upon looking at ancient dictionaries, I see that a stock was an article of dress, worn about the neck. Now, why should people meet here, to barter away these articles? There could certainly be but little profit in such an operation. I have hence concluded that it was a mere friendly ceremony; and that it was the custom when two persons met, after a long absence, and wished to compliment each other, for them to hurry to this 'exchange,' and accept the ornaments from each other's necks."

"Probably long-established enmities might have been made up in this way, and this bartering of personal adornment have taken place in the presence of mutual friends, in sign of complete forgiveness of the past," suggested the Professor of Mental Gymnastics.

"The same thing has occurred to me," said the other; "particularly as I find hints that these exchanges, as they called them, were often accompanied with peculiar ceremonies. For instance, the ancient writers make frequent mention of bulls and bears. Now what could have been the object in having these animals there, unless for the purpose of sacrificing them, in order to give dignity to the occasion?"

The two men then gradually wandered into the discussion of a late and curious phenomenon — no other than the discovery of a small native tribe, some of whom had wings of a few inches in length, growing between the shoulders; not of sufficient length, indeed, to fly with, but serving, in some degree, to assist and lighten their motions while walking.

"I have of late wondered," said the Professor of Mental Gymnastics, "whether it may not be that, for thousands of years past, the human race has been in a state of gradual but constant progression; increasing in size, power and mental activity; commencing at a low point, and destined to acquire still more extended attributes, as, in the course of centuries, this continual development advances; and whether, in fact, these winged men may not betoken the approach of a new stage in the same direction, whereby in due time, though probably long after our day, all men may become winged. I throw this out as a new idea, and one perhaps worthy of speculative attention."

"Nonsense!" said the Professor of Ancient Languages. "It is not a new idea, by any means. It was first broached, three hundred years ago, by the celebrated Winklewink. Then, as now, the idea was considered too ridiculous to be entertained for a moment. All the remains of mankind, that have ever been discovered, assure us that our race has always maintained an uniform average standard of height; while as for any additional mental development, the writings of the ancient Americans have not been equaled, as yet, by any of their successors. Look at that little dwarf who, somehow, owns half the shipping and houses of Tooxo," continued the Professor, unaware that I was present. "Look at him, the next time you meet him, and then tell me whether you can believe that the ALMIGHTY could ever have made a whole race in such a form, and then have called it after His likeness! The idea is too preposterous. Any child could tell you, that such a little dwarf, so far from being the representative of a class which has once existed, is merely an eccentricity of nature; and I say the same of these winged men. They are merely certain accidents of nature — monsters, as it were; just as we have had double-headed camels in our fields, and four-legged pelicans in our barn-yards. They are chance exceptions to the general rule of humanity, and can never themselves establish a rule."

I listened no longer, but slily slipped aside, and gained the street. What a terrible thing it was to be so constantly reminded of my difference from other men! I had wealth in abundance; acknowledged talents; unimpaired health; was noted for my liberality in responding to every demand of charity, art, or science; and yet, go where I would, I could hardly turn a corner or enter a room without overhearing some disparaging remark, or some sneering expression from men who had no claim to consideration for any thing beyond their seven or eight feet of stature! What, then, was wealth, or health, or talents, to me? I would have given up half of these, would have consented to wander henceforth over the earth as a beggar, could I only become like other men; and through coming ages, be able to partake of their development, whatever that might be.

Crushed in spirit and soured in disposition, I passed along the streets; joining in the currents of the crowd, or creeping beneath men's shoulders, as I strove to walk in opposite directions. And so, passing through circles of exhibition-booths, and stealing between lines of soldiery, I wended my way, intent only upon reaching my own home, and concealing myself in its seclusion. For a time I was moderately successful; but all at once, a sudden approach of cavalry from a side-street caused a change in the direction of the crowd. Unable to extricate myself, I was borne along with it; and at length, almost crushed to a jelly, I succeeded in escaping from the confusion, by plunging into the open door of a traveling-trader's tent

Observing my disorder and confusion, the trader politely assisted me to a seat, and allowed me to remain until I had recovered myself. And then I took occasion to glance around, intending to recompense him for his courtesy, by purchasing some of his wares. But I saw nothing, except a small shelf of little bottles.

"And what are these?" I said.

The trader feebly smiled. It was a gloomy smile, moreover, telling of disappointment and heart-sickness.

"Why should I inform you?" he said. "You will only ridicule my discovery, as others have done."

But I assured him that, from my lips, he would

encounter no ridicule, whatever might be the nature of his wares; and after a while, I induced him to speak.

"These little bottles," he said "contain the results of more than twenty years of toil. It is a preparation invented by myself; and it has the wonderful faculty, when taken into the system, of suspending animation for a long or short period, as may be desirable; at the end of which time the patient will awake in full health and strength, as he had lain down. He will awaken, indeed, no older in body than when he had gone to sleep; for however long may be his repose, he will lose none of his life. His life will only be postponed, that is all. In common sleep, the body all the while grows older; but in this, its functions are so suspended, that, during years, the system will suffer no manner of loss or waste. You go to sleep at thirty years of age, and sleep for ten. When you awake, though ten year, have elapsed, your animation has been so completely suspended, that you find yourself still possessing your constitution of thirty years; and in reality, have still the ten years of life to enjoy. You may not believe me, sir, but my invention has certainly the power which I have claimed for it. No one yet has believed me, but on all sides I have been treated with ridicule. And yet, sir, I assure you that I am no quack, and would deceive nobody. This invention has cost me many years to perfect, and has proved itself to be all that it is asserted to be."

Still feeling somewhat incredulous, I looked the man steadily in the eye, but could see there naught but sincerity. He bore not the slightest evidences of deceit, or of being engaged in the trade of quackery; while there were, in his face, certain lines denoting superior thought and intelligence. I felt already half convinced.

"But admitting all this to be so," I said, "what can be the benefit of this discovery?"

"It has many uses," he said. "The man of science may wish to peer into the operations of nature, during future years; while without this preparation, he would be obliged to live his life through in one coil, as it were, and at its end, of course, be no more capable of awakening to observation. The politician may wish to live his life in future years, instead of now, in order to observe the result of his theories of government. The poor man may desire to sleep, while his land increases in value, so that he may awake and find himself rich, without having been obliged to wear out the best portion of his life in toil. I myself, by way of experiment, once suspended my animation for five years; and when, at the end of that time, I awoke, there was not one gray hair the more upon my head. A single drop will cause sleep for a year, five drops for five years, and so on in proportion."

I was still somewhat incredulous, but I remembered that there can be such a thing as being too unbelieving. The world had scorned my invention, and yet, for ages, I had been a living testimony to its truth. Might I not, then, do an equal injustice in ridiculing the results of this man's scientific labors?

"I must not forget to add," the man continued,

"that, during the time animation is suspended, the body itself is preserved from injury. The liquid endues it with a peculiar property, whereby the action of the atmosphere upon it is restrained; and even insects, and the beasts of the forest, will not prey upon it. The sleep which is produced is as secure as it is sound."

Having but an hour before been scorned and insulted, my ruffled feelings put me in the mood to attempt any experiment whereby I might compose my weary soul to temporary rest. And I resolved to try the value of this man's invention. It might be a worthless deception; but then, what would be the consequence, beyond the loss of the inconsiderable gold-piece which I would pay for it? It might be of such powerful nature, that I might never awaken; but after all, what great affliction would the loss of my life of scorn and degradation be to me? And on the other hand, it might prove to be all that had been said about it; and after a year or two of sleep, I might awaken to find the world grown wiser and better, and no longer willing to measure man by height or breadth of chest or strength of arm, rather than by the soul within his breast or the talents within his brain; and then, what joy it would cause me to find that I had at last been yielded my proper position, among my fellow-creatures!

And so, moved by the strong impulse of the moment, I grasped one of the little bottles, threw down my purse in payment, and hurried away.

Through the city, which every moment became more and more crowded, as strangers from the country and neighboring cities came in to attend the great festival of the day! Through the suburbs, usually so quiet, but now thronged with living streams, all journeying cityward! So I passed along to the open country. I stayed not for coronation or military review. I had seen these by scores, and the ever-repeated pageant had no charms for me. My only desire now was to hasten away, and try the merits of the wonderful liquid, while the fever of experiment was yet fresh upon me.

Still I hurried on, through the suburbs, until I had gained the open country. There for a moment I paused to take breath, and looked around. I stood upon the top of a slight elevation, and, at a little distance below me, lay the great city of Tooxo stretching away towards the south for miles — a goodly prospect of palaces, parks, warehouses and cathedrals — and overtopped by hundreds of domes, towers, and minarets. For an instant or two I gazed upon it, with a new interest; for if the wonderful liquid which I held in my hand should be effective, a year or two would elapse before I could again stand there, and look upon that fair prospect. In the midst I could see the great square, with the coronation-throne in the centre, beneath a crimson canopy, and to be mounted by a flight of fifty steps. From every direction the populace was streaming into the square, in crowds; and in one of the broadest approaches to it, I could see the head of the coronation procession on its march, with its flaunting regimental balloons, and its crashing music half deafened by the tumultuous cheering of the excited crowd. And away off to the south, was the open sea, studded with vessels. How many of those were mine! I could count my sail-vessels by fifties; and of twenty huge atmospheric ships, which lay in port, at least a dozen belonged to me. And of the great rows of warehouses which lined the wharves, the tallest and broadest were my own. All this property I should, probably, not see again for a year. And what would be the excitement throughout the nation, when, month after month passed away, and I did not appear to claim my own! And how much greater the wonder, when, at the end of the year, I should suddenly reappear, and drive back the crowd of persons who, by that time, would be quarreling for a share of those possessions!

Fearing lest I might waver in my determination, I now turned away in order to complete my project. It had, at first, been my design to lock myself up in a room of my country-seat, and there partake of this magic sleep. But now a new idea made me change my purpose. Search would, of course, be made for me; and when I was found in my own house, stretched in apparent lifelessness upon my bed, what if my death should really be conjectured, and, in my trance, I should be buried; and finally awaken, only to suffer a thousand deaths in the sealed tomb? No; I must seek out a spot where the foot of man could not come near me, and where, secure from molestation or injury of any kind, I could await, in tranquil safety, my gradual awakening to life again.

About two miles from my country-seat was a high, rocky cliff. For three hundred feet, it loomed up almost perpendicularly into the air, and, at first view, was apparently inaccessible. This is what I should have thought, had I not been often induced to pick my way along its ledges in search of my little life-bestowing weed, which, in this part of the country, happened to grow only upon those rocky slopes. During one of these expeditions, I had discovered a small natural cave, about half-way up. With but a narrow opening, which was almost hidden by external projections, it gradually increased into a roomy apartment as it ran back. Here, then, I determined to make my experiment; for here I concluded that there would be perfect safety, from any chance of observation or detection. I alone knew of the existence of the cave, or the approaches to it. From above, it could not be reached at all; from below, only by a strangely tortuous path. Near as it was to the city, it is probable that, for centuries, no person but myself had ever tried to climb those sides; for the attempt appeared dangerous, while the almost bare rock offered no inducement in the way of fruit or flowers or verdure. Even the stone itself was unfit for building purposes, and would probably never be touched; while the solid sides of the cavern would defy the shocks of earthquakes to disturb them. And therefore, in the fullest confidence of security, I laboriously climbed the ascent; and at last, after an hour of toil, stood within the cave.

Here, then, I prepared for my long sleep. I first removed from the interior of the cave all insects or vermin which might injure me during my helpless state; for I considered it best not to trust too strongly to the promises of immunity which the trader had held out to me. Then I piled up a few loose stones, in order more effectually to conceal the mouth of the cave, and prevent even the birds of the air from entering to make it their habitation. After which I spread out my cloak upon the rocky floor, and, lying down upon it, wrapped myself warmly in its folds. And then, drawing forth the little bottle of liquid, I uncorked it, paused for a moment in irresolute fear, and finally, mustering up all my courage, at one draught drained the bottle to the dregs.

Almost at once I could feel that a gentle languor was softly stealing over me. I knew that it was the commencement of the effects of the draught; but one of its qualities seemed to be the stimulation of hope, and I felt not afraid. A happy, even temper was produced within me, and I lay awaiting the result of the experiment as calmly as though I were merely about to take a night's rest. And while I thus lay, and felt the drowsy influence upon my senses slowly increasing, I chanced to rest my eyes upon the label of the bottle, containing its directions for use.

Horror upon horrors! I had forgotten to observe the relative proportions of the liquid! Instead of the single drop, for a single year, I had drank the whole — enough to lay me into a sleep of thousands of years ! At the dreadful discovery I tried to arouse myself, and struggle against the drowsy influence, but it was too late ! My limbs had already become paralyzed; and in a moment more my senses left me!

When I awoke, it seemed as though I had slept but an hour. At first, I was inclined to curse the inventor of the liquid potion, for his deception upon me, whereby I had been put to much toil and inconvenience, without arriving at any practical result. My next impulse was to fall down upon my knees, and return thanks for being delivered from the fate of an almost eternal unconsciousness.

In doing so, an astounding fact overwhelmed me, for I discovered that I was entirely naked. But this excited only a momentary surprise. I at once conjectured that the artful trader had sold me a liquid which had the effect to drug me, whereby he had been enabled, during the past hour, to track my course, and stealing upon me, unaware, to plunder me of all my raiment. What gave cogency to this supposition was the fact, that the entrance to the cave, which I had carefully closed, was now open, all the loose stones having been rolled away. I resolved, consequently, to wait until night, and then carefully make my way to my own house, and there rehabilitate myself; and to beware how, in future, I allowed myself to be made the prey of designing impostors.

I crept to the door of the cave, and looked out. Good heavens! What did I see? Where was the great city of Tooxo, with all its towers and domes, its palaces and cathedrals? Far as the eye could reach were thick forests, covering up all indications that a great commercial port had once there existed. And what had become of the ocean, which had rolled its tide close up to the former gay and lively streets? The ocean had disappeared; and where stately ships had once lain at anchor were now great forests, stretching miles away, until lost in the horizon. And then, passing my hand across my forehead, the truth flashed upon me; the potion had but too well done its work. I had slept for centuries; perhaps for cycles. And during all that time, my clothing had rotted off my body; the vast empire had gone to decay, as empires had gone before; the cities had been deserted and fallen to ruin; the forests had reasserted their claim to the ground, and stretched their wild arms about the vestiges of wealth and refinement; and the little coral-worm had all the while been at work, and had extended the continent far southward — how many leagues — who could tell?

And where was now my vast fortune? It seemed but an hour ago that my ships had covered the sea; my warehouses lined miles of the shore. Now all was ruin and desolation. I was again a beggar upon the face of the earth; even worse conditioned than the beasts of the forest. They had their coats of fur, and their holes to live in; I was naked, and without any means of subsistence, or any place which I could call a habitation.

But at last I aroused myself, and proceeded to descend from the cave. The path by which I had ascended was now so altered, that I could recognize no single feature of it; but by carefully picking my steps, I at length managed to reach the bottom in safety. There a piece of good fortune befell me, for I found sufficient wild fruit growing to satiate my appetite; and moreover, a certain large-leaved plant, with which I contrived to manufacture a loose covering for my exposed limbs. Somewhat encouraged by this good luck, I took heart, and pursued my way with more cheerfulness.

And I resolved at once to journey to the southward, in search of the ocean which had so mysteriously receded, and, upon gaining which, I had some hopes of falling in with my fellow-men. My first day's journey led me over the site of the great city, Tooxo; but so dark and dense grew the vegetation, that I could see but little that might serve to tell the wayfarer that civilization had once there existed. At intervals, to be sure, I came across broken masses of overgrown ruins; but these were now only shapeless piles, nor could I discover any means of determining to what building they could have belonged, or in what portion of the old city I stood. All was ruin and confusion.

Then I journeyed on, still advancing in a southerly direction. I knew that I was where the tide of the great ocean had once ebbed and flowed; but the earth itself bore no indications of the change.

There were little streams and high mountains, granite rocks and trees of an hundred years' growth; but not a shell or grain of sand to denote its oceanic origin. The change was as complete as though the continent had been planted there at the very commencement of the world.

Nor were these changes confined to the earth alone. When night came, I saw new alterations in the sky. There were different spots upon the surface of the moon. One of the stars, forming the Southern Cross, had shifted towards the West, so that the Cross had become like a wooden crane. And another of the Pleaides had entirely disappeared. Was I really upon the same world; or had I been conveyed during my sleep, to another one?

Still onward I journeyed. By the increasing heat, and the altitude of the sun, I could tell that I was approaching the equator; but yet the dark forest seemed to have no limit, and day after day passed without a single human being appearing to gladden my eyes. There were strange and paiatable fruits to serve for my subsistence, and thus I kept up my strength, and felt no want. I saw numbers of singular species of animals, but none of them seemed inclined to molest me. I was as wild as they, and they probably feared me as much as I dreaded them. I saw many places where forest glades, and rich prairies, and cooling streams, and delicious wild fruits combined to form lovely nooks, where I might have lived for years in idle sylvan luxury; and there had been times, during my past life, when I would have liked nothing better than to have pitched my lot in some such spot, and there idly dreamt on for centuries. But now I tore myself away in haste. The universal solitude and desolation filled me with such a longing for one more glimpse of my fellow-creatures, that I would have been content to become a slave to them, and submit to any degradation or contempt, if I might only thereby enjoy the privilege of knowing that I was not alone in the world.

And at length, upon the twentieth morning of my pilgrimage, the sound of the roaring surf burst upon my ear. Madly I plunged forward, and gained the limit of the forest; delightedly I looked upon the ocean, stretched out in boundless expanse before me, glittering in the rays of the bright sun, and, in all things, as unchangeable as the sun itself. I fell upon my knees, and poured forth my thanks in an outburst of emotion; in all my life I had never experienced such a moment of intense happiness.

Suddenly, while I remained in this ecstasy of transport, I heard a loud cry, and felt myself rudely grasped. I turned, to offer resistance, but at once saw that all resistance would be useless. I was in the hands of a being more powerful than I — a being of ten feet in stature — black as a negro in complexion, but having a singular beauty of expression and intelligence in his countenance, and having long wings, which drooped nearly to his heels. At his cry, a dozen others like himself flew down from different points, and formed a close circle about me.

They were not beasts, I saw at once. They were men, but men endued with higher attributes than I possessed. All at once the whole truth flashed upon me. The learned Professor of Mental Gymnastics had been right in his theory. During all the past centuries, men had continued to progress; and the scanty tribe of what had once been called the accidents of creation, had gradually developed into one universal race. I saw, with dismay, that my condition had become still further lowered by their advance; and, that if I had before been looked upon as a human deformity, I could now no longer be called even a man. Even if my own perceptions had not assured me of this fact, the wondering expressions of the group about me would have satisfied me of it. To them I was a curiosity, a hitherto undiscovered animal. The few human attributes which I possessed were insufficient to give me a claim to rank among the men of the present race. I was no more like them than, thousands of years ago, the ape had been like me; and now they gazed upon me with the same curiosity with which I would then have looked upon an ape, and regarded all my attempts at conversation, in a language so unlike their own, as the mere unmeaning chattering of an animal.

I knew, of course, that I could suffer no harm at their hands. Had I been an animal of any known species, I might have been slain for food; but I was too great a curiosity not to be kept alive. I consequently prepared my mind for attentions of a different character, and, most probably, in the line of exhibition for pecuniary profit. And so it proved. When the strangers had sufficiently gratified their immediate curiosity, I was tightly bound, and carried away; and in a few days, found myself domesticated in a large city.

In a city as large as Tooxo had been, and like it, thronged with temples, academies and palaces! In a city built and inhabited by winged men, of wondrous height and ebony complexion, like unto my captors! In a strong cage, in a public room of that city, exposed to curious gaze, with other cages, containing wild animals, flanking me on either side; and opposite to me, as a wonderful curiosity, the skeleton of a horse! But of all these, I was the most powerful attraction; and thousands daily flew through the open roof, and, lighting in front of me, stared at me for hours.

For a while my life was a burden to me. I had no hope of escape, could cherish no expectation of manly treatment. Every action, indeed, assured me how little trust I could put in my slight likeness to my fellow-men, and how little they would be disposed to regard me as one of their own race. Their solemn, speculative, gaping scrutiny; their laughter, at what they considered my grotesque motions; the air of patronage and curiosity with which they pushed nuts and meat and fruits through the bars of my cage; all assured me how hopeless of recognition my claims to manly nature must ever be.

At first I was sullen, and would only eat when driven by hunger; but soon a better feeling came over me. It chanced that, one day, among the

fruits and grasses which were thrust into my cage,
I recognized a few leaves of my little life-giving
weed. I eagerly seized and devoured them. The
word then, of course, flew around, that an article
which the strange animal liked had been found; and
ever after that, my cage was plentifully supplied
with it. Having thereby the means of preserving
my life, I reflected, that, though escape might be
impossible, yet sullen discontent would do me no
good ; that by cheerfulness of conduct, I might not
only increase my happiness, but also gain new favors;
that, after all, there were many of these powerful
winged men who were beggars, and would gladly
exchange their hard lot for the comforts which I
enjoyed; that if these strange people found much
about me to wonder at, I also could amuse myself
in observing them; and that thus, in finding such
endless incitement to my curiosity, I might lead a
life of tolerable comfort.

And thus, resigning myself to my fate, I further
reflected, that if I could learn their language, I
might detail to them the circumstances of my past
life, and gain many advantages. And with this
intent, I went to work. By attentively listening
and observing how their actions corresponded with
their conversation, I speedily picked up a few words.
To these I gradually added others, pretty much in
the same manner as a child picks up his mother-
tongue ; and thus, in a few months, I began to flatter
myself that I could talk with my visitors with
tolerable ease. And one day, I resolved, that, upon
the next morning, I would make my first attempt.

Just as I came to this conclusion, I heard a loud swell of many voices in the building, and saw a few men bringing in a bundle closely bound. And I gathered that the excitement arose from the fact that another animal of my species had just been discovered.

"Put it in along with the first one," said the director of the exhibition; and accordingly the bundle was brought forward, unbound, and thrust into the same cage with myself, where it crouched in the corner as though in mortal fear. It was late in the afternoon, and had become so dark that I could not readily distinguish the form or features of the stranger. And before I could find any method of satisfying my curiosity, the exhibition came to a close, and the cage was locked up, leaving us in still greater darkness.

All night I lay awake, wondering whether any being of my race had discovered my receipt, and thus, like myself, had lived on for ages; or whether there were still left upon the earth, nations which had not progressed like others, and to which I might escape some day, and find myself once more among my equals. At times I spoke to the stranger, but he answered only in gibberish; proving that he either talked a different language, or, perhaps, like the brutes, had no settled language at all. At times, too, I ventured to touch him; but the only response was a low growl, which warned me to refrain from further experiments.

So passed the night; and at length, as the first glimmer of dawn began to glow through the open roof of the building, I began indistinctly to see my companion. He sat crouching in the corner of the cage, and glaring at me with a fixed and somewhat idiotic expression. He was naked, and, doubtless owing to long years of exposure, his body had become almost covered with hair; so that, even to myself, he appeared more like an animal than a man. I felt that with such a being, I was destined to enjoy but little pleasant companionship.

Gradually, as the day brightened, it seemed to me that I had seen him before; and as I traced feature after feature, the truth suddenly flashed upon me. It was my twin-brother, who sat mowering before me. And yet he was not like my brother, as I had seen him last — a man like myself, full of strength, activity and intelligence. He had become debased almost into brutishness. Far from my control and example, he had not continued to cultivate his natural intellectual powers; and though he had mechanically continued to eat of the source of life, his mind had been suffered to become enfeebled and to die away, until but little beyond the mere semblance of life and manhood had been left to him.

How had he contrived, during so many thousands of years, to avoid all those perils of land and sea, against which the little weed, powerful as it might be in other respects, could not guard him? Over what lands had he wandered? And how did it happen that now, at last, we so curiously met again, and in the same captivity?

And why, indeed, should he, a man of lively intellect, have suffered his mind to go to decay? Embittered, like myself, against the human race, had he withdrawn into solitude, and there, from the mere want of association with others, been unable to keep his intellectual development in its proper tone, and thus gradually lost his natural powers? Or had the change been a more sudden one, and been owing to remorse for the wretched piece of revenge which his passion of the moment had induced him to execute upon me?

As I reflected upon this last supposition, my anger, which, though buried so many years, had not been dead, burst forth in fever-heat, and I grasped him by the shoulder, and shook him with a force which he could not withstand.

"Where is she?" I cried, forgetting at the moment how many centuries had elapsed. "What have you done with her? Tell me, that I may go and find her."

No answer; but as I released him, he muttered incoherent ravings, and then settled down again into his beast-like attitude, and there remained gazing at me with the same watchful idiotic glare as before. I tried a new manœuvre, and proceeded to supplication.

"Brother," I cried, "we have lived long together. We have shared the same joys and sorrows. We should not quarrel now. Only tell me what you have done with her, and I will forgive all that is past."

No answer yet; but seeing a few leaves of our little weed lying strewn about the floor of the cage, his eye lighted up with pleasure, and he began to pick them up, and chew them with a sort of mechanical frenzy. Upon this, my wrath burst forth again. It seemed like a double insult to me, to sit there, unconfessing, unregretting that he had wronged me; and yet, all the while, to avail himself of the priceless secret which I had taught him.

"Tell me !" I cried, again seizing him. "Tell me all, or you shall die, though forests of plants grew around you !"

Still no answer; but drawing himself up, he pointed his forefinger towards me, with a sneering, contemptuous expression, which flesh and blood could not have endured. And yet there was probably no sneer or contempt intended. It was only an idiotic gesture, without thought or meaning. But at the moment, it seemed to me as though he had meant all that his action implied — that he had recognized me, and was tormenting me with the misfortune which he had brought upon me; and at once I lost all self-control. There chanced to be a loose iron bar lying on the floor of my cage. Transported with fury, I raised it in the air, and even while he sat with his forefinger pointed at me, brought the weapon down crashing into his brain.

He fell at my feet — dead ! The life which had been preserved so many thousands of years had fled in an instant. No mere herb could avail to save, after such a blow as I had given.

For the instant, I felt overwhelmed with the consciousness of the dreadful deed which I had committed. But I had then no time to weep or to curse my lot, for at that moment I heard the keeper opening the hall. I had merely time to turn the body of my brother, so that the wound in his head might be concealed, and he appear as though he slept; and then the front of my cage was taken down, and the exhibition of the day commenced.

In a few moments, over fifty people were standing in front, and gazing at me; and remembering my determination to attempt conversation with them, I suddenly inquired:

"My friends, what year of the world is this?"

At this unexpected speech, there was instant commotion. One or two women, of eight or nine feet in height, fainted; a dozen or two flew out at the roof, in hot haste; and many men turned pale, and staggered back in affright. But as I gradually reassured them, by a few pleasant words, and let them know that, in spite of my wonderful quality of speech, I was perfectly harmless, the crowd again collected about me; and one who, by his appearance, might have been one of the wise men of the city, undertook to reply to me.

"What do you want?" he said.

"I wish to know how old the world has become," I replied.

"How can any one tell?" he responded, in a loud tone, and apparently as desirous of impressing the crowd with his profundity as of enlightening me. "We can only tell that our nation is several hundred years old, and during that time, has been gradually elevating itself from barbarism into civilization; but no one knows how many years have gone before that. But who are you?"

I then proceeded to tell how that, it might have been thousands of years ago, I was a human creature, a citizen of the great seaport of Tooxo, and had there fallen asleep, and had only waked up to find myself seized and treated like a wild beast; and I demanded my release. But the wise man only shook his head.

"We can hardly believe such a story as that," he said to the crowd about him. "In the first place, though our knowledge of the past has been yearly increasing, yet we have never heard of such a place as Tooxo; and it is probable that no such place ever existed. In the next place, there have been no remains ever found, to indicate that mankind was ever any thing different from what it is now. Moreover, it would be attaching a derogatory idea to the work and intention of PROVIDENCE, to suppose that HE would ever create such a small, white-looking, wingless object as that, and call it after HIS own likeness."

I thought of the time when the Professor of Ancient Languages, in Tooxo, had expressed kindred sentiments, and I groaned aloud.

"I grant that it is a singular thing that he can speak our tongue," the wise man continued. "But what does all that prove? Not that he is a man, but merely that PROVIDENCE, for some wise purpose, has created a brute with somewhat superior intelligence; and that the brute thus created has had the cunning to listen to and learn our language, in order to impose this singular fiction upon us, and thus endeavor to claim relationship with our nobler natures."

While he spoke, soft music began to break upon the ear; and, through the open roof, I could see numbers of people floating in the air, some remaining almost stationary upon their spread-out wings, and others engaging in a singularly beautiful dance. All were clothed in white, and new additions were constantly made to the party; while new strains of music continually arose from different quarters.

"What does all this mean?" I said. "Is this a festival-day?"

"It is a day the tradition of which has descended for many thousands of years," answered the wise man; "a day which has always been celebrated with mirth and brotherly love, in all lands, I believe. For on this day, it is said that our CREATOR became a man like unto ourselves, and for us commenced to live on earth."

"Christmas day!" I exclaimed. And as I turned aside, and saw the dead body lying at my side, I wept. Of what avail had been all the years I had lived? On another Christmas day I had attained my great secret, and had hailed the discovery as a glorious one, because I had imagined that I would have many more years in which to purify my soul, and make me more fit for heaven at the last. And instead thereof, I had been growing, year by year, more hardened in heart; and at last, upon a Christmas morning, had ended a career of selfishness by murdering my own twin-brother !

"Listen !" I exclaimed, turning to the crowd. "It may be that I deserve my fate, but my story is none the less true, for all that. Were he, who now lies there, only alive and in his senses, he could speak up, and also tell you who we both once were. But he's dead — dead by my own hand — and cannot be my witness. But hold !" I suddenly cried, in a passion of ecstasy. "There stands one who can vouch for the truth of my story ! Ask her, and I will abide by what she says !"

For, among the crowd of spectators, I recognized my long-lost wife, who, all this while, by our common secret, had retained her hold on life. With her, as centuries before, the principle of new development had continued on in steady progress. She was now nearly eight feet in height, and darker in complexion, and, like the rest, had drooping wings; but in all else, in expression and in features, was unchanged. Though thousands of years had passed, I knew her in an instant.

"Call her! Let her tell!" I cried, not thinking it possible that, even if she recognized me, she might shrink from acknowledging as her husband one who only had the social position of an ape. "She will tell you whether I have ever been a human being or not."

She turned. I saw her advance towards me. Hope swelled in my breast. I screamed aloud with joy. I frantically rattled the bars of my cage.

And I awoke; awoke to find my wife—still small and fair-complexioned and wingless, as I had first married her—bending over me. It had all been a dream; and Apollonius Septrio, and his secret, were but the phantasies of a disordered brain.

"Wake up, dear Will!" said my wife, giving me an affectionate shake. "You are dozing, and the syrup is boiling over; and if you do not stir it, we shall lose it all, and the children will not have their Christmas candy."

I rubbed my eyes. Yes, there was the pot—which contained no elements of an abstruse analysis, but simply a little boiling syrup—running over at the edge, as it had done when I first commenced to doze. I looked out of the window, and saw the old sexton, lantern in hand, still plodding on through the snow, and hardly a step from where I had first seen him. Yes, all this dream of events, of thousands of years, had occurred in a second or two of time!

In a few words, I told my wife the substance of my vision. She smiled, and pointing behind her, said:

"Why, indeed, should we care for such long life? Shall we not live again in these?" I looked, and there stood our children.

Hark! at that moment the bells struck up! They were ill-tuned and cracked, and moreover were set to no particular air, but jingled to-and-fro according to the strength and disposition of the old sexton and his juvenile aids. But somehow, on that night, there was a musical sound to them, for they seemed to speak of peace and good-will to all the world!

"It may be," said my wife, gazing up with an expression of sweet serenity irradiating every feature, "it may have been no dream that you have just had. It may be prophecy."

"Prophecy?"

"Yes. It may be, that upon some future Christmas day, I shall really wear wings," she said. "But it will not be in this world, but in another and a better one, I hope. And if that day does come," she continued, "I hope that you, too, will wear wings; and that together we may live in that better world, never to be parted; and there continually gain new developments in the eternal progression of love, and joy, and holiness!"

Prior Polycarp's Portrait.

CHAPTER I.

IT is my intention to narrate every circumstance of the story, — freely, and without attempt at concealment or extenuation. At the time, it caused me many a heartburn; now that advancing years have gathered so much more closely about me, and I have become interested only in my professional ambition, I can afford even to laugh at the matter, as an amusing retrospect.

It happened upon Christmas-day. It would have been a very sad trial and disappointment to me, if I had been obliged to pass the evening in the loneliness and obscurity of my own lodgings, with no other society than my morbid thoughts; and yet, for a time, it seemed unavoidable. When, therefore, early in the morning, there came a dainty little note from Mabel Cuthbert, inviting me to dine with her at the Priory, my heart was wonderfully lightened from its depression, and my spirits gave a sudden exultant bound into sunshine. It was a pleasant little invitation, without the slightest tinge of stiffness or formality, — genial and winning, rather, in tone, as of one writing to a very near and trusted friend, and not to some mere chance acquaintance of the day. And it informed me that I was to be the only guest; Mabel and myself, — those were all.

I was more disposed to feel pleased, in fact, than I had imagined the mere invitation to a Christmas dinner could ever make me. It was something, indeed, to escape from the loneliness of my bachelor quarters, with only my landlady, Mrs. Chubbs, to skirmish around, serve up my poor little chicken for me as the mere ghost of a festivity, and all the while keep a vigilant eye upon me, that I should leave a goodly portion of it for her own subsequent delectation. It was a great deal to avoid the subsequent brooding reflections, when every darkening shadow would be sure to strike into my soul, each moment becoming more and more fretful with the bitter pang of loneliness. But now that I was to avoid these troubles, it seemed to me a great deal more than any thing else, that my invitation should be to the Priory. For, during the past two years, the Priory had remained a closed residence for anything in the way of formal entertainment. Ever since the Squire's death, his daughter Mabel had lived there in the strictest seclusion, going nowhere, and caring little about seeing any one. In fact, I was known to be almost the only person whose visits seemed to be at all looked for or encouraged; it having happened that at the Squire's death I had been the attending physician, and hence had acquired some vested right to continue my visits upon the footing of friendly interest. Now, therefore, that the seclusion seemed drawing to an end and some faint indications appeared of a return to the outer world, it was very pleasing to me to see that I was still the first person selected for social favor, and that I was considered worthy of encouragement for something other than my professional character and qualities. And moreover, — for I may as well confess the fact at the very beginning — I dearly loved to be at Mabel Cuthbert's side, and always felt my heart bound wildly at the slightest hint of any preference for me.

Pleasantly humming a tune to myself, I started off on a little round of medical calls, lasting until afternoon. When I returned, I found Mrs. Chubbs in my office, washing the windows with great appearance of zeal. It was an unusual performance for her on Christmas, or, indeed, on any other day; and I felt that the sudden fit of cleanliness was merely a pretense to open communication with me. I was not mistaken.

"And so you are going to dine at the Priory, Doctor," she said. "And in course, you will be the first person to know all about it."

"And how, Mrs. Chubbs, could you have ascertained that I was going to the Priory?" I responded severely. "Surely you have not given yourself the liberty to read my correspondence?"

There was little need, indeed, to put it in the form of a question, inasmuch as upon the corner of Mabel's note, inadvertently left by me open upon the table, was the broad impress of a soapy thumb. I held out the note towards Mrs. Chubbs, as I spoke, in token of the perfect knowledge that gave me authority to reprove; but she was not to be put down or thrown into confusion as easily as that.

"And what if I have read it?" she said. "Do you think, Doctor Crawford, that if a patient comes after you, and I have charge of your office, and he says where are you, and I say I don't know, and he says find out, and I have to look over your desk to see if you have left a paper or so about when you will come back, and he says look further yet, and I come across a note and think may be it will tell where you are gone, and when I read it, find it is only where you are to go this evening, — do you think, then, that I can forget all about it again, and never remember anything of the past or of what is going this day to be found out at the last, Doctor Crawford?"

With a red face, Mrs. Chubbs descended from her perch, gathered up her pail and step-ladder, and stumped off out at the door, leaving the cleaning for another season, and, in her dignified departure, knocking the end of her ladder so violently against my skeleton-case, that I could hear all the bones inside rattle. And I, crushed and discomfited, and giving little further heed to what seemed to me her random, purposeless remark, kept silence, nor thought to ask what it was, that, at this last, was to be found out, and all about which I was to be the first person to know.

Rousing myself after a little, I prepared my toilet for the evening, — then again took up the note. For the first time I happened to notice, that through some inadvertence, the hour for dining was not mentioned. It might very well be five, — Mabel's usual hour; and yet, to-day it might be later, being a special occasion. I was a little nonplussed, at first, but finally settled the matter satisfactorily in my mind. I would go at five, — and would inquire at the gate-lodge for further particulars. If the dinner chanced to be later, I would ride on and visit old Mrs. Rabbage, returning to the Priory at the proper hour. Old Mrs. Rabbage would most likely believe that my white cravat and dress coat had been put on in especial compliment to her case; and if there were any real virtue in the imagination, it might do her rheumatism more good than all my other attentions. Therefore, at half past four, I climbed into my gig and started.

It was a brisk, cheery day, not too warm or cold. The sky was somewhat heavy and overcast, with prospect of becoming more so; but the atmosphere was bright and lively with falling snow, descending in large dry flakes, not offensively driving into one's face with tempest blast, but dropping lightly and softly, so that I could almost feel company in their steady coming; watching how they slowly melted away upon the bearskin robe tucked snugly around me, and how, beneath the gradual deepening of the fleecy deposit of those that descended in more favorable places, the ground and the hedgerows gradually turned to light blue and then to white. And jogging thus along, in wondrous pleasant frame of mind, contented with myself and all the world, I met Parkins, the brewer, driving home in his own light wagon.

"Whither away, Doctor Crawford?" he said.

"To the Priory, Mr. Parkins,—to dinner. Not a large dinner," I added, in explanation. "Only myself, I believe."

"Aha, to the Priory? You're in luck, Doctor. Was telling Mrs. Parkins that we ought to have you down at our place; but now that you are going to do so much better—Good dinners, always, at the Priory while the Squire was alive; and, likely as not, yet—Well, one thing, Doctor; you will be the first person to know all about it. I suppose, however, we'll all know, after a while."

"All about what, Mr. Parkins?"

But before he could answer, his horse had started, and in an instant was half a hundred feet off. Parkins was not much of a driver, though he imagined the contrary In fact, he generally contrived to get run away with three or four times a year. At the present moment, though he parted from me with elbows squared out and with a cheery "gee-up," and altogether great affectation of wielding a gallant rein, I could not resist an impression that the horse was moved with an instinct of Christmas oats ahead, and was in a hurry to get home and was moderately running away, and that Parkins could not have checked him, if his life depended upon it. Be that as it may, the consequence was a sudden separation between us that momentarily increased; and so my question was left unanswered.

"At any rate," I now said to myself, not attaching any more importance to the brewer's observation than to Mrs. Chubbs, "there is one matter, at least, about which I will hope to-day to know something."

I have already intimated that it was the great happiness of my life to be at Mabel Cuthbert's side; and now, of course, it will be understood that I was thinking of my hitherto unavowed affection for her. For months I had endeavored to stifle it, but in vain. It was a love that had no cessation, — allowed me no rest; surely then it was about time that, even if I knew nothing else, I should have some knowledge as to whether my affection might be prospering, — whether I was doomed at the end to relinquish all my hopes, or whether they would gradually brighten into sweet assurance. And what better day than the present, with its genial and inspiring influences, to learn at least something that would direct me to a knowledge of my fate? What better time than Christmas-day, with its cheery unrestrained greetings, to catch some unguarded indication peeping forth here and there, to tell me what I might expect?

That my hopes were well founded, I had gradually schooled myself to believe. To the outer world, unacquainted with all the circumstances of the case, it is true that my love for Mabel might have seemed pretentious, — my attentions, a presumption. She was scarcely twenty-five, — I was nearly forty. She came from a long and honored ancestry, — I could not go further back than to my grandfather, himself a village doctor. But, on the other hand, looking at the matter in the prosaic yet none the less practical light of worldly fortune, the Crawfords had been long accumulating, and my own possessions were not

inconsiderable; while the Cuthberts had been gradually losing in estate, generation after generation
parting with a field here and a quarry there, until
at least half the landed property was gone. Half
of the remainder even, was at that moment imperiled;
inasmuch as a chancery suit about the title to some
five hundred acres of its family estate was now,
after twenty years slow progress, drawing near its
close, with the chances, so far, greatly in favor of the
outside contestants. Moreover, as has been already
said, for the past two years Mabel had remained
in strict retirement, seeing few persons and in no way
exposed to the admiration of the outer world, during
which time I had been nearly her only visitor, —
coming almost daily in the light of a true and valued
friend. At one time I had taught her what little
French I knew, and often we had read to each other.
It seemed, therefore, as though such exclusive inti-
macy must bear some fruit. I knew that I was
always received with warm pressure of the hand and
a sunny smile. Did that mean love, or was it mere
friendship? I could not tell for certain, indeed;
though at times I gazed earnestly into her eyes, in
search of some fleeting, unguarded expression that
might, of a certainty, betray the nature of her feelings. But all the while my wishes had been teaching me to hope for and believe the best; and it
seemed as though there could not be a better time
than that Christmas-day to ascertain, beyond a
doubt, the real strength of my self assurances.

Chapter II.

THUS jogging along in hopeful, though not altogether unanxious train of reflection, about five o'clock I reached the Priory. It was not an imposing building. In its best estate it had been one of the smaller and least known religious houses of the kingdom; and since it had been secularized, every change in its extent and outward appearance had been for the worse. The quaint old bell-tower had been taken down, and the bell removed to a distant parish church. The chapel had fallen into decay, and finally been cleared away as an useless appendage, not necessary to be restored. The refectory had been cut into several smaller rooms; and in doing so, it had unfortunately happened that much of the heavy carved oak wainscoting had been destroyed. Much of the symbolical ornamentation sculptured upon the outside of the building had been chipped away by a vandal owner of the place during the last century, under the idea that it was unsuited to a private residence. And so, little by little the Priory had fallen away from much of its former pleasant estate;—in some places brick taking the place of stone, until it became a mere quadrangular building, without especial type or character, — such a building as might have been erected within the present century, after a design giving up everything to space, and sacrificing all ornamentation to utility.

Adding to all this, the fact that gradually much of the land belonging to the Priory had been alienated, until there was now little left besides lawn and garden, and that the knightly title that had been enjoyed by its earliest civil owner had drifted off in some other direction, as titles will sometimes mysteriously do; and it will be seen that in her inheritance, Mabel Cuthbert had not become a great heiress or social power in the county. But for all that, the place was still known as the Priory, such being the permanence of English tradition; and, as will be seen, certain traditions lingered about it, with a pertinacity that defied all influence of outward physical change to banish them.

Stopping for a moment at the gate-lodge, I looked around in every direction, but found no one. The occupants of the lodge had evidently departed upon some Christmas frolic, and the gate stood wide open for any one to enter who might be inclined. Therefore I drove through; somewhat reluctantly, however, not wishing prematurely to present myself before the house, in case I had mistaken the hour. But upon reaching the end of the Priory building and before emerging into the exposure of its full front, there I saw Roper the butler, standing at the side porch. And I beckoned him to me.

"Dinner at five, as usual, Roper?"

"At seven, to-day, Doctor, — being Christmas."

"Ah! then I had better make a professional call or two, and then return."

"Better come in now, Doctor Crawford, and wait. It is not very likely that Miss Cuthbert will see you do so. She is in her own room at the back of the house, lying down and will scarcely come out until seven. I will send the gig around to the stable and smuggle you into the library, where she seldom comes, and will not announce you before it is time for you to come in the usual way."

It was very tempting, and for the moment I gazed around irresolutely. Not so very irresolutely, after all, perhaps; for I must have had in my mind, from the first, some premonition of the inevitable issue of any conflict on the subject. The sky was becoming more overcast, — the snow was descending more heavily and was now deeper under foot, somewhat clogging the wheels and discouraging any tendency to further admiration of its pretty crystal whiteness, — old Mrs. Rabbage's rheumatism would be none the better or worse, whether I came or stayed away, — through the half open door I saw the red flicker of coalfire in an open gate, reflected upon the wall of the hall outside; — in fine, I hesitated and was lost.

"I think, — I suppose I had better do it, Roper," I said with a sort of half cough and an expression of voice as though I were reluctantly yielding to some requirement of duty. With that same impress of reluctance stamped upon every motion of my body, I slowly climbed down from the gig, threw the reins to a stable boy whom Roper beckoned up, shook the few snow flakes off my coat, and allowed myself to be escorted through the hall and into the library.

It was a cozy, old fashioned little room. With the dining room adjoining, it had been cut off from

the long refectory.   In this operation, as has already
been stated, much of the carved wainscoting had
been torn away; but the loss had afterwards been
partially replaced with heavy hangings of Spanish
leather, and the original graining of the ceiling had
happened to be retained, so that there remained much
pleasant basis for picturesque effect.   This had been
increased by a broad fireplace of antique design,
and all the paintings upon the wall were sufficiently
smoke-dried and discolored as almost to defy scrutiny, and thus add to the general impress of high
toned antiquity.   Though the room was called the
library, it did not rejoice in many books; for the late
Squire was not a man of literary proclivities, while
the studies of those who had gone before him were
mainly confined to treatises on horses, dogs and
hunting.   In fact, there was merely one small case
of books, and those of such unprepossessing character to the general reader that they were seldom
opened from one year to another.   But upon a small
stand between the windows were a few volumes
belonging to Mabel, in whom had sprouted the earliest recognizable evidences of family culture; and
upon the broad oak table in the middle of the room
lay the morning papers and a few of the most popular periodicals of the day, — Mabel's own reading.
   Throwing myself into a deep cushioned chair, I
took up the Cornhill, and was about to lose myself
pleasantly in its pages for the next two hours, when
Roper reappeared.   While standing at the side
porch, he had been in a sort of deshabille, — in no
way clad differently from the inferior beings around

him. Now, as the assumption of his official duties
drew near, he had thrown himself into the undress
uniform of black coat and pants.

"Wouldn't you like a little something for lunch,
Doctor Crawford?" he said. "Just a little pastry,
or a trifle of some such kind, to prepare for dinner?"

It seemed to me a very apt suggestion.

"I am not sure, Roper, but what, after all, I
would," I responded, again assuming that hypocrit-
ical tone of irresolution which I had adopted when
entering the house in preference to riding further;
though, as then, I knew very well what was the
fore-ordained result. "As you say," and it was only
afterwards that I remembered he had not said it, —
"the road hither is a pretty long one, and the air
has been a little nipping and — yes, Roper, on second
thoughts I am inclined to believe that I might manage
to eat a mouthful or two."

Roper grinned, — I am sure I do not know at
what, — and turned to go.

"I will bring the things in here, Doctor," he said,
"for the dining-room table is getting made ready
for dinner. And besides, you are more likely not
to be disturbed here."

With that, he cleared away a portion of the papers
from the library table, then disappeared, and soon
returned, bearing a well laden tray which he set
down before me. There was, indeed, a goodly array;
some jelly and pastry, the remains of a venison pie,
delicate biscuits, olives, and indeed enough to con-
stitute a varied and ample meal for a professed
epicure. If this were Roper's idea of a lunch, what

must the coming dinner be? Thinking incidentally upon that, I resolved that for the present I would refrain as much as possible from allowing too much scope to my appetite, and sat down with intent at rigorous self denial. Possibly, however, I did not fully live up to my prudent resolution. Owing to the long drive, my appetite was more than ordinarily keen, and somehow seemed to increase with the first few mouthfuls. As generally happens in such cases, therefore, I was led on by small degrees into utter abandonment of my good intentions, and ended by making a very full and excellent repast.

Towards the end, I began to find my hunger giving way to thirst, and wondered that Roper had not furnished me with any wine. A mere thimbleful was all that I would require,—just a mouthful, indeed, to wash down the venison pastry and take away something of the dryness of the French rolls. There was not even a goblet of water; and altogether, it was a very strange state of affairs. It was, of course, merely a case of momentary forgetfulness on the part of Roper; but then, it did not seem right that he should ever have forgotten. For the instant I felt a little insulted, as at designed neglect. Roper should really have known better, inasmuch as I was such a frequent visitor to the house, and my taste for proper treatment must be so well recognized.

But while thus inwardly expressing to myself my discontent, I chanced to observe a bottle resting upon a small carved corner shelf near the door. A short, stout bottle, holding, perhaps, a trifle over a pint. It had a yellow seal, and even across the room and through the gathering gloom of evening, I could see that the tops and sides of the bottle were thickly coated with dust. Doubtless a bottle of very superior wine; and now it flashed across me that Roper must have intended it for myself. Nothing more probable, indeed, than that he had brought it in with the tray, and finding it crowded to the danger of being upset by the swaying of the dishes, had lifted off the bottle while passing, and placed it upon this little shelf, intending afterwards to return for it. And of course, nothing was more easy than, in the end, to have forgotten it altogether. As though to prove the truth of my conjecture, a small silver corkscrew lay conveniently at the side of the bottle.

I crossed over and carried the little treasure of a bottle back to my table, then held it up to the light. The glass was dark and thick, and the dust seemingly darker and thicker, so that I could form no fair judgment of its contents. I could merely ascertain by the weight and the faint line of demarkation at the top of the neck, that it was full, which so far was satisfactory. After all, the only true way to judge of the contents of a bottle is to taste them; and in this case it seemed plainly to have been intended that I should do so. Accordingly I pulled out the cork, and there being no glass at hand, I took a copious, gurgling draught from the bottle itself.

It was a very fair wine,—as near as I could judge, port. I have never professed to be anything of an expert in wines; still, I can tell good port from gooseberry, and whether a wine is thin or fruity. In the present case, I found the wine rich and palatable; with something of a strange tendency to acidity, however, as though it might have been kept a little too long. I had read that after a certain number of years, a wine begins to lose in excellence; and it struck me that this little bottle might have been emptied, with more advantage to its proper enjoyment, a few years earlier.

Still, thinking the matter all over, I felt glad that it had not been so disposed of, for in that case I would not have had the drinking of it; and whatever might be its present defects, calculated upon some artificial standard of absolute perfection, it was a much better wine than any to which I was accustomed, and admirably served its purpose in washing down the pastry, now becoming dry and tasteless. Therefore I placed the bottle lovingly beside my plate; and when my throat had been duly moistened, I felt able to eat more venison, and with the dryness of the venison, to take another draught of the wine. So continuing, turning from neck of bottle to pastry, and from pastry back again to neck of bottle, there came at last a moment when the wine refused longer to run, and somewhat to my astonishment I felt that I had drunk it all.

I was not displeased or disheartened thereat. I felt, indeed, that I had had enough. The pastry was not all gone, but already it had lost much of its attraction for me, and as for the wine, I cared not for a single sip more. I was satiated, pleased with myself and contented with all the world. Satisfied appetite had put me in a tranquil and happy frame

of mind; and I could lean back in my easy chair,
fold my hands before me, and dream away an hour
or so, with scarcely a care.

One thing, indeed, troubled me a little, at the first.
The wine had evidently been intended for me, but I
had been guilty of the impropriety of drinking it
without invitation. Now that my needs were
assuaged, I began to think that it would have been
a little nicer for me to have waited until Roper had
placed the bottle before me. Though he might altogether have forgotten to do so, and I had continued
to the very end to prick the coating of my throat
with dry pastry, it would have been better so, than
to have shown such eagerness to help myself. And
yet another fault. I had drank the wine out of the
bottle's neck, instead of ringing for a glass. This,
of itself, was rude and unbecoming; exhibiting not
only a lack of due deference for good wine, in the
proper use thereof, but also giving my action something of the semblance of shame faced concealment.
How should I repair these errors, and, in some measure, restore my shattered self-respect?

There was nothing in fact, to do, but to replace
the little bottle upon the corner shelf and thereby
avoid immediate betrayal of its misappropriation.
Accordingly, I restored it to its former resting place,
first pushing the cork down even with the rim, and
I laid the cork-screw again beside it. This done,
I sank once more into the easy chair, and resumed
my uninterrupted flow of tranquil thought. My
fault repaired as far as for the instant I could do so,
I was no longer to give the matter a single moment

of concern. What harm, after all, had I done? I had merely drank some wine that had been intended for me, and, through forgetfulness, had not been offered. Whatever license had here been shown, would never anywhere give offence. Mabel would never hear about it; and Roper, upon discovering it, would utter no criticisms, inasmuch as, under similar circumstances, he would have been certain to do the same. I should avoid the wondering glare of his fishy eye, by leaving the house before he discovered that the bottle had been emptied; how he might afterwards look, need concern me little.

Thus comforting myself, to the re-establishment of my mental equilibrium, I settled down still more snugly into my chair, again took up the Cornhill, turned over a leaf or two, and, I think, must have dropped off into a passing doze. I conclude that it must have been so, from the fact that I had not seen Roper re-enter the room. A slight rattling of plates aroused me; and opening my eyes I saw Roper at the table, gathering up the appurtenances of my late lunch. He piled the china upon a waiter, and then staggered to the door. Opening it, somehow, with the back of his knuckles and holding it open with the side of his heel, he squeezed through, turning as he did so, for a parting observation.

"This is the great day at last, Doctor Crawford."

"What day, Roper?"

"The day when we are to know all about it; — the day for the opening of the twenty-five year old bottle."

Chapter III.

THE door closed behind Roper and his laden tray, and I jumped up as though I had been shot. A cold chill ran down my back, — then the blood rushed to my head with fever heat. I wished that I were away, — in the middle of China, — ten feet beneath the surface of the earth, — anywhere, rather than in the upbraiding presence of that unlucky bottle. I felt that I could have jumped down a well, — gone up to the stars in a balloon, — submitted to any torture or persecution, rather than have been led by cruel fate into the Priory on that Christmas-day.

Yes, — I recollected the whole story now. It had happened years ago, when I was a mere growing lad. I had known it at the time, though perhaps it would have made little impression upon me, if I had not heard it talked over, unremittingly, for two or three years after. Then it had all died away again; but as there are men who keep the calendars of heat and cold and changes of the wind from year to year, with no apparent object or result, so there are other men who make it their business to note down registry of anything in the least singular or unusual, with purpose to bring it all up again at some appropriate future time. Some one of these persons, doubtless, had made minute of the bottle, and now within a day or two, as the time drew near, had opened his budget of expectations, and again awakened the curiosity of the whole village.

It was a little over twenty-five years before, that he whom they called the "Old Squire"—the grandfather of Mabel—had died. He left his estate, in the natural way, to his descendants. Attached to his will, but forming no part of it, was a simple direction that a certain accurately designated bottle of wine should be put away in a safe place, and left untouched for twenty-five years from the coming Christmas, at which time it should be opened by the then owner of the Priory. Naturally the mandate caused much gossip and speculation. There were a few—a very few—who laughed, and pronounced the thing a mere whim and joke of the "Old Squire," not worth a second thought; but the majority considered differently. The more the matter was canvassed, the more wonderful did it seem, and the wider and less bound down to probability became the range of speculation. It was the expressed belief of some that the wine was a newly-discovered elixir, which should restore departed youth, and thereby give to the House of Cuthbert the gift of unfailing life; though the advocates of this theory, it must be confessed, were few, and principally among the ignorant and the lovers of the supernatural. Others thought that inasmuch as the "Young Squire"—Mabel's father—had not the credit of being very strong minded or exacting of his rights, the "Old Squire" had accurately calculated twenty-five years as the time necessary to impoverish the estate, and had made arrangements for replenishing its fortunes at

the end of that period. This might be done by a
scroll in the bottle, revealing the spot where treasure
was concealed. Such post-mortem protectory devises
were not unknown in English history, it was alleged;
though no one, at the moment, could place his
finger upon any well authenticated instance. Still
another class argued that it might not have been
necessary to point out any especial place of deposit,
inasmuch as the treasure might be in the bottle
itself. A few large diamonds of sufficient value to
redeem the estate from any ordinary liability could
easily be secreted in the bottom of the bottle, snugly
packed around so as not prematurely to betray themselves, and thus lie hidden until the opportunity for
their disinterment might arise.

As it turned out, of course, the theory of those
few comprising the sensible and reflecting class was
the correct one. The bottle held no treasure; simply
its modicum of good port wine. The Old Squire
was an eccentric man, vastly fond of dealing in sur-
prises and mystifications. It had doubtless happened
that in some moment of jovial companionship with
an especially excellent bottle of wine, he had regretted
that his descendants could not enjoy the fellow of
it; and in the impulse of the moment had endeavored
to procure them that pleasure, by solemnly dedicat-
ing it to a life of twenty-five years in expectancy.
Possibly he had then forgotten all about it; more
likely he had remembered it with a chuckle from
time to time, enjoying the anticipated mortification,
and only sorry that he could not be there to see.
As it happened, he could not have contrived a better

way to keep his memory green; the speculations
over the bottle having accomplished this for him far
better than if it had been a bronze monument. And
now to me the secret stood revealed; it was wine,
not at all improved by age, — only that.

Only that, in essence; and yet to me, in its consequences, perhaps a very serious thing. Expectation now stood agog throughout all the village, —
it would be known that I had been summoned to
attend at the uncorking, — I would be expected to
reveal the long hidden secret; — and what, alas!
was I to say? I could not refuse to say anything,
making affectation of new mysteries; for Roper, also,
would be at the opening, and would expose the
truth. I would not dare to own that I had myself
emptied the bottle, for in every way the consequences of the confession would be disastrous to
me. Ridicule and suspicion would become my
portion ever after. I would be pointed out as the
doctor, who, at a private house, had taken upon
himself surreptitiously to purloin and by himself
drink a whole bottle of the family wine. Who after
that would trust me in their houses? And what professional confidence could afterwards be reposed in a
doctor who would be reported as being in the habit
of emptying a whole bottle of wine at a sitting, not
in the justifiable conviviality of the dinning room,
but in the morbid seclusion of his own privacy?
Moreover, would not the advocates of the diamond
theory express disbelief in the story of any wine at
all being in the bottle; and claim, instead, that I
had pilfered the estate of its hoarded brilliants,

robbing the fair unsuspecting heiress for my own enrichment?

The atmosphere of the room seemed stifling, — I could scarcely breathe; and seizing my hat, I sought the open air for more collected reflection. As I passed out, I could see that Roper stood at a little window, and gazed after me in some astonishment. Well, indeed, he might. The snow was falling faster than ever, and was already over my ankles. The wind was increasing, the sky dark, and it was certain to be a tempestuous night. I had no overcoat, — my thin boots were little fitted to plough through the deepening drifts; why, then, should I leave the comfortable bright coal fire and wander through that outside stormy blackness? But, at the moment, I cared not what Roper thought; I was only intent upon composing my own distracted mind, and it seemed as though I could better do so, while wandering at will down the broad avenue of oaks than while pent up in a close room.

And what, — so my troubled thoughts step by step carried me on, — what in addition would be the consequences of my error, in the matter of my hopes of Mabel? How, in that, might not that unlucky bottle thwart me? What if, despite my comfortable assurance of full success, Mabel's feelings of mere friendship or real love for me were at that moment so nearly balanced, that any little circumstance would turn the scale, and she should believe that the village laughter which would assail the collapse of the bottle mystery had attached in part to herself; and that, therefore, looking upon me as the author of the annoyance, she should definitely turn her heart from me? What if, inclining already to allow me the freedom of a betrothed, she were to look upon my sequestration of the bottle as an arrogant anticipation of rights of ownership to come, and so were to harden herself conclusively against me? What if there were a hitherto undetected basis of suspicion in her nature, and in common with some others she were to disbelieve that the little bottle had contained only wine and were to accept some theory about papers or property therein retained for my own advantage? Look at it in any way I might, I could see nothing but injury, gloom and ruin to come from the confounded bottle.

Thus reflecting, I found myself at the end of the oak avenue and before the stables. My horse stood just inside the door; and by the light of a lantern the ostler Joe was rubbing him down.

"Let him be ready the instant I want him, Joe," I said. "I may have to leave here at a moment's notice, — to visit old Mrs. Rabbage, may be. In fact, if you hear nothing to the contrary, send the gig round at eight."

"Just so," responded Joe. "It shall be ready. And Doctor — "

"Well?"

"Isn't this the day for the bottle? Shall we not now — "

I turned away and strode back to the house. Was there any one in the village, over a year old, who was not on the tenterhooks of expectation about that miserable mystery? Oh that I dared frankly tell Mabel all about it! But even if I dared, I should probably have little opportunity, so near at hand was now the dinner hour, so small the chance that I could see Mabel for long before. Oh that I were already betrothed to her, so that I might be able to make my confession freely, with full assurance of being forgiven upon the spot! Confusion upon those wasted opportunities of French and reading lessons, during which I might have spoken, and in my faint-hearted foolishness had not done so! Oh that I might even now find occasion to rectify that stupid delay, so that when the dreaded disclosure of my imprudence was made, I should be forgiven at once and with a smile! But alas! with that disclosure so close at hand and Roper ever hovering near, there could be no time for love avowals.

With that last train of thought, suddenly there came upon me, as by demoniac suggestion, an idea so strange and fanciful, that even now, as I reflect upon it and try to impart to it some element of sense in its justification, I am at a loss to account for its possession of me. But for my distortion of mind at that moment, I could never have entertained the idea for an instant; but for my agitation driving me to stretch out hither and thither wildly for relief, it might never have come to me at all. It was the idea that I might yet make my proposal and in such manner that it should precede the dreaded disclosure and be known only to Mabel and myself. I might write out my offer of heart and hand; and — I might put it in the bottle!

It was a wild scheme; and at any other moment

than that of my agitation, I could never have countenanced it. And yet, even the most insane ventures sometimes meet success, the very oddity of their conception drawing attention from what would otherwise be considered their unworthiness. At the first flash of that thought, indeed, I felt that I must discourage it; the very next instant it assumed shape, cogency and reliability. There was no time, indeed, for prolonged self argument upon the subject. Between the conception and the adoption of the idea was such a minute division of time that the whole thing seemed almost like a flash of inspiration. I was standing with one hand raised to my forehead in whirl of puzzled thought when I conceived that strange purpose; my hand was still brushing across my temple when the purpose had fixed itself, and taken the signification of long shapen resolution.

Yes, I would place my offer in the bottle; and this seemed destined to be the happy effect. Mabel would open the bottle, and would find in it a folded paper. This would not in the least surprise her, inasmuch as one of the theories about the bottle was that it contained not wine but some written document. She would unfold the paper and hold it up to the light. The first few words might startle her, as not like any thing that she had expected to find, but she would control herself and read further in search of explanation. Gradually the whole purport of it would dawn upon her; — so gradually, indeed, that she would have full time and opportunity to compose herself. When she realized my meaning, she would be silent a moment, while I awaited response; and during that moment at least, she would forget all expectation she might have had about any different secret in the bottle, or, if she remembered it at all, would do so with such confused and mingled perception of the past and present, that no instant annoyance or disappointment would be felt. If my appeal for her affection was unsuccessful, — which, indeed, I could scarcely bring myself to believe, so kind and winning of late had been her manner, — she would refuse me more in sorrow than in anger; so that, in that moment of pity, she would at once forgive my rash error about the bottle, and the one presumption would atone for the other. If she accepted me, she would surely pardon everything, for the love that I had brought her to confess. I pictured the whole scene as in a mirror. She would sit for an instant with her hand before her face, as in tumult of undecided thought. But, in a moment, I would be allowed to see the answering smile stealing into view from beneath her fingers; and then, as though concealment were no longer to be dreamed of, she would let her hand fall and the sweet glance of responsive affection shine full and radiantly into my own eager face. That would be my answer, and surely it would be sufficient. And yet, perhaps, she might do more. For fuller token of her acceptance she might pluck a flower from her bouquet, and with affectation of playful spirit, extend it across the table; and I, taking it from her outstretched hand, would place it in my button-hole. And there was almost a humorous side to the picture, I considered; for there would be Roper standing stiffly beside us, and, in his dull way speculating upon what the bottle may have contained, and yet a thousand miles off from the real truth. He would see a paper drawn out, and he would wonder whether it was the key to a hidden treasure; and would little dream that it had unlocked the long concealed treasure of my heart. He would watch the passage of a flower across the table, and would deem it a mere idle compliment of the moment; nor even know that it was the well recognized symbol of the interchange of heart for heart.

Transported with my scheme, and growing each moment more eager to put it into effect, I hurried back to the house, disregarding more than ever the darkness and the falling snow. In a minute I reached the hall door, entered and sought the library.

Roper had been in and had lighted up the sconces, and now the gloom of dusk that I had left behind me was replaced with the brightness of wax candles. A soft glow fell upon wall and furniture, bringing out pleasant tints upon the hangings of Spanish leather and affording picturesque contrasts of light and shade. But I could not now stop to admire mere artistic effects; my first glance was towards the bottle, in fear lest it might have been removed. It was still there, however; and the old eyes of Roper, in his going in and out, had failed to notice that the cork had been meddled with, or the gathered dust displaced. Once more I seized the bottle, drew its cork,—then looked around for sheet of paper.

There was none at hand; for, as I have hinted, the library was one in little other than name, nor in any light could it be called a study. Not to be baffled, I drew out from my pocket a small blank book, in which I was wont to write prescriptions. The paper was thin and coarse, but there was no time, now, for consideration of that matter. Already the clock was upon the stroke of seven, and I must be speedy. The form and setting of my appeal must matter nothing ; the words themselves were the only thing to be considered. I laid the little book upon my knee, and with blunt pencil, hurriedly scrawled my declaration of love.

Grant to me, dear Mabel, — so I wrote, — all that kind consideration which is so richly in your gift, while I dare to convey expression of that love which appertains to you and you alone. Not merely now, indeed ; seeing that no prior portraiture than yours has ever been engraven on my heart. If I have long delayed in making this poor record and recital of my love, it has not been from lack of fervor, but rather that I have not dared believe that you would acquit me of presumption in my claim for your forbearance. Give me one smile in sign that your forgiveness of my daring has been sealed, and that my heart may at last be delivered from the bitter pain of its suspense.

"It is rather a neat thing after all," I said to myself, with sweet satisfaction, as I folded the paper and stuffed it into the bottle. " Better, perhaps, than if I had indulged in labored rhetoric, seeing that this may seem to come more imploringly than the other, from the heart."

I clapped the cork back into place, held the neck of the bottle for a moment in the flame of a candle, pinched the melted wax into form, and restored the bottle to its old position upon the shelf. Scarcely had I done so, when I heard the rustle of silk, and Mabel entered.

Chapter IV.

NEVER had Mabel appeared to me more beautiful than at that moment; never had I been more impulsively attracted towards her. For nearly two years she had remained in deep mourning; but now seemingly, was about to return to the world. The lustreless black was banished, and in its place was a pale silk of some new tint that I had not yet learned, admirably harmonizing with her rich complexion and bright sparkling eyes. Throughout her whole costume, were other departures from the sombre attire of grief, in the form of adornments whose names or purport I could not tell, and which not too obtrusively lent their assistance in making up the whole picture of grace and beauty. Not for me, indeed, in my ignorance of woman's ways and tastes, to decipher all that now combined to embellish her loveliness; it is sufficient that, though in their detail I was unlearned, I knew that, in their cultivated accord and arrangement, they added new lustre and attraction to what had before been so precious to me. Gazing upon her, as for the moment she stood silent and composed in the doorway before advancing to welcome me — grace in every line and perfection in every feature, from soft wavy hair to dimpled chin, it seemed as though I must have fallen at her feet and there, in more tender words than any I could write, have avowed my passion. Then, for an instant, there came a flickering shadow of despondency upon me. Could it really be that all that beauty was for myself alone? It was with an effort, indeed, that I recalled her late gracious manner and her kindly glances, and reassured myself with the conviction that all was well.

"I need not wish you a Merry Christmas, Doctor Crawford," she said, advancing; and, in the plenitude of her usual pleasant mode of greeting, holding forth both hands. "To you, so full of kindliness of heart and the satisfaction of good works, every day should be a merry — or at least, a happy one."

"No day happier than this, Miss Mabel," I said; and again came the scarcely restrained impulse to avow myself. How hard, indeed, to resist clasping her in my arms, as there she stood, and not release her until she had promised to be mine forever! "No day merrier than this, when I see you looking so well and happy. And you have given me the first opportunity to tender you the Christmas greetings. Should I not be thankful for that?"

"It is a very little thing, indeed," she said. "And who so thankful as myself that I have so kind a friend, and upon whom I may call at will, to share the joy I hope to feel in this new Christmas-day? Sit down, dear Doctor; for perhaps Roper will give us yet a little respite from the more formal duties of the occasion, and I have something that perhaps I should tell you."

"Proceed, Miss Mabel." And I seated myself on the sofa at her side.

"It is first, to thank you yet again, for coming

so speedily and promptly at my poor invitation. To-day, as you see, I am throwing aside open evidence of past sorrow, and preparing once more to take my place in the outer world. And could I do so with greater satisfaction than in looking for the cheery presence of my first, my best, almost my only friend ? "

" Ah, Miss Mabel! " I could only say.

" And then again; to whom else could I look for assistance — perhaps advice — in the great duty thrown upon me to-day ? You know what that is, Doctor Crawford ? You are aware what I must do to-day ? "

" I think — that is, I have heard — "

" Yes, I see you know something about it — the bottle. As you are aware, it was left by my grandfather to be opened in twenty-five years from his death, by his heir and on Christmas-day. To-day is the appointed time. Can you not realize that I must feel some nervousness about it — some desire not to be alone, but to have the attending presence of a near and valued friend; if not for assistance, at least as witness of what may be found or may happen, so as to avoid misconstruction through this gossiping neighborhood around me ? "

" And yet, Miss Mabel, if there should be nothing in the bottle, — if the matter were merely a quaint jest of your grandfather — if it should turn out that the bottle had since been opened through some mistake — "

" But that could not be, dear Doctor. It has been kept under close lock and key until to-day. Only

this morning has it been taken out, in readiness for
opening, and been placed carefully aside in this
library, so as to run no danger of being mingled
with any other wines."

" Yes, — yes, indeed, Miss Mabel.   Yet if — "

" And as to what may be in it, Doctor, I have
really very little expectation of the marvelous.
There are some who speak about new fortune to be
found; and some, of life-giving secrets.   I place little
faith in any such anticipations or vagaries as these.
There may, after all, be only wine.   The most that
I can hope for, is some paper bestowing gift of little
value except as affection or association might give
it worth."

" Anything that might be offered to you, Miss
Mabel, surely would be of little value compared
with what is most worthy of you."

" Thanks, Doctor; but really, you are so compli-
mentary this evening!   Are you always so, on
Christmas-day ?   Well, that is what I really think;
all the little that, at the most, I can hope for.   But
now, shall I tell you what will insist upon coming
into my mind, in spite of all I can do to drive it
away ?   It may seem very silly to you; but then you
must know that the Cuthberts always have been
silly upon that point.   It is the Cuthbert vagary;
and we hold to it as tenaciously as some families
retain their alien or unpopular religion or politics."

" And what then — "

" This, Doctor.   You must not laugh at me; but
really it seems as though Prior Polycarp had something to do with the mystery of the bottle."

" And who — "

" Not know about Prior Polycarp, the head of this house when it was a religious institution ?   And yet, now that I think of it, I do not know that I have ever spoken to you about him, and there are very few other persons sufficiently interested in the history of the place to be able to inform you.   He was the last Prior, bringing the annals of the Priory down to the date of its breaking up in the time of Henry Eighth.   His portrait hangs in the dining room, where you must often have seen it without thinking to inquire who it was.   Probably you took it for an ancestor, in spite of the ecclesiastical costume and the tonsured head.   The picture is almost the sole relic of the religious furniture of the place.   He was not an ancestor, of course, but yet might be called a relative.   When the Priory was confiscated, it was sold to Sir Guy Cuthbert, my far off ancestor, and he happened to be a brother of Prior Polycarp.   This relationship was so far beneficial to the monks, that they were not rudely turned out, but were suffered to depart at their convenience, while a few of the most infirm were allowed to inhabit the cloisters until their death, the whole of the Priory not being immediately altered for secular purposes. Among these was naturally the Prior, who continued to reside in the place as his brother's guest.   As may be imagined, this leniency made a more pleasant state of feeling between the old and new possessors than generally prevailed in these cases of dispossession ; and certainly, the two brothers remained in perfect accord and affection until their deaths, which happened within two weeks of each other. And it must have been owing to this fact, that after his decease Prior Polycarp continued to show his good will towards the family."

"After his death, did you say?"

"Yes. The matter, however singular, cannot be doubted, there were so many instances of the fact. I cannot mention half of them, indeed; but will try to entertain you with a few. There was the incident of the siege, in the time of Charles First, for example. The besiegers had not yet invested the place, but were stealing up towards it from a distance, hoping to take it by surprise. Sir Geoffrey Cuthbert — the then owner — was asleep, apprehending no evil. Suddenly he was awakened by the tramp of footsteps to and fro along the hall. Rising to ascertain who was the disturber, he could see no one at all; yet all the same the footsteps continued, even at his very side, going off a few paces and then returning, with evident desire to lead him to follow them. At last he was moved to do so, and thereby was led through the hall and up the stairway, and thence out upon the roof, whence all at once he saw the rebel forces stealing up at not more than half a mile off. The small garrison was immediately called to arms and posted properly, and so the surprise was turned into a siege; and two weeks after, the King's forces brought relief. And it was always thought by us, Doctor, that it must have been the Prior who made the mysterious footsteps, and for the purpose of giving information to Sir Geoffrey."

"And then?" I said, too much surprised at her

fixed belief in that family tradition to utter any comment, and preferring to lead the way to further confidences.

"Yes; then there were other instances. There was the case of Morton Cuthbert in the time of George Second. He had been Sir Morton; but, in some way that I could never understand he then lost the title. He lost the estate too, for a while, and probably at the same time and by the same process. Afterwards he regained the property, but the title was gone forever. For two years he was an exile; and during that time, the new owner — he whom we have always called the Pretender — lived on the place. At that time there was a belfry on the top of the building, and in it, the bell that was wont to call the monks to prayers and the refectory. When they were dispossessed, the world had grown less religious, and the bell was only used for the call to dinner. It was a bell of very sweet and silvery tone, the glory of the neighborhood. But when the new occupant first had it rung, — it was at a great feast which he gave to celebrate his accession, — to the amazement of all, the bell rang false, its pleasant tone was gone, and a harsh rasping sound was in its place, — the note, indeed, of a cracked bell. It is said that when a servitor climbed up to see what was the matter, he saw old Prior Polycarp standing beside the bell, and deadening the sound with his outstretched hand. This might or might not have been so. It is certain, however, that the Prior must have had something to do in the matter; for when the Cuthberts again came into possession, lo! the bell rang true and distinct and silvery as before, so that the country people were drawn hither in crowds to listen closer to what seemed to them a miracle."

As may be imagined, I listened to all this in astonishment. Mabel was not naturally a credulous person. But, after all, how easy is it to be credulous in matters reflecting honor or distinction upon family history! And how readily we can cheat ourselves into believing circumstances that seem to indicate the protection and favoritism of higher influences thrown around us! For the moment I considered whether, when Mabel became my wife, it would be my duty to argue with her and convince her of her superstition; nor, indeed, could I quite make up my mind whether it would be proper to do so, or whether I had better let those stories about Prior Polycarp remain uncontradicted, as phantasies that gave her pleasure and could do her no harm.

"And therefore you see, dear Doctor Crawford, how easily I can incline myself to believe that the old Prior has something to do with this bottle, thereby practicing some intervention in our affairs and for our good."

"But you forget, Miss Mabel, that this bottle has not come down from the Middle Ages. It has been merely reserved by your grandfather, and within twenty-five years."

"That is all very true, dear Doctor. But may it not be that the Prior, for certain purposes of his own, had put it into the heart of my grandfather,to seal up and dedicate for a long life a bottle with merely wine in it, or even an empty bottle, — intending himself thereafter to make use of it as a repository for some important secret? Even you cannot certainly say that the bottle may not in the beginning have contained merely wine and been afterwards opened and some paper substituted."

"No, Miss Mabel; certainly I cannot say that," I rejoined, a little startled at her coincidence of thought. "And if — that is to say, — if the bottle was found to contain not a secret of the past, but merely — that is to say, something that you did not suspect, would you — would you be very angry?"

"Why, how could I ever tell, Doctor Crawford, until I saw what was in the paper, and knew whether it was proper to be angry or not? But it is little use now speculating upon the matter, for here comes Roper to summon us and we shall soon know all about it."

Roper, indeed, at that moment appeared, dazzling in white waist-coat, cravat and gloves, and threw open the door leading into the dining room; and offering my arm to Mabel, I escorted her from the library. As has been said, the dining room also had once formed a portion of the refectory, and much of the heavy graining of the ceiling had been suffered to remain. Like the library, there were rich hangings of Spanish leather, and in many respects the style and furnishing of the two rooms were similar. Where in the one stood bookcases, in the other were great mahogany side-boards weighed down with rich treasure of old family plate. There was, of course, an ample display of other heavy plate, over which the chandelier thickly set with wax candles shed a soft and pleasant gleam. Around the walls were a few family portraits; among which I now observed, placed so that it faced my allotted seat at table, the picture of the Prior Polycarp. He seemed to be a pleasant faced man, with rosy features and rather convivial expression; and as we took our places, and the wax candles slightly flared with the motion of our bodies, a fitful gleam was cast upon the old man's countenance, causing the smile to deepen and a certain roguish twinkle to gleam in his eye, almost with the potency of a wink, the whole effect of it, moreover, seeming to be directed upon myself. It was a good omen, I thought; the old Prior thus beaming acquaintance upon me as though welcoming me into the family.

A pleasant apartment and a cozy little Christmas party, indeed. There must have been occasions in the olden times when the table had spread the full length of the room, affording space for large family festivities. Now, however, it had been shortened in proportion to the requirements of merely Mabel and myself; so diminished, indeed, that, as we sat at opposite ends, we could have touched hands across. A very snug arrangement, in every respect; and, except for the somewhat elaborate garniture of the table in honor of the day, vastly suggestive of future comfort. How probable was it, that Mabel and myself were destined thus to sit in cozy contiguity for all the future years! How suggestive was it all, of our approaching domestic felicity!

For a while there was little to be said. What might be called the heavy work of dinner engaged our attention, and the presence of Roper skirmishing around us in all that solemnity of state apparel was not propitious for ease of conversation. But even then, my thoughts ran freely; and as I gazed at the beaming smile upon Mabel's face and basked in the sunshine of her sweet winning manner, I gave fuller vent to my sanguine hopes and felt that my happiness was all assured. And in this connection, I remember that it became a play of fancy to watch the flickering of the candles upon the picture of the Prior Polycarp and from the contraction or expansion of his smile, to draw my auguries of the future. At every pleasant expression from Mabel I found myself looking up at the portrait for-ghostly assent; at each good wish uttered by myself, I there sought kindly confirmation of my hopes. Little did Roper know how, as he stood magnificently beside the table and made the candles flare higher or lower with his ceremonious flourishing of the silver covers, he widened or narrowed the Prior's welcome and approbation of me, and thereby alternately elated or depressed me.

At last the time arrived for Roper to put on the dessert and take his departure; which he did with a series of flourishes that wreathed the old Prior's face with plenteous increase of smiles. Then Mabel filled her own little wine glass and nodded to me. Up to that minute, she had indulged in merely a sip; though I had done much more, as indeed was expected of me. For, as it was not known that I had already finished a small bottle of port and I could not confess the fact, it seemed not too exacting to demand that I should do fair duty to the light

sherry, claret and champagne that graced the border
of my plate. It was a little too much for me, however; and I could feel my head buzzing and my
tongue becoming unloosed; the more so as the longer
I looked at Mabel and watched the kindly play of
her expression in even the most commonplace
remark, the more assured I felt regarding her affec
tion for me, and the more exhilarated at my success
But sedulously I restrained all appearance of elation,
nor could any unwonted excess be at all detected,
unless from my increasing garrulousness and tendency to merry and trifling thought.

"Will you let me pledge you many a merry Christmas?" Mabel said. "It is a day so full of joy
and hope that we must needs do more than merely
use it carelessly — we must take solemn possession
of it with grave and dignified toasting of each
other."

"A day of hope, indeed, my dear Miss Mabel," I
responded, bowing towards her. "A day for every
good word and deed."

"For peace and comfort and forgiveness to all the
world, dear Doctor Crawford. I can say this truly to
yourself, as always first in the appropriate keeping
of it. For I know how, in your ministrations you
bring peace and comfort wherever you go."

"And the forgiveness. Miss Mabel?"

"Why as to that, Doctor, I know your kindness
of heart, as well as the favor in which you are held
by all men. What is there that you would have to
forgive?"

"Everything—and everybody, my dear Miss

Mabel." And with that, the wine mounting still higher in my head, I broke away from the serious strain in which we had begun, and wandered off carelessly into spirit of idle jesting. "My landlady, who in every way cruelly wrongs me, must be forgiven ;— and—and there is my rival, the homœopathic doctor. Shall I tell you what he did three months ago ?"

"Yes, tell me, Doctor," she rejoined, a little surprised at my new tone, and scarcely knowing how far I meant what I said.

Then I told how that I had been in the apothecary's shop, buying jalap; and how that the homœopathic doctor being also there had said "give them a bucketful of it, Doctor Crawford." How that I had made no immediate reply to that fine irony, but had afterwards remembered that I should have retorted, "better that, than a millionth part of a grain in a bucketful of water." How that thereafter I watched the shop to see when the homœopathic doctor was present, and on such occasions always went in and purchased jalap in hopes that he would renew the sarcasm, whereupon I should have been ready with my retort. How that for want of such opportunity I had been very angry at the homœopathic doctor; but now, at her request and instance would forgive him. And how that she must properly appreciate the fact, inasmuch as it was a great and unexampled thing for an allopathic doctor to forgive a homœo- pathic doctor within three months, for anything.

"And have you not also some little matters to forgive, Miss Mabel ?"

"I do not think — I scarcely know — "

" Not even the Vicar's wife ? " I asked.

And then I went on, in the same loose, rambling, half serious way to tell her how I had heard of the sarcasm of the Vicar's wife, about Mabel's favorite mission among the Hottentots. How that it was unjust, inasmuch as the Vicar's wife was still more urgent in a mission among the Afghans. How that I had forgotten what the Vicar's wife had said ; but that, whatever it was, there must have been somewhere a good answer for it. How that I would have her prepare a set of answers for any emergency, and then lie in wait for the Vicar's wife and by cunningly engrafted allusion to the Hottentot mission draw forth an innuendo, and then at once let fly an arrow from the collected quiver and annihilate the Vicar's wife upon the spot. Who, having been annihilated, could then, as a matter of course, be forgiven for her former attack, and thereby the true purpose of Christmas-day be fulfilled.

All this was very foolish, indeed, and I knew it at the time; but I seemed to have no power, at the instant, to stop myself. The wine was too far up in my head for common sense to restrain me, and I know not how far I might have run on, or into what other foolish excesses of speech I might not have been led, but for a glance at Mabel's face. The old Prior, I may mention, appeared to frown at that moment, but the glance at Mabel was enough for me. There was a puzzled, uncertain expression, — a seeming doubt as to how far I spoke in jest or earnest — and whether it was all good fun to be laughed at, or mere drivel of a vacant mind much to be pitied. I knew that in a moment she would be driven to the latter theory and feel grieved; and at once, before it was too late, I arrested myself.

"But all this is foolishness, my dear Miss Mabel. Forgive me for trying to make you laugh, when perhaps you were wishing to speak seriously. You were saying —"

"Yes, Doctor," and now at last she smiled pleasantly, being doubtless relieved to find that I was not really becoming vacant of mind. "Not to speak seriously, perhaps; and yet I would look upon the day as given up to different kinds of forgivenesses than for such poor slights as those of which you now speak. Rather let it be dedicated to the making up of great injuries, and the restoration of family peace where it has been for a long period injured. It seemed so singular — so coincident with my reflections upon the day, that only this morning I should have received a certain letter written nearly a month ago! Do you remember one Captain Stanleigh — once of the Guards?" '

"I think I do not — I am sure, indeed —"

"Possibly you do not, for it is long since he has been at the Priory; and when he was here, it was for only a few days at a time. The truth is, he always quarreled with my father to such an extent, that, in the end, my father almost turned him out of the house. And yet he did not mean to quarrel, after all; it was only his silly obstinacy."

"As how —"

"In this way. Captain Stanleigh was our cousin;

but, though of our blood, always professed to disbelieve the story about Prior Polycarp befriending us so mysteriously. He did not deny that such interventions might happen; for had not similar things occurred in other old houses? But Captain Stanleigh had taken an idea that we were not in any degree of kindred to the Prior; and therefore, why should we be assisted by him? It was not Sir Guy Cuthbert the brother of the Prior who was our ancestor — the Captain insisted — but one Mark Cuthbert from the other side of England, a mere equerry of one of the noble houses and no relation to the Prior. Upon this point my father and Captain Stanleigh violently disputed, and I must confess that I took my father's part; the whole point turning upon the question as to whether, at that time, we were of noble blood, or whether we had obtained the title afterwards and by purchase. And the quarrel finally raged so violently, that all intercourse was broken off between us, and Captain Stanleigh went off to the West Indies."

"Such family estrangements are always very sad," I said.

"Are they not, Doctor Crawford? But now comes the better part of the story. This morning I have received the letter about which I speak, in which the Captain regrets the past, expresses himself with great respect and affection for my father, acknowledges his own perversity and my father's correct views about the Cuthbert descent, begs for a restoration of the family harmony, and promises me a speedy visit."

"That is all as it should be," I said.

"Yes, Doctor; it is the proper thing, indeed. All family reconciliations must naturally be pleasant. In this case, there is one peculiar feature about it. — I must premise that, apart from a mere re-agreement it might happen. — I can tell it to you, Doctor, as such an old friend — the probability is, that, in this reconciliation with Cousin Tom, — with Captain Stanleigh, I should say, — there will come a renewal of our engagement."

"Good Heavens!" I cried within myself, and falling back in my chair as if struck. "And my proposal in that confounded bottle!"

Chapter V.

A mist seemed to gather before my eyes, — cold chills to run through my frame in every direction, — a palsy to bind me hand and foot. It was as though I had been stunned and pierced and buffeted with every variety of sensation that ever the human frame is subject to, and that the misery of it lasted a full hour or so. Yet it could have been for only a second or two, for when I regained resolution enough to raise my face and gaze around, I found that all things remained unaltered. Mabel had not in the least noticed my agitation, which could scarcely have been the case if it had lasted for any considerable length of time. Indeed, at that moment, her face was partially turned away, watching for Roper, who, at touch of bell, was now emerging from the next room. In his hand he held the unlucky bottle, which at her direction, he placed upon the table at her right hand, but so awkwardly that it toppled over upon its side.

"Be careful, Roper."

"I thought, Miss, that it was heavier," he responded, retiring slowly, and all the while eying the bottle as though already mysteries were gathering about it, in foreshadowing of some wonderful result.

"Certainly it feels lighter than it did," said Mabel, gently weighing it in her hand. "And really, it has less appearance of holding wine than once it had.

Actually, now that I try to look through it against the light, there seems to be a folded paper in it. I never noticed that before. Look for yourself, my dear Doctor Crawford. Does it not also seem to you — "

"Doubtless there is a paper in the bottle, Miss Mabel. Which being so, is it safe for you to open it now, — or at all, indeed? Better let me take it away with me and have it opened in the presence of your lawyer. It might contain some dreadful family secret, which it would not be proper for you to know, — at least just now. We would thus spare you the pain of it, if necessary; and afterwards, if the proper time should ever come — "

"The proper time is now, Doctor Crawford," and I noticed that she spoke with appearance of a little pique. "There can be nothing about my family that I should fear to know."

"But at least, my dear Miss Mabel, let me open the bottle for you. These things sometimes fly apart in the most unexpected manner; and if through any misfortune, you should cut your fair fingers — "

For I thought that if I were to open the bottle, I might affect to do so with great effort to overcome resistance, requiring me at the least to rest it upon the floor and under the shadow of the table cloth, where unseen, I might succeed in plucking out my miserable little note, and pretending that there had been nothing inside after all, except a modicum of old wine that must have evaporated through the cork. But even in that scheme, fate seemed to work against me.

"Thanks, my dear doctor. But you must remember that the injunction of my grandfather was to the effect that the bottle must be opened by the heir. And after all, as you can see, I must have some aptitude for such a business, since the corkscrew goes in so very easily. Look, too,"—and here she gave a pull, — "how readily the cork comes out!"

It came out, indeed, — and of course not at all to my surprise, — as easily as an almond from its shell. And there sat Mabel, in some momentary admiration at her own dexterity, with the bottle in one hand, and the corkscrew and cork in the other. Looking towards the bottle, I could see that my unhappy offer had unrolled itself, and had projected one little corner through the neck, as though eager to bring on the dreadful crisis. What, now, was I to do? To seize the bottle from her hand and fly with it wildly from the house? This seemed all that was left for me; and alas, it was more than I dared attempt. Meanwhile, Mabel laid down the corkscrew, placed the bottle before her upon the table and tried to peep within.

"Yes, there is surely a paper here," she said; and with graceful motion she pulled it out and tried to spread it flat in front of her. "And see, dear Doctor! There is writing on the face of it, and on the back, some mysterious symbols. That alone should prove the antiquity of the paper, should it not? Were not such signs used in the Middle Ages? Come around to me, Doctor, and tell me what you make of it all!"

"Yes, — in the Middle Ages — and on Solomon's

sword — and — oh, Miss Mabel! this becomes frightful. Better not read further, but throw the paper into the fire upon the spot! What should cabalistic characters have to do with you, except for harm?"

Even in that moment of my agitation, indeed, I could scarcely repress a smile, so closely does the influence of the grotesque sometimes envelope us. For I saw, at once, that the cabalistic characters were the mere beginning of a prescription that I had once dotted down in my note-book and forgotten,— a line or two of technical contractions mingled with the customary symbols for drachms and penny-weights.

"To burn it, Doctor! Why no, it would be foolish to do that; without, at least, first looking at the other side. But see! There seems, unfortunately, to have been some remnants of wine left in the bottle, and the paper is all discolored. Scarcely a word here and there remaining unobliterated. How careless in the Prior not to have chosen a cleaner bottle for his message! Can it all be lost, do you think? Is there anything at all to be made out of it?"

"We will see, my dear Miss Mabel," and hope began to dawn within me, — the hope of extrication from my trouble. Yes, the carelessness with which Roper had let the bottle roll over upon its side had had this one good result for me, that the thin paper had become here and there blotted with wine-stains, so that only a few words remained decipherable. "We will see, Miss Mabel; perhaps we can read a little of it."

She spread it upon the table, we bent our heads closely over and she began.

"Yes, Doctor, — a little; yet after all, only here and there a word. '*Grant, — consideration,— gift, — appertains — prior portrait — record — recital — quit — claim — sign — seal — deliver —*' That is all of it that I can make out. What can it mean, Doctor Crawford?"

"It would seem, indeed, to refer to some important legal document," I responded. "But where, indeed, is the document to be found? This paper does not seem to tell that. May not the words '*prior-portrait*' be the key that —"

"The very thing — the very, very thing!" cried Mabel. "There has always been a tradition in the family, of a recess behind the Prior's portrait, for concealment of treasure, though no one has ever believed enough in the matter to look for it. Let us now search! Oh, my dear Doctor! How kind you are; and how wise, too, to guess at once what might have troubled me in vain! Yes, let us search."

The smile of anticipation that wreathed her face was possibly not half as radiant as the smile of relief that now I wore. I felt, indeed, that, by a lucky chance, I was saved. No further interpretation of my miserable note would now be looked for; and whether the old Prior were to have any thing concealed about him or not, was a matter of indifference to me, as long as I was out of my difficulty. It was with a light heart that now, first taking the paper from Mabel's hand and, as if in abstraction, crumpling it into my pocket, I jumped upon a chair and began

to fumble about the Prior's frame. It was with no
lighter heart, indeed, — for nothing now could happen to disturb me, — but with unutterable astonishment that, after a minute of unguided wandering,
my fingers struck upon a concealed spring and the
old Prior slowly slid one side, and left a small cavity
disclosed behind him. As he rolled past the line of
the chandelier, new reflections fell glancing upon his
good natured face, and it seemed to me that he
smiled more broadly than ever before. It was with
a cry of delight that Mabel called to me to hand
down to her the parchment roll that lay inside, for
she knew at once what it must surely be.

"The old — the original deed of the Priory!" she
exclaimed, hugging the dusty roll close to her breast.
"It has been lost for two generations, and no one
has thought that it would ever turn up again!
Father so wished that it could be found, and he
would have been so glad to see this day!"

"Glad, indeed, Miss Mabel," I responded, perceiving at once the value of the instrument. "For this—
this gives you the victory in that terrible chancery
suit. The whole five hundred acres will at last —"

"What do I care about that, dear Doctor Crawford?" So, in the inconsiderateness and insufficiency
of her spirit of calculation spoke this heedless young
lady respecting a conveyance that, as it afterwards
turned out, assured to her the title to all those disputed acres, with a quarry, two mills and a tract of
valuable forest land. "What matters the old chancery suit, now? Better than all else, can you not
see that this deed proves our title as coming not from

Mark Cuthbert, the equerry, but from Sir Guy Cuthbert, the brother of the Prior? Ah, what would Cousin Tom now dare to say about it, if he were here!"

"He would dare to say nothing about it at all, but would be glad to let the whole matter drop, on the original terms," said a quiet voice close behind us.

Turning, we saw a tall young fellow standing just inside the doorway, and leaning against its post. He had stolen upon us unperceived, and was regarding us with a certain affectation of solemn stolidity, his mouth drawn down and his hands clasped penitently before him; but all the while unable to repress the spirit of fun that gleamed in his bright hazel eyes. I knew, of course, that this must be Cousin Tom.

"Captain Stanleigh, I believe?" said Mabel, slightly inclining her head. "You must excuse me if I am not altogether certain, it being so long since — "

"Yes; Captain Stanleigh, at your service. You must excuse me, as well, Miss Cuthbert, for coming upon you so suddenly and unexpectedly. I arrived only this morning, and took the train at once. The anxiety to see old friends, — yourself, I may say, perhaps — and Roper — and — and Prior Polycarp, who, I hope, is still strong enough to take his nightly promenades, though how he could ever make such a lively tramping with those thin sandals of his has always passed my compre — "

"It would not need a very wide divergence from the straight path, to pass your comprehension, Cap-

tain Stanleigh. But you forget that there is a
gentleman present who may not care about listening
to your foolishness. This is Doctor Crawford.
Doctor Crawford, this is my cousin, Mr. Thomas
Stanleigh."

"I am very happy to be able to meet Doctor
Crawford. I recognize the name as of one learned
in medicine — and — and all that, indeed. You are
giving me a great pleasure in making his acquaintance, Cousin Mabel."

"You must know that Doctor Crawford was one
of my father's oldest friends, Cousin Tom, and since
his death has been my best friend, as well. Indeed,
I do not know how I could ever have gotten along
without him, so kind and considerate has he been in
all his attentions, — a second father to me, indeed."

"Nothing, certainly, could give me greater pleasure than to learn that Cousin Mabel has found a
friend so eminent for kindness — and distinction —
and so on. You need never fear, Mabel, that I shall
not always value the opportunity you have given
me to make such a pleasant acquaintance. Perhaps
Doctor Crawford being such a friend of the family
can tell me what I know you would not think to
mention, Mabel — whether of late the Prior has
walked the passages with his dinner-bell over his
head, and — is it possible that, after all, I have not
got it right, Mabel?"

"You are as silly as ever, Tom. And you oblige
me to explain to Doctor Crawford that you are not
always so foolish. He has come a long distance,
Doctor, and must be very hungry, and it always goes

to the brain and makes him flighty. It is a Stanleigh peculiarity."

"Mabel is right, Doctor Crawford. I am not always as silly. Leaving, therefore, all such talk aside, let me in all seriousness thank you for your uniform kindness to her. Be assured that her friends always shall be mine, and that I will ever be glad to meet them. I hope, therefore, that in future you will not look upon me as a stranger, but will feel that you have gained a new friend and admirer. That must be so, Mabel; must it not? Doctor Crawford shall always find a warm welcome with us; shall he not?"

"Certainly, Tom. We could never feel happy if we did not know that there was at least one person who, at any time could be sure of a sincere greeting at the Priory."

All this while I had been standing before them, — confused, embarrassed, but more than all else, filled with astonishment. I had not sought to say a word, — could not, perhaps, if I had wanted to, have found space to put in a remark among that running stream of compliments, — might not have been heedfully listened to if I had done so, seeing that they cared not to hear me speak, and that their conversation, though ostensibly directed towards myself, was practically meant for each other. In any other condition of mind than that of my prevailing self-mortification, I might have felt amused at watching how speedily the difficulties of those two young people found solution. They had parted nearly two years ago in quarrelsome spirit, — they had met again with affectation of ceremonious reserve which might possibly, one would have hoped, wear off in time. And lo! throughout all, the glad light of loving welcome and heart yearning reconciliation had shone unrestrained in each other's eyes; and in a minute, almost unwittingly to themselves, the sorrow of the past estrangement had been all forgotten and their engagement been renewed. All this would have amused me, indeed, but for my own sense of humiliation. How weakly had I allowed myself to encourage hopes that I should have known must be baseless and unreal! How foolishly had I thought that Mabel's frank, open welcomes at my approach could have been the outpouring of anything other than a friendly spirit! How sad and bitter to think that in myself could have been such spirit of self-deceit, as to dream that for me would ever shine forth that light of love which glowed in every feature as now she glanced stealthily upon the chosen one of her heart beside her.

"The gig is here," interrupted Roper, as I stood silent, thinking how best I might frame words of response to all their kindly commendations.

"It is not time? Surely you will not leave us yet?" said Mabel.

The eyes as bright as ever with spirit of kindly welcome, — the hand extended as warmly in friendship as of old; and yet, somehow, I knew at last the difference with which her eyes and hand would have welcomed Cousin Tom. And I felt, moreover, that however high her appreciation of me, she would not be greatly displeased to have me go.

26*

"Thanks, Miss Mabel," I therefore said. "You are very kind; but a doctor's time is not all his own. I have a patient yet to visit to-day,—old Mrs. Rabbage, whose rheumatism—and therefore must tear myself reluctantly away."

And with that I bowed myself out and left them to themselves. I have said that as I look back upon that scene after so many years, I can treat it philosophically, and can even smile. But it is not always so, perhaps. Though I am now old and have long surrendered thoughts and dreams of love for certainty of fame and fortune, yet once in a while, on Christmas-day, if I chance amid the evening festivities, to hear the wind and snow outside, as on that afternoon at the Priory, my memory will carry me sadly back, and I will lift the curtain of my retrospection and once again look upon that parting scene. The open door, always flung back so cheerily in my welcome, and now seeming to creak gruffly upon its hinges in enforcing my departure,—the blackness of the night outside, ten-fold as dark and forbidding as ever before, beneath the increasing violence of the tempest blast,—driving snow and cutting cold wind,—this is the outside picture. Within, as the door closes behind me, one parting glimpse of an earthly paradise,—a warm room bright with cheerful coal fire and clustered wax lights,—not too sombre shadows mingling with the prevailing brilliancy and by pleasant contrast, throwing out their suggestions of homelike peace and comfort,—the old Prior gazing down with abundant wealth of smiling visage, no longer upon myself but upon two persons who stand below him, silent, for the moment, in the happiness of their reconciliation, Tom with his arm already gliding around her waist and Mabel with her hand lightly resting upon his shoulder —

" Why so pensive, Doctor ? " at this moment some one laughingly asks.

Then I drop the curtain, with a forced smile, and in a minute am myself again.

St. Nicholas and the Gnome.

St. Nicholas and the Gnome

Chapter I.

"I DO not exactly comprehend you," said the Gnome. "That you, who can so easily travel up and down the wide world and at your own sweet will can see every thing good and pleasant that is to be found therein should now — "

"It may indeed be," interrupted St. Nicholas, "that I am becoming morbid and prejudiced and far from looking upon the matter in its right spirit. That may all very well be so. And yet, so annoyed and disappointed have I been with all the changes and perversities of the last few years, that it seems no more than natural for me — "

"But still — " objected the Gnome; and then he paused. In fact, though he had his argument all laid out in his own mind in shapely manner, he scarcely knew how to present it properly for the other's consideration. For as yet he knew little about St. Nicholas' real nature, or how most suitably to appeal to it in matter of disputation. In truth, they had been only a short while acquainted with each other. After his usual custom at that season of the year, St. Nicholas had taken his team to the extreme north, in order that it might invigorate itself with a breath of its native air and gain new flesh and strength by crunching the Arctic mosses. He had encamped upon that sterile plain, across which only glaciers seemed ever to have moved; and he must have had quite a shepherdlike appearance, as he leaned against a jagged slope of rock and watched his reindeer at their browsing. When the little Gnome had first popped his head out of the rock crevice to note who might be the intruder, the Saint had taken him for some wild animal, inasmuch as all that in the beginning appeared, was a round, shaggy head, with hooked nose and sharply pointed furry ears. When the whole body had at length emerged and stood upright, in its roughly built suit of fox skin, the Saint had felt compelled to recognize him as an intelligent being; but even then there had been some hesitation between them as to who should make the first advances toward acquaintance, so widely different were their styles and so unexpected the appearance of each one to the other. At last they had spoken, drawn together by some common sympathy; the Gnome being impelled toward St. Nicholas by attraction of rotund, pleasing jollity, and St. Nicholas taking to the Gnome through a certain winsome earnestness that spread itself across every feature of the quaint little face. But for all that they were not as yet fully acquainted; and though for a while they had talked together, there had not been any such mutual exchange of confidences as might lead to unembarrassed intercourse. Therefore it was that the Gnome, now hesitatingly beginning his remark stopped; and it was left to St. Nicholas to take up and carry on the greater part of the conversation.

"I understand all that you would say," he remarked. "To you who keep so quiet and secluded" —

"You may well affirm that," interrupted the Gnome; "for I am scarcely out of my nook in the bowels of the earth from one end of the year to the other. It is a very large treasure I am obliged to guard. Gold and silver ornaments for the arms and legs — a silver embossed shield and helmet — a cup half filled with diamonds — pearl head-dresses — gold vases and a jewel-encrusted sceptre — piles of ancient coin and many other priceless articles besides — gathered together in distant ages and from diverse countries and I know not by whom, yet all the same committed to my watchful care. — Well, go on."

"To you who keep so quiet and secluded," pursued St. Nicholas, "it must seem a strange thing that I who can so freely use the light and sunshine and the power of locomotion should not enjoy them more. And, indeed, it was not always so. Years ago, there was no gayer being on earth than myself, and more abundantly than all other times did I take pleasure in my Christmas Eve. It was so joyous, in fact, to drive from house to house, leaving bountiful favors at each and making everybody happy along my route. But now" —

"Now?" said the Gnome.

"Now, indeed," continued the Saint, "not only does it seem that the world has altered and grown practical, making it harder work for me to satisfy people and cause them to be even moderately happy, but other things have been greatly changed, so that my efforts are made at much increase of bodily exertion and at times my pleasure becomes almost a toil, my life as empty as a toy balloon."

"And how is that?" the little Gnome inquired.

"Firstly, I may say," was the desponding answer, "because of certain new and abominable styles of architecture coming in, making it exceedingly difficult for me to go my rounds as quickly as heretofore. Narrow flues, you must know — and little thin chimneys meant only for furnace-pipes, themselves an unwarrantable innovation — and tin tops to cure the smoke, as though the smoke were not needed in the chimney to cure hams — and altogether a variety of new-fangled notions that may be valuable in their own way, but all the same make it exceedingly inconvenient for me to slide down into the bed-rooms. True, I might get in at doors and windows; but who, after all, would respect me, if I departed from ancient customs?"

"It might be — I cannot tell how it would be about that," said the Gnome. "And what else?"

"Then the tin and asphaltum roofs — you can scarcely conceive what an annoyance they have already proved to my poor reindeer, who heretofore, on the shingles or Dutch tiles, could generally calculate upon a little moss and even grass to nibble at, while I made my visitations below. But now, with the new fashion of things, they might easily starve to death."

" What more ? " asked the Gnome.

" There is a creature called Kriss Kringle who has begun infringing within my domains; and with his pertinacious spirit of intrusion and with much blowing of his miserable little trumpet in his own praise, has succeeded, in many places in weaning people from their respect for me and attracting them into an allegiance to himself. He affects to despise the old-time filling of stockings, and hangs his pretentious gifts upon pine trees, surrounded by short candles which are liable at any moment to topple over and set the whole thing in a blaze. Moreover, many people are now beginning to confound us and to call me Kriss Kringle; which, not being my name, is an insult to my person."

" That is very bad," said the Gnome, " and more than the other matters which perhaps do not amount to much. I know very well that I should greatly dislike to have a rival power coming into my territory and insisting upon helping me keep watch over my treasure. What further ? "

" This — and to my mind it is the hardest thing of all to bear. You would scarcely believe it, but there are people who begin to imagine that I have no real existence — that I am a myth, a mere abstraction, a creature of the fancy. Tell me now," St. Nicholas exclaimed, in the earnestness of his argument seizing the Gnome by the arm, " do you think that it is a nice thing after driving about from sunset to sunrise during the whole of a long winter night, leaving goodly gifts in almost every stocking — and the children have learned to hang up pretty capacious stockings, too — not to get a particle of credit for it? To have boys and girls grow up thinking that they are very wise, and to begin disbelieving in me and allowing their fathers and mothers all the merit for the gifts? Yes, to have those parents not only meanly take to themselves the credit of all the presents, but even to pretend that it has been so from the very first, and that even the pretty toys with which I had filled the stockings of four and six year old youngsters had been the products of the paternal purse?"

"It is not a nice thing, indeed; nay, it is very bad," said the Gnome.

"And that," St. Nicholas continued "is why I feel dispirited and disgusted with the world — so barbarous are its new designs and practices, so bitter the indifference, incredulity and ingratitude of men. That is why I would retire from active labor — would even change places with yourself — will perhaps, this night, for the first time in many centuries, remain here in quietness and repose and altogether abandon my Christmas rounds."

"Nay, I would not do that," responded the Gnome; and he looked sadly upon St. Nicholas, pitying his distress and wondering what could be done to relieve it and bring about a happier frame of mind. The dispirited air with which St. Nicholas bent over in persistent gazing upon the snow-clad ground — the usually merry face now drawn out long and woebegone — the jolly paunch seemingly shrunk almost to concavity — the clay pipe remaining twisted in the hat band, its unused condition affording the best proof of its owner's despondency — all this touched the heart of the Gnome. Were he to consult his own pleasure, it would be that the Saint should remain by him; but he felt that it was not the right thing to consent therein.

"I would not do that," he therefore said. "You must know, indeed, how dearly I would be pleased to retain you here. It is very seldom that I see anybody with whom to talk. Men do not come past my cave in this desert waste; and if they did, it is scarcely possible that I should see them, so seldom do I put my head above the surface. If there are other gnomes, they are all in distant portions of the earth, each probably guarding his separate treasure; and therefore we never meet or even know of each other's existence. But were I to retain you here, surely it would be at neglect of your duty or at the expense of some expectant person's happiness, and to-morrow, doubtless, you would be sorry that you had yielded to your sense of injury. Are there not chimneys of the old favored style still remaining, down which you can descend after the time-honored manner? May there not yet be living those who believe in you and are grateful for your attention, and will not refuse to call you by your right name? You cannot surely travel all over the world; why not, therefore, select such portions of it as still continue faithful to you?"

"You are right — I must go," St. Nicholas answered, lazily raising himself from the ground. The earnest words, coupled with the winsome expression of the Gnome, convinced him that there was a

27*

duty not to be neglected in his long established manner of life; nay, he felt that were he now to neglect it, the society of the Gnome, far from proving a pleasure to him through the night, would be a reproach. Therefore, he roused himself; yet it was with faint semblance of alacrity. There was that repose in all nature around him that predisposed him to lassitude. There was no breath of wind — no movement of the low pine tufts. The little white reindeer were now asleep around his motionless sleigh — even the northern light that glowed over the far away horizon was for the moment stilled; the spears of electric brightness that had shot half downward from the overhanging arch remaining with undeviating length, like celestial stalactites. All things listless and quiescent; and he, of all, must prepare to move away, departing upon an errand that he had learned to hate and leaving a companion whom he had begun to like. But a sudden thought struck him.

"If I go to-night," he said to the Gnome, "will you go with me?"

"I?" responded the other in wild astonishment, "you know I cannot leave home. I have my trust to perform. For many centuries have I guarded the treasure and still must guard it. There is tradition that some day a griffin will come to ravish it from me, if possible; and if I am not here to defend it —"

"For centuries you have been awaiting the griffin," said the saint, "and he has not come. For centuries longer he may not come. I ask of you only this night. I will not go alone upon my doleful round through an ungrateful world. Accompany me and I will go as usual. Is that too much to ask? You have sometimes wished for opportunity to see the world; now the opportunity has come. What say you?"

"And will you bring me back to-morrow?" the Gnome inquired.

"To-morrow, at dawn."

"And will no one see me, wherever I may go? For I have heard that the people of the world are different from myself; that they are larger and whiter; that they have softer faces and do not carry these long pointed and furry ears; that they are all handsome, indeed, even as yourself, St. Nicholas. I would not like to meet anybody who would hold me up to scorn for my personal appearance, so homely and uncouth beside your own; I, with my shrunken body and you with that portly and so gracefully carried paunch; I, with my hairy, black skin and you with face so white, except where for its crowning beauty and for proper contrast, it is delicately touched off with tints of red in the very centre. I would not like to have my feelings thus hurt," said the innocent little Gnome.

Saint Nicholas softly stroked his face, feeling vastly gratified, inasmuch as he was aware that the Gnome meant it all.

"I am as I was created, that is all;" he modestly replied. "We cannot take any credit to ourselves for the way we are made. But as for yourself, being with me, neither of us will be visible to any one whom we may meet."

"Then I will go with you," said the Gnome, hesitatingly. It was with mingled gladness and fear that he consented. He was pleased at the unlooked for opportunity to see the world, yet he dreaded the leaving behind him a neglected duty. But it would be for only a night; after that he would return to his watchful task in the bowels of the earth, there to remain for centuries longer, perhaps, without seeing a strange face. And it would be a comfort to him then, to think over all that he had seen and heard among the haunts of men.

Chapter II.

GIVING the Gnome no time to retire from his
resolution, the Saint slung his pack upon
his back, then whistled to the reindeer, which,
awakening, fell methodically into their allotted
places before the sleigh. A moment more and St.
Nicholas and the Gnome were in the seat, snugly
tucked in with bears' robes. The lash was lightly
applied,— the reindeer spread out their hoofs, for
an instant passed along the ground, then lightly
skimmed its surface, then rose into the air, the
Gnome for a moment clung nervously to the side of
the sleigh, then released his hold as he felt that
there was no actual danger, and so the journey was
begun.

Across a frozen sea where the ice lay piled in hummocks almost mountain high, — over a sterile land
whose only effort at creative labor was the great
glacier from whose mouth the ponderous icebergs
broke off and so drifted adown the ocean currents, —
over other frozen seas and barren landscapes, with
here and there bleak mountain ranges and pine surrounded lakes set as icy jewels among inaccessible
steeps, coldly reflecting the moon from their motionless surfaces, — swiftly down to more temperate
climates where the rugged pine gave place to elm
and maple, but where all the same the breadth of the

whole land lay ice-bound and snow-covered, — over
and along a beautiful river whose wintry fetters were
worn more lightly than had been seen further
north, so that, as the travelers journeyed along its
entire length, they could gaze down and see how
the thick ice at its source gradually grew thinner
and less hard and white, until at last when nearer
the mouth, the dark water broke through with here
and there a pleasant ripple and further along gathered strength and threw off the icy fetters and sent
them whirling away, grinding each other to fragments in impotent rage; so the swift route of St.
Nicholas and the Gnome carried them onward. At
last, — it was near the mouth of the ever broadening
river, where the icy covering had all been thrown
off and the waves were dancing in celebration of
their deliverance, — there appeared a throng of dis
tant lights, studding the darkness over many miles
in extent; to which the Saint animatingly pointed.

"See," he said, " the city, our destined field!"

The Gnome gazed eagerly downward. He had
never seen the like before. Sometimes he had looked
up from his desert burrow and watched the stars
gleaming in the steel cold sky of that Arctic region
and had tried to number them. Like those stars,
these lights now under foot, seemed countless; but
there was this difference. Those stood all calm and
motionless; these were mostly the same, yet of them
there were many that moved as with life — some
glimmering in slow but not less perceptible passage
along the thoroughfares — some swiftly darting
across the encircling waters of the city, and far

away, here and there, a single light appearing and disappearing with regular sequence as it revolved upon its tall base.

"We will descend," St. Nicholas said. "Mark whither I am directing my course. I well know the route, indeed. Between the steeple in front of us below and the neighboring bell tower — taking our angles from them and thence drawing the line to yonder illuminated clock — so that we cannot well go wrong. There, at least, is a place where we shall not fail in welcome and appreciation."

"You know the house, then?" remarked the Gnome.

"As I know my own home," the other answered. "A pleasant little house, set lovingly in the midst of its own extended garden, only two stories high, with tiled and moss grown roof and chimney so capacious and redolent of well smoked bacon that it is a luxury to descend. There have I visited for fifty years past — at times each year — then again with intermission of a year or two, — as of late, indeed, when failing to get around in time. Always finding there a hearty welcome; the fire suffered to go out, the hearth swept up, the very cat upon that night remaining indoors and lingering around the fire-place as though with prescience of something happening; all things, indeed, seeming to be arranged with expectation of my coming. We will descend, now, gently as a feather, lighting upon the roof as softly as a snow-flake; so making our anticipated visit to the household, yet careful not to awaken it."

Now more tightly he drew the reins and guided

his team into a descent, gradually checking their pace as they dropped down. Not regulating the action aright toward the end, however, as it happened; for, of a sudden, the descent was arrested by a hard shock that set the reindeer capering in wild confusion, half overturned the sleigh and sent the Gnome and St. Nicholas out headlong upon a tinned roof.

It was the roof of the celebrated Bon Ton Hotel, finished two months before, unknown to St. Nicholas, and with its ten stories stretching up so loftily, as naturally to have caused mishap, by checking too suddenly a descent adjusted for a lowlier building. To make sufficient space for the hotel, the little two-storied house had been swept away and the neat garden all built in, as well. The new erection was an object of especial and exceeding city pride and the public papers spoke glowingly about it. After their manner they described its six hundred windows, its mile and a half of passages and its seventy-two miles of lead pipe; and when, in pursuit of further statistics, they dilated upon the many thousand tiles that made up the paving of the corridors, the popular enthusiasm could not have been surpassed. Nowhere was mention made of the building's size in simple feet and inches; and this, perhaps, was consequently only known to the owner. But the impression, from all other descriptions, was naturally as of vast extent; and with that the people felt obliged to be content and admired accordingly. To St. Nicholas, however, the substitution of this great edifice for the little old house so consecrated to him by older recollections was no cause for congratulation.

"Was I not right," he said, scrambling up and ruefully rubbing his short, fat legs, where the skin had been taken off by the concussion, "in telling you that I should not desire to come out to-night? Look, now, at this! Where is the home at which I visited for fifty years — the boy whom I loved as he grew up from the early beauty of childhood into a strong man — whom then I loved equally for his noble, manly soul? Where is the young girl whom, year by year, I saw developing into new beauties of heart and culture? Gone; and in their place this human hive!"

"Be not dismayed at that," cried the Gnome coming upon his feet with smiling countenance, rubbing his bruises as well, but affecting to make little of them. "Your friends you may see again elsewhere — who knows? Or, if not, then in this human hive, as you call it, you may make other friends," he added, a little too cheerily, perhaps. For, having never been enough away from home to note the difference between places, he had no conception of the power of association; and certainly, in his obscurity, he had not learned how hard it is to make friends and how wise it is, consequently, not lightly to give them up when made. "Therefore, try not to be downcast, but let us descend."

"And how?" demanded the Saint, disdainfully pointing to the nearest chimney pots. "Through there, indeed? Are such things worthy of one who for centuries has accustomed himself to" —

"Through this, rather," responded the Gnome, opening a capacious scuttle in the roof and thereby disclosing a convenient ladder. It was wonderful, indeed, in that moment of his chief's dejection, to see with what capable energy the little Gnome took the direction of things. "There is proper access to the building — why seek for chimneys as though nothing else would do? Come, follow me."

With that he bolted down into the scuttle-hole — not descending feet foremost in the ordinary fashion of men, but plunging in head downward as he would have gone into his own rock-crevice, rabbit-like, his feet for a moment twinkling in the air and then his whole body sliding out of sight. St. Nicholas followed somewhat sulkily. His first impulse was to retire altogether from the hateful scene and return at once to his own home. This, however, he could not do without abandoning the Gnome, who, for the time, was his guest and would have been in sore distress if left alone among strange scenes. Therefore he, also, after a moment, passed through the scuttle, slowly clambering down in the usual method, and in a minute the two explorers stood together at the foot of the ladder.

Looking around, they found themselves in a long, plain hall, with uncarpeted floor and white-washed walls. Along each side were ranges of doors, making it evident that a number of small rooms opened into the hall. At each end a single gas-bracket projected from the wall, emitting a dim and somewhat insufficient light.

"What next?" muttered the Saint. He had not

recovered from his testiness, by any means, and now spoke with some assumption of indifference. If the Gnome were inclined to enter upon any experiments — so the Saint seemed to imply — let him do so and take the consequences of resulting failure or unpleasantness. As for himself, he would mutely follow, but bear no part or liability in the matter.

"What now, indeed?" cried the Gnome cheerfully, still taking the direction of affairs. "Why, surely, there must be people all around us. And among them some who need your help and would be grateful for your kindness. It matters not where we begin; shall we strike out at random?"

With that, he pushed open one of the nearest doors and entered, followed by St. Nicholas. The two found themselves in a small, poorly furnished room. Upon the bed and fast asleep lay a tall, slim negro. His frizzled hair was broadly puffed out on either side and his moustache carefully waxed. These adornments seemed to have suffered no discomposure in his sleep; and it was evident that as a soldier will slumber with his arms in his hands, in like manner long practice had taught the negro to maintain his chief physical charms undisturbed by midnight tossings, in constant readiness for sudden call of duty. Upon the wall hung a green velvet coat, a yellow vest and pantaloons with chequerboard figures many inches broad. Across two nails lay a silver-headed cane; thrown over which, as a convenient bracket, was a choice collection of purple and orange colored cravats. It was evident, however, that these adornments were all reserved for holiday seasons when duty did not interfere, for on a neighboring chair lay spread out the costume of toil — the badges of servitude in the shape of black broadcloth coat and pantaloons. On an adjoining table lay the sole mitigating elements of that sad oppression, — a linen shirt, short and somewhat ragged, indeed, as to its hidden portions, but gorgeous in front with broad display of stiffly starched cambric frills.

"The Head Waiter," muttered the Saint; at once, from long practice enabled to determine accurately the rank and occupation of the sleeper.

"And what, therefore, from our bounty shall we give to him?" the Gnome inquired, unconsciously in his awakened interest identifying himself with St. Nicholas' anticipated liberality.

St. Nicholas shrugged his shoulders and grimly smiled. It seemed scarcely worth while, indeed,— he thought — to select for beneficiaries such lowly objects as these. Yet, as for a moment he glanced down, he saw that the Head Waiter was smiling in his sleep,— his face dilated widely with pleased anticipation of the wearing of the green velvet coat. Noticing this, the Saint relented. Surely it would be cruel, indeed, not to add something to this happiness, since so easily it could be done. And being so, it was a curious thing to observe, how as the ripple of his accustomed pastime began to flow in upon him, the soured air of discontent for a moment faded away from St. Nicholas' face. He even smiled a little with something of his olden beneficence of aspect.

"I will at least lighten the servitude of his official costume," said the Saint. And with that he drew from his pack a brilliant breastpin composed of a single stone somewhat larger than a pea and fastened it conspicuously upon the sleeper's finely frilled shirt front. Though there was no light in the room, excepting that which shone in from the outer hall, the breastpin glittered in that reflected ray like a planet.

" You are so wealthy !" said the Gnome, in open mouthed astonishment. " In all the treasure I am guarding, there is no diamond such as that."

"A California diamond, but sufficient for the purpose," the Saint responded. Then seeing that the Gnome did not comprehend, he was about to explain the difference between the true and false. But on second thought he paused. Why impart a knowledge that in its possibilities might even make the Gnome suspicious of his own treasure and render him unhappy with cruel doubt of its real value? Therefore he refrained; and merely said, resuming his surly tone :

" Well, have we now done ? Hardly is it worth while, indeed —"

" Nay, we have perhaps scarcely commenced," the Gnome cheerily responded. " This may do very well for a beginning. But there must somewhere be others who are equally worthy of our bounty and possibly may more closely attract our sympathies. And here is another stairway. Let us descend and see whither it may lead us."

28*

Chapter III.

So they began to descend, the Gnome blithely leading the way and St. Nicholas moodily following at a pace or two behind. First passing down a steep, narrow and roughly finished stairway, they found themselves at the bottom in a long hall —in all respects like that which they had just abandoned, except that it was carpeted and bore appearance of more perfect finish. Then came another stairway, wider and comfortably matted, and after that again a hall still better finished than the one immediately before. So with progression from one story to another; finding each stairway a little wider and each hall more elaborately furnished than the former one. It was like descending from a bleak mountain top, wherein, almost imperceptibly, the snows lessen and give place to dense pine forests and these again to open groves of ash and maple and fertile fields appear instead of the former desolation ; so gradual and undeviating was the passage from the unadorned life beneath the hotel roof to the esthetic culture of the stories below. And at last when nearly two-thirds down the Gnome arrested himself. It seemed to him that now they must have descended far enough to be assured of newer and more pleasant association, and he pointed to a door over which gleamed a light from within.

"Let us enter there," he said.

" As you will," St. Nicholas indifferently responded.

The Gnome touched the door, which slowly began to swing back before him. Peeping in, preparatory to entering, however, he saw a sight that troubled him a little. A small symmetrical pine tree stood in the center of the floor. Among its boughs, as the basis of adornment, were pendant balls of colored glass, amidst which were suspended a copious array of gifts. Short wax candles blazed from every branch and shed a pleasing and festive gleam upon the other decorations. It was a very pretty scene, and the Gnome would have liked to dwell longer upon it. But resisting, he closed the door again with hasty pull, fearing greatly the effect upon St. Nicholas, should he, also, behold those evidences of a rival visitant.

" What now ? " cried the Saint, coming up just in time to feel the door shut in his very face.

" There is no one there," the Gnome apologetically answered. " But yonder is another room, also showing its light, outside. Let us enter there. We cannot always find apartments vacant."

It was with some perturbation that he made the new suggestion. What if that other room, also, had its Christmas tree ? What if in every room these evidences of Kriss Kringle's more enterprising handiwork had already been obtruded ? But the essay must be made at every risk. And when they had entered this new apartment, the Gnome was relieved to find his apprehensions groundless. No intruding pine-tree there. No occupant to the room, indeed ; other than a little child, scarcely six years old, coiled up in quiet sleep in the middle of a large, sumptuously furnished bed, her tiny head and arms scarcely visible at first sight among the frills and laces of the downy pillows.

"The Pet of the House," said St. Nicholas, once again with his practiced sagacity defining the lot and station of the little sleeper.

Now the Pet of the House had that evening been present at a juvenile fancy party given in the main parlor of the hotel and she had begun her social life by being the acknowledged belle of that infant assemblage. For three hours she had been Marie Antoinette; and though, of course, not yet sufficiently versed in history to enter upon her part with any knowledge or conception whatsoever of the original, she was not deficient in some vague, childlike comprehension of being looked upon as a leading character among her many companions and thereby entitled to more than ordinary share of homage. This homage she had exacted and accepted with an assumption of quiet self-sufficient serenity and composure vastly gratifying to the taste of all the mature spectators; and thereby, with that childlike and unreasoning acceptation of royal dignity, mingling smiles and laughter with haughty condescension, she had chanced, perhaps, to act her part as fully to the life as if she had been of proper age to study the character from the page of history. Though her royal honors were now all laid aside, the glory of them still hung around her. On a chair beside the bed was spread out her embroidered train, with its complement of rich gold thread and laces; and on the nearest table rested the tiny powdered wig that, with the child's flaxen curls gathered up beneath it, had formed the head-dress of the day. These relics of queen-like state had carefully been so disposed that to the last moment of wakefulness the child might continue to enjoy them as evidences of past triumphs and might gaze upon them again with the morning's earliest glow.

During the evening the Pet of the House had, of course, been lavishly feasted, and cakes, ices and macaroons, with here and there a stolen sip of champagne, had been abundantly pressed upon her; so that at the last it happened, very naturally, that the attentions paid to the childlike Queen had greatly disturbed the first slumbers of the Queen become again a child. Hence, doubtless, the presence of the paregoric beside the royal head-dress. Headaches and tossings for a time; — these had been the painful allotments of the little head and limbs. But youth is strong and soon throws off its unsatisfactory burdens, and for young trespassers upon its laws nature is swift to prove both kind and forgiving. Therefore it happened that at the hour when St. Nicholas and the Gnome entered, the headache had been subdued and the tossings composed and the Pet of the House was enjoying pleasant, undisturbed slumber. Yet as the devastation of the tempest will sometimes remain visible in the bright sunshine that follows, so, amid the tranquil smiles and regular breathing that marked the slumber of the little child, could be seen the faint pouting of the lips and the single tear glittering upon the rounded cheek. A tear upon one cheek, the fellow tear to which had just been brushed away by the chubby right hand that rested upon the pillow close beside the seraph face and remained half closed, as though retaining the captured tear in its infantile grasp.

The Gnome looked on, wondering and speechless, but filled with earnest thought. Were all the sons and daughters of men as beautiful as this? He had never before met with a young child — seldom, indeed, had he beheld a human creature. He had seen the young of white bears, walruses and seals and had thought them very pretty, after a degree; but this child with its ribbons, laces and curly hair and all those adornments that help make infancy interesting seemed a thought more pretty than any of them. What revelations of novelty and interest were constantly being made before him! And what a scene of loveliness everywhere seemed this world upon which he was for the first time entering! Again came the wonderment that St. Nicholas should ever dream of treating it with despite or should give up any opportunity of mingling with and enjoying it. So thinking, he turned to look upon him, expecting still to find the usual indications of discomfiture and ill-humor. But to his surprise, he saw that the face of the Saint had cast off its morose aspect — was clearing into sunshine like the sky after a summer's shower — seemingly was taking some reflection of his own admiring, grateful thought. Noting this, the Gnome became vastly cheered at heart and full of courage for any suggestion; and therefore, still identifying himself with the other's liberality, as though in common ownership of the fund, he said:

"And what, from our store, shall we give this one?"

"All things and every thing that a child can wish for," said St. Nicholas. "Do you not see," he added, pointing to the little stocking that hung beside the fire-place, "that here is one that is faithful to me? Do you not see how, even now, with dreams of my coming, she lies with face turned this way, so that at her first waking in the morning her glance shall rest, not upon foolish adornments of the past night but only upon my own good work in her behalf? Let us to work, Gnome. For once, that demon, Kriss Kringle shall not prevail."

Perhaps St. Nicholas spoke severely. It is the habit of a true saint, indeed, to look upon all rival saints as demons. But his face was so bright and cheery that the Gnome had no heart to make comment upon his words and stooping down he assisted in selecting gifts from the already opened pack. Punch and Judy gazing enraptured upon each other out of the separate corners of the box — tin kitchens complete with stove and pans and hams hanging upon the wall, not to speak of the black cook herself with skirts tucked up, using her long-pronged fork over the frying-pan full of painted fish — a curly sheep that bleated and a hairy cow that lowed — a narrow case filled to the very ends with black minstrels, who, at the pulling of a string beat the tamborine and thrummed the banjo and turned their

white eyes from side to side in eager waiting for the
answer to the time-honored conundrum — all these
and much besides were put into the tiny stocking or
attached to it outside. Nothing too good, indeed,
for the child that has not bowed the knee to Kriss
Kringle. Once St. Nicholas drew forth a box of
green and yellow candies and made as though he
would put that also by the stocking, but looking
around he chanced to see the paregoric upon the
table and he shook his head and restored the candies
to his pack. But instead thereof, he produced a
beauteous doll with every gift and appliance of
modern ingenuity and design — with gold embroidered shoes and silver dress, with drooping laces and
silver-threaded bodice and with its fair locks built
up into labored pile, more artistic and grand, even,
than those of Marie Antoinette — a graceful doll,
with face flesh colored to the life and piquant in
expression as though a human soul actually lurked
behind — a doll that could open and shut its eyes
and upon uplifting of the arms would speak. With
this he crowned the huge pile of gifts, then at last
buckled together his sadly shrunken pack and lifted
it again upon his shoulder.

“I begin now,” he said, “to feel glad that I have
come.”

“Is it so?” cried the Gnome, for the moment a
little foolishly elated with the result of his experiment, as though to himself were all the credit.
“You see, then, that I was right. Perhaps if I knew
it, I am always right. Never after this deny that I
am good for something. And always when in
trouble take a gnome’s advice.”

Chapter IV.

SILENTLY, as fearing to disturb that infantile slumber, St. Nicholas and the Gnome stole out of the room. There was elation in each heart, though from different cause. The Gnome continued vastly pleased at the triumph which had attended his advice; though, constrained by exceeding good nature as well as by a little native tact, he forbore any longer to express his thought, not knowing, indeed, how far St. Nicholas might further listen to it in moderation. On the other hand the Saint felt his heart aglow with transports that it had not known for many days. It was something, indeed, to have prevailed over Kriss Kringle in the race for human preference; this alone was a subject for deep self-gratulation. But far more enjoyable than that — which after all was a selfish triumph at the best — was the knowledge that there was still an unseen influence pervading the world in his favor, leading to something like the old-fashioned allegiance, and that the time was not past and might never entirely depart, in which he could bestow his annual favors and find them accepted and appreciated with the accustomed gratitude and fervor. Yet he also maintained silence, not knowing, perhaps, exactly how to express his thoughts to the comprehension of the other; and so the two wandered side by side down the broad passage. With a change, however; for now St. Nicholas instead of lagging moodily behind, kept even pace with the Gnome and again assumed the direction of affairs.

Now down another flight of steps and still another — so anew from story to story the two descended. And as in following yet further the mountain slopes the traveler may leave the temperate zones and finally arrive at excess of tropical vegetation in all its wild luxuriance and beauty, so in their descent through the Bon Ton Hotel, St. Nicholas and the Gnome continually reached new developments of lavish and superb adornment. Rich carpets beneath the feet, deadening the sound of heaviest footfall,— bright fresco paintings in arabesque upon the walls,— the dim, half-turned down light, gleaming from massive chandeliers,— at each end, mirrors covering the whole extent and appearing to repeat the scene to indefinite endless distance — to all this the descent at last led. To St. Nicholas such things were already familiar; but to the Gnome they presented all the zest of novelty. Truly he had never beheld the like of this; and for the instant he lamented that he should ever be obliged to go back to his service in the rocks. In a moment, however, he recovered himself. Let the future take care of itself ; why should he not enjoy the present, without the bitter mingling of useless repining ? After all, was he not better off than most gnomes, who, doubtless, never had any opportunity to move away from their ceaseless monotonous trusts ? Therefore, bracing up his mind for unimpaired enjoyment of the pleasant present, he threw back his head and cheerfully strode down the corridor at St. Nicholas' side. Had it been possible for any one passing through at that hour of the night and meeting the two strangers to penetrate the invisibility that enveloped them, he would have been vastly amazed at the spectacle. St. Nicholas, short and fat — seeming shorter and fatter than he really was, by reason of his thick white furs and the broad basket that he carried at his back, — the Gnome so much shorter still that he scarcely reached to his companion's shoulder and waddled as he strove to bring his little thin legs up to the other's more rapid pace, — in figure thinner than the Saint, and with his sable furs forming strong contrast with him, — keen and inquiring of expression, and altogether partaking of the grotesque, through the unaccustomed combination of little bright, weasel-like eyes, sharp nose and pointed furry ears ; — these two formed a couple never before seen in hotel hall and who would have filled a stranger with astonishment and awe. But they remained unseen and plodded on for a moment silent and uninterrupted. Once, only, the longings of the Gnome found vent, as he considered whether he might not mingle the pleasures of the world and the requirements of his duty together.

"It is a novel and a beautiful world," he sighed. "Could I only bring my treasure here to guard" —

"Could you do so," St. Nicholas interrupted, "you would be obliged to maintain it in such unceasing conflict against the violence and craft of men that the incursions of griffins would seem to you merely child's play."

So the Gnome, for the moment, said no more, and they passed onward through the midnight stillness. Not altogether through perfect silence, perhaps. There were two call-boys with ice-water quarrelling in the main hall and threatening each other with their pitchers. A group of chambermaids sat loudly giggling, in the deep recess of an end window. The office clerk came passing onward to his room with stately tread. Three belated travellers with four porters in the rear sat down upon their trunks in the main hall to talk over their adventures, while a waiter who had brought up the wrong keys went back for the right ones. Two waiters bearing material for a midnight supper noisily jostled their laden trays together; and mistakingly seeking entrance to the wrong room brought forth uproarious expostulation from the unduly awakened occupant. And a porter who had been keeping Christmas eve a trifle too freely came stumbling along with armful of boots, picking up new ones at each door and unconsciously dropping old ones, blazing his path thereby through the long hall, like Hop o' my Thumb with his crumbs through the wilderness. With these trivial exceptions, the main hall of the Bon Ton Hotel was wrapped in tomblike silence.

It is easy to get lost in the Bon Ton Hotel. Men have been known to spend many hours endeavoring to extricate themselves from the tangled maze of its interminable passages. But by wisely following the more direct corridors and keeping in those which were broadest and noting their position by the line of chandeliers, St. Nicholas and the Gnome escaped all vexatious complications and succeeded in confining their route entirely to the more attractive portion of the house. For a time they resisted all temptations to stop, though they passed many doors similar to the last and with appearance of lights burning inside — choosing rather to await some subtle inspiration to direct them. At length the inspiration appeared to come, for suddenly St. Nicholas pointed to a door at the end of the hall, not in the least differing from other doors along the same range and said :

" Let us here enter."

" Do you know," said the Gnome, with a smile of cheery assent, a little loth as yet to give up the sceptre of direction, " that I was about to say the same thing myself? It seems to me, also, that here we may find something to interest and entertain us. Yes, let us enter."

With that St. Nicholas touched the door, which, gently opening, admitted them. They found themselves in an apartment so similar to that of the Pet of the House that it might easily have been mistaken for it, except for some alterations dictated by individual taste and thereby varying it from the customary pattern of the place. Though the hour was now so far advanced, the occupant of the room had not yet retired, but was sitting by the open grate fire, seemingly buried in deep reflection. Evidently her half-completed toilet for the night had been suspended by no ordinary interruption of thought, for she remained motionless as a statue, her long, wavy hair hanging loosely down her back, a shawl thrown around her shoulders, her naked feet thrust into embroidered slippers and lightly balanced upon the fender, her arm raised from her knee to support her face half concealed in the upturned palm.

"And what from our bounty shall we give her for this new Christmas day?" said the Gnome.

At the question, St. Nicholas approached her with gentle step, and looked over her shoulder; with intent, perhaps, by a nearer view, to gain some inkling of her tastes. Then, for the first time, he saw that she held in her hand a little miniature; upon which, as her gaze turned from the fire, she dwelt fixedly, and, as it would seem, with tender interest. At the Saint's first glance, his face already becoming so cheery broke out into newer and more expansive brightness, and with all the eagerness of sudden unanticipated delight he seized the Gnome by the hand.

"It is they!" cried St. Nicholas. "I have found them at last."

"And who are they?" responded the Gnome. "And they being found, whoever they are, what from our store of bounty shall we" —

"Can you not imagine, Gnome? She, the daughter of the house that stood here; the house that I had so longed to see and that has given place to this. He, the lover, who two years ago was constant to her and must be constant still. Coming daily, with the favor and authority of all who had any claim upon her; seeing that, though poor in worldly goods, he was gifted in heart and intellect. Even then I foresaw that the friendship between the two would ripen into betrothal; and now that I view her with his portrait in her hand, how can I believe other than that it has so come about?"

"It would seem so, indeed," answered the Gnome.

"A fine young fellow, indeed, with heart overflowing with love and with a brain that will some day make him famous. As full of science as a Noah's ark is full of animals. Why, he could dig down into your cave, and from the very look of the rocks each side could tell you how long it has been there, how long it took to form. Nay, if your treasure had always belonged there as a portion of nature's store and had not been brought from elsewhere, he could tell you from a long distance off just where it lies."

"A dangerous person to have around one, I should think," said the startled Gnome.

"Further than that," St. Nicholas continued, "he could look into some rock, created at a time when griffins were more plentiful than now, and could pick from the solid wall a talon here and a scale there, and tell you for a certainty whether there were any griffins yet alive or not."

"That were a better thing to do," said the Gnome. And he wondered whether griffins might not be really extinct, and whether, if so, the fact could be known to science, and whether he might not then leave the treasure unguarded, as no longer exposed to evil influences and take up his abode in the bright world of sunshine and enjoyment. "Yet if this maiden loves him and is so much beloved," he added, returning, like the sensible Gnome he was, to the business in hand, "why is she unhappy? Why are there tears upon her cheek?"

"Tears! Can it really be?" exclaimed St. Nicholas; and with that he moved around further toward the young girl's right hand, for as yet he had merely been standing behind where he could only see her face in partial relief. And now he noticed that the tears actually stood in her eyes; and, as he gazed, one transparent drop loosened from her long eye-lashes and rolled down and breaking, spread over the face of the miniature. She brushed it tenderly away with her laced handkerchief; then, for a moment, laid the picture one side. A moment more of silent contemplation of the fire, — then she gathered up out of her lap a small bundle of letters, all in the same handwriting. These, one by one, she glanced over rather than deliberately read. They seemed, indeed, to need no careful reading, so familiar to her must have been their contents. One of these — perhaps not better than the others but regarded merely as type of all — she placed aside to save, then made a motion as though to lay the others on the fire. If her purpose therein was destruction of the letters, her heart failed her, for she withdrew her hand and the letters again fell spread out in her lap. And then, leaning back in the chair and covering her whole face with her hands, she broke forth into more undisguised weeping, the hot tears stealing between her fingers and falling upon miniature and letters alike.

"This is serious, indeed," said the Saint, "and I cannot pretend to comprehend it all at once." He stood aside; and for a moment, with his finger beside his nose reflected, then spoke again. "I cannot believe that the lover has played her false; there is truth itself written in every feature — truth and unswerving constancy. Truly, I am at a loss for the meaning of all this."

"May it not be," said the Gnome, and he spoke hesitatingly, as one whose experience was so limited that it was scarcely worth while offering an opinion, "may it not be — listen now. I am very poor. Of the treasure committed to my care, I own nothing; all I own is my fur suit and my lodging in the rock. At times I crawl up and look at the stars and watch the birds and the seals at their play, and this is all my amusement. Yet I am content. My life is a happy one, upon the whole, and I ask no more out of it. But I have sometimes wondered what would be in my mind if the treasure belonged to me. At the first thought, indeed, it would seem that if I were content with nothing, I could not be less than content with much. And yet" —

"Yet, you would say?"

"It seems to me, on the other hand, that the very incompleteness of the treasure, about which now I care nothing, would then distress me; and that being thus rich I could not be happy unless I made myself more so. I would desire that the gold vase should have its double and that the copper cup that holds the diamonds should be full to the brim; that all the silver coin should be exchanged for gold;

that the jeweled sceptre should have its true accompaniment of jeweled sword. I would be restless and miserable beyond conception and would find my contented nature changing unless I could fulfill my whole desire. And, doubtless, if I had children I would learn not to secure simple tastes or lives for them; but I would wish to mate them with other gnomes, if such there be, whose wealth of treasure might equal or even surpass my own."

"And then?" St. Nicholas demanded, seeing that the other hesitated.

"Well, that is all, I think, excepting this, that I would suggest from it. If man-nature is any thing like gnome-nature, might it not have happened that the man who was so amply contented with his small house and garden, while he believed it worth little, now that he has become rich should have learned to nourish other and more brilliant ambitions than heretofore? This, too, not merely for himself but for his child, so that "—

"I see it all," cried the saint. "Yes, it must be so, indeed. There can be no doubt. Come now with me. Since she is here, the others cannot be far distant. The night wears on apace and we have much still to do."

"And she," said the Gnome, "this favorite of your true friendship, — shall we leave her without one gift to signify our presence?"

"See, she sleeps," responded the saint. The young girl still sat reclining in the cushioned chair, but her hands had softly fallen from before her face and now rested in her lap. Nature, for the time, had conquered grief and her eyes were closed in quiet slumber. There was no sign of sorrow or turmoil now upon that tranquil face — rather a smile of sweet contentment; except that in the flickering fire-light a single tear glittered like a jewel upon one cheek and spoke of the trouble that lately had been. "She is at rest; I will give her the choicest gift at my command — a pleasant dream — a dream of coming reconciliation and reunion."

He waved his hand lightly over her forehead, beaming the while gently upon her upturned face. At once her smile became more intense and radiant, — her eyes half opening for the moment, not in wakefulness but rather from the inner straining of the soul urging her to meet one coming to her with equal love in his heart, — her lips feebly murmured words inarticulate, but doubtless words of welcome.

"Tell me this," cried the Gnome, scarcely pleased at what he saw. "You are not deceiving her with a dream of what may never be? Not giving her a pleasant vision from which she must awaken to new miseries rendered more burdensome by reason of the one transient contrast of happiness? That were a cruel thing, indeed, to do."

"Have no fear of that," said the Saint. "It would be a wrong to her for which I could not forgive myself. If I bestow upon her the blessing of a sweet dream, it is because I hope, through my good management, to have it continued for her increasing happiness, in her rewakening. Now let us go."

Chapter V.

THEREFORE they turned away; but not through where they had entered. There was another door at the side, and St. Nicholas directed himself thither, rightly judging that it must lead to other apartments of the family. Passing through, they came at first into a large parlor, and after that into another bedroom, in which slept two persons.

Approaching the bed, the visitants gazed down upon it. Two persons, as has been said, occupied it,—a man and a woman,—both past the middle period of life, though not as yet showing marks of old age. To the woman there was a round, pleasant face, well filled out with health and ruddy withal — the face of one whose life had been an easy one from the beginning. Had poverty or distress been its lot, at any period, for a series of years, it would have left its traces in thinness or in care-engraved wrinkles, or more than all these, in that worn, suffering expression of anxiety which long battling with the world scarcely ever fails to bring. Yet all the same there was token of present sorrow upon that face — not far enough continued, indeed, to produce permanent impress, but which, perhaps, might yet have that result if unduly protracted. A thoughtful, disturbed expression — a sorrowful falling of the lips — wakefulness that could not be conquered nor would yield to calm philosophy — a mute look of despair in the wide-open eyes — a turning toward her companion with some sort of apprehension, as though ill at ease in his society and constantly dreading outbreak — nay, that certain sad indication of disturbance, a tear yet undried upon the cheek.

"Tears — tears everywhere," St. Nicholas muttered. "Upon the cheek of infant, maiden and mature age. This certainly should not be so upon Christmas day."

Then he turned to look at the woman's companion. A bluff, gruff, roughly cast man, at the first sight — seemingly one who was always ready to invite dissension, the sharp quills of his moral nature all standing up on end, in alertness to meet attack. This grim face, full of hard lines and angles as though it had been carved out of thickly knotted wood, in any condition of being might have seemed well calculated to treat the world aggressively, riding it tyrannically and remorselessly down and over ; now, in the accessory adornment of a long cotton night-cap with frayed tassel, it appeared almost appalling. And yet, more closely examined, it was not naturally a face to be afraid of, but rather under better circumstances to love. There were finely, even delicately cut features, lips that showed by their curve that they could be trained to smile ; in fine, it was the face of one who should attract rather than repel and surely would have done so, if from long habit or assumed system the better nature had not been overcome. Such as he was, the doubt and sorrow and nervous tremor of his wakeful wife gave him no disturbance, for his eyes were closed and his mouth open and in common with the saints of the earth he was sleeping the sleep of the just.

"How shall we manage him?" said the Gnome, thus somewhat varying his question.

"It may, perhaps, be a harder task than I had anticipated," said St. Nicholas, after a moment of silent inspection. "Yet hitherto I have not failed in more desperate undertakings. If he would only awaken"—

"I will arrange that for you," cried the Gnome.

And stooping down, he ran the furred prickly point of one of his ears into the right ear of the sleeper, who thereupon, at the unusual tickling, jumped, choked and sneezed and almost at once became wide awake.

"What now?" he gruffly said, turning towards his wife, whom he naturally believed to be the person who had disturbed him.

"I did not say any thing," timidly she answered, "except—I would like to say it now, for it is long past twelve, is it not? Merry Christmas, dear."

"Bah! What is Christmas?" he snapped back. "Only a time when I must empty out my pockets for people I don't care about, that is all. As for the mischief of it,—don't you know that the Board is closed on Christmas day? Almost every day for the last six months at the Stock Board I have made nearly a thousand dollars, while to-day it will be not a cent, of course. Suppose all the brokers are cut off from like profits; can't you figure up the gross loss to the business community, by reason of closing the Board for this one day? A good, round sum, I can tell you. And all for Christmas."

"I don't know any thing about that; of course, you can tell best. But there was a time when you"—

"Yes, before I knew any thing about the world; I am wiser now."

"We were so happy, then;" she persisted. "Perhaps it is better not to become so wise, if it takes away all the pleasure of it. You and I, dear,—and—and our child; and now she—she is so wretched—and"—

"Will get over it well enough, just as other girls get over it. And I tell you what;—sending that fellow off and letting her know that she must never have any thing more to do with him is the best move I ever made. What is he, after all, with his foolish care for science? If he could tell how best to get a railroad through the mountains without too much tunneling, indeed, it would be worth while. But what is the good of learning about all the rocks that lie five miles deep in Maine or Georgia? Who cares for them, indeed?"

"And yet"—

"Yes, I know all that. We have enough for both, you would say. But no one ever has enough; no one, no matter who he is, can ever have enough of any thing for both of anybody else. Let the young fellow give up his foolishness and come into my office and learn to make a little money for himself; and then, perhaps, after a year or two, something may be done. There, enough of that, now:

I don't want to hear another word about it, ever. Are you ever going to let me go to sleep, old lady, or ain't you?"

With that he drew his night-cap a little closer over his head as if for necessary protection from her expected expostulations, turned upon his side, opened his mouth with a preliminary snarl and in a moment was once more fast asleep.

"Wake him up again, Gnome," said St. Nicholas.

The Gnome once more bent over and with the furred tip of his long ear tickled the sleeper upon the side of the face. Again the sleeper puffed and sneezed and gave a violent start, this time leaping into a sitting posture, and clapping his hand hastily to the side of his face, gazed round at his wife.

"It wasn't she this time, anyhow," he said. "I thought it was a fly ; but, of course, it could not be a fly at this season of the year, either. Whatever it was, its pretty certain I can't get asleep to-night. I might as well read my letters, I suppose. "

Up to that moment the room had been only dimly lighted, but now the old man reached forth his hand and turned the light on at full blaze. Then he sought for his spectacles upon the table beside him, put them on and was ready for work. And with this intent, he stretched forth to secure a package of letters that lay upon the same table. But at the same instant, St. Nicholas drew from his ever-ready pack two folded papers and laid them on top of the pile of letters.

"Let me see," said the old gentleman, lifting off one of the papers and opening it. "From Gurgle

& Wallopy, I suppose; about the margin in Great Western — Why, bless my soul! What's this?"

Inclosed in the envelope, was the painting in miniature of a boy of about eight years old; a beautiful boy, with long flaxen locks and erect, lithe figure and open, generous expression and undoubted manly bearing.

"It is your picture turned up again," said the wife. "Though how" —

"That's the queer thing about it," he exclaimed. "I supposed it had been lost years ago. Well, well; what a meek, milk-and-water looking young fellow I was, to be sure !"

"Not so, dear. A very pretty boy, indeed. So they all said. Brave, manly and generous; and in all things " —

"In all things better than I am now ?" he interrupted, turning upon her with some suspicion of her trying to interweave an unpleasant, uncomplimentary truth.

"I didn't say so, did I ? Of course, you must be different now ; that is to be expected. Certainly a man must be other than a boy. If you were only now a little more trustful in kind fate — somewhat more ready to believe, as formerly, that there was a good Providence over us — Do you remember what a queer little tot I was then, only two years younger than you ? And how, even then, you used to call me your little wife and say you meant to marry me some day and that I should have a carriage and two horses?"

"And I kept my word, didn't I, old lady ? You

have the carriage and two horses, do you not?" he responded, a certain flicker of good nature interweaving itself with his habitual grimness.

"Yes, we have it. Perhaps when it came, we took it too much as matter of course, caring little about it and having so many other things to make us happy. Do you know, it seems to me that it is only since we became rich that we have felt ourselves anxious and in need? Before we learned how valuable were the old house and garden, there were no more contented people than ourselves in all the world. How little, then, we thought of money for itself, rather than for what it might enable us to do for others! You were so cheerful and well pleased with every piece of kind fortune, no matter how small. And as for our child —"

"There, there; I knew of course that you were coming to it," interrupted the other, "she and he always on your mind and scarcely ever out of your mouth. Really, it cannot be — you must know that as well as I do. He has nothing at all; and as for us, it is only lately that I have learned how much more we ought to have to be as rich as we should be. Trust a man for that. And go to sleep now — it is already near morning. Did you say Merry Christmas to me a while ago? Well, Merry Christmas back again; and so, good night."

He said it with a sort of sullen snap, as though he were not used to it and considered it a childish performance and went into it only to please her. Perhaps that was his thought. And yet as he spoke, somehow a wrinkle or two smoothed out of his forehead and a trifle of more generous feeling seemed apparent for the moment in his expression. He sighed softly to himself, also, as he took the picture again and gazed upon it before replacing it upon the table. A milk-and-water young fellow? Well, no, not exactly that. There was really something nice about that face — he might admit it now, since he was so different that the admission could scarcely be called personal praise. He could remember now, very dimly, how as a boy, people seemed attracted by him; now they appeared inclined rather to flee away. This was because he had had to fight his way, of course, and had not learned to make himself too agreeable to most people. It was not natural, indeed, that the grown man could ever remain bright looking and simple hearted like the boy. And whether it was pleasant or not to feel so changed, it could not be helped and he must abide by it. But again he sighed and for a few moments he lay still, with his hands clasped behind his head, in deep and somewhat disturbed train of thought.

"But this is not Gurgle & Wallopy's report," he muttered at length, arousing himself. "Surely their letter must be somewhere here."

Again he stretched forth his hand, lifted a paper, opened it and uttered an exclamation of surprise:

"Another of those old pictures!" he cried out. "I thought, wife, that they had all been lost."

"I thought, indeed, that this had been lost at our moving," she said. "I am so glad it has turned up again. It is the picture you gave me when first we became engaged. Oh, how handsome it is!"

Very handsome, indeed! The full length miniature of a young man of twenty, — erect, pure-hearted,
confident of his future and full of manly impulses
and aspirations. The figure of the lad of eight
grown to man's estate, yet not having as yet lost his
identity ; the candor, generosity and purity of the
boy remaining intact and visible upon the likeness,
with the full strength, purpose and daring of manhood superadded. As the woman now gazed tear-
fully upon the picture, the husband also looked on ;
and, before he was aware of it, his accusing conscience
was aroused and forced him into self-betrayal.

"Surely I never looked as well as that !" he said.
"So different from now."

"Yes, it was a likeness then, — never any better,"
she answered. "Do you remember when you gave
it to me? We were standing at the well in the
country; and you placed this in my hand and told
me that at last you had the place in the counting-
house and we could look forward to an assured
future if we were moderately prudent. It was not
much, indeed, that you had, and I had nothing at all;
but how happy we were for many years, creeping
upward in the world and making the most of the
little we had ! We used to read together in those
days, and you wished that you could study more,
and regretted that necessity compelled such other
labors, and said that if ever you became rich and
our little girl —— "

"That young fellow, eh ? At it again, old lady ?"
he said, this time not unkindly.

"Yes, dear, all about him again. For you know

that he is worthy, and, but for the accident that he is not rich, you would have nothing now to say against him. You have already almost promised him. True, there has been no word given, but you have let him come again and again for two years past and when away he has been allowed to write and it has been all but a complete promise between them. Turn him not away, now. If once we could trust so firmly in our not certain future, can you not put faith in theirs, with honors of the world so ready to be showered upon him, as well as all the help we can give and not in the least miss it from ourselves? You have been unkind to your child this last day. Believe me, she will not soon get over it. Is it so easy to recover from that kind of blow? Suppose, when you had given me your picture, my father had said that you were not rich enough; what would I have done?"

"You?" responded the husband, essaying a laugh. "Why, you would have come all right in a week and forgotten me, I suppose. But I" — "with a tremulous little cough, "I believe that I should have broken my heart."

"Then do not let his poor heart or hers be broken with the same cruel disappointment. I have been at her side this night and she is sitting up in tears and deep despair, refusing to be comforted. Could you but see her, your resolve would surely melt, I know. Dear husband, you have asked me what I would choose for Christmas present. You have offered any thing that wealth can furnish — jewels and dress or whatever else the soul could crave.

Give me none of these,—I care not for them. What peace could they ever give me, with our child lying broken hearted at my feet? For sole Christmas present, give me our child's happiness! Let me go to her this minute and tell her that when you spoke unkindly to her you were in jest or in some trouble of the moment and that you meant it not!"

For a minute or two, he remained silent. One might have thought that he had not been listening to her. And yet, there was a gathering moisture in his eyes and one by one the wrinkles still seemed to smoothe themselves out of his rugged forehead. In his right hand he yet held the portrait of himself at twenty and while she spoke he had been dreamily gazing upon it. At the beginning, indeed, with the same cold curiosity with which he had looked at it, upon its first discovery; then with gathering interest and something akin to an expression of mournful regret. It had been rightly said, a moment past, that the mature man cannot look altogether like the boy; and yet it is none the less true that if the man be endowed with noble character, some of the physical traits of the honest-hearted boy may remain. Therefore, though that little portrait spoke not of advanced age or darkening face or increasing baldness of forehead or here and there a wrinkle, yet in the older man there should still have been something of resemblance to it, were it merely in its pleasant, engaging look, winning eye and impress of serenity and peace.

An hour ago, the face that rested upon the pillow had borne little of such likeness, indeed. A hard, stern face, as has been intimated, repulsive and unsympathetic, fierce, aggressive and repugnant — seeming to bristle with offense and sordidness. But now, as the man sat and listened to the pleadings of his wife and gazed upon the picture in his hand — that picture of his better past life — and felt how true would be her reproaches were she unkind enough to make them, — felt, indeed, his own heart reproach him more severely than she could ever be driven to do, — felt how little she would have had to plead with him for any thing in the former days of confidence and love; there came forgotten, crushed out sympathies of soul, struggling to the surface. And with their new expression, something of the purer and better man crept into his face; and already it seemed as though, with renewal of long lost tender graces, the hidden likeness of his former self would be renewed.

"If I answer yes, old lady," he responded, affecting a jesting humor he did not feel, "will you then say nothing more and let me sleep?"

"Ah, dear!" exclaimed the delighted woman, "now I know that you are going to be kind again, even as in the old times."

"Then go; and before you do so — a merry, merry Christmas to you! And now, give me your Christmas kiss."

For a moment they wrapped their arms about each other — these two old people — with all the loving fervor of their long past youth.

"Do you know," she said, releasing herself, "that this seems more like the Christmas of our youth than any thing that has happened since? Can you remem-

ber how, when children, we would awaken early to
see what St. Nicholas had brought us? It was a
joyous time for us; and yet, if the value of what
could be given were the true test and measure of
joy, surely never was heart more lightened than
mine is now, at having that gift of our household
happiness placed within my keeping. It almost
seems as though St. Nicholas himself had come again
to guide our hearts and impulses right."

"True, it might seem so," he said with half a sigh;
"for certainly, old lady, something has come over
me to-night to make me yield more easily to you
than I should have thought possible. But after all,
the fancies of our youth must be left apart forever.
There is no St. Nicholas."

"No — I suppose there is not — there never can
be," she said, as in slow pondering, "the dreams of
childhood can never be restored. And yet, what
if childhood, in that respect, were wiser than age,
and there were actually truth in what we learn afterward to call untrue? What if there were really a
kind St. Nicholas standing invisibly beside us, guid-
ing our thoughts into more noble channels than they
find throughout all the rest of the year — teaching
us —"

"Go to — you are a foolish woman," he interrupted.
"And now, take up your gift of happiness, as you call
it, and bear it away to the other room, lest I repent
and recall it."

She smiled and kissed him once again; then sliding
from the bed, slipped through the door into the
other room to tell the joyful tidings — awakening

thus the child from the pleasant dream that the Saint had given, but leading her into a lasting reality of happiness, whereof the dream truly had been merely a transient shadow. And he, the husband, lying back upon his pillow, no longer thought about his stocks and bonds; but picturing out his other better days, felt his face again become genial with youthful innocence and generosity and his heart glowing with a serenity it had not known for months. The portrait was once more growing very like, indeed.

Chapter VI.

"WILL he keep his word?" said the Gnome, as he and St. Nicholas slowly left the room.

"He will do so," responded the Saint. "Even were he to repent of it, scarcely will he now depart from his promise. That to him will be sacred, even as a mercantile guaranty given in the outer world. And now, what more can we do to-night?"

"Nothing, I should think," said the Gnome. "Hardly could you hope for such another triumph as that, to-night. And see! the day is near at hand, and we should now depart."

In fact, already there came a faint glow of dawn stealing in at the end window of the hall, confusing all the light and making the artificial brightness within grow dim. Then came a servant along the hall, putting out each gas-jet, so that the light of day seemed to pour in from the end window with stronger power, and having it all its own way, made every thing almost as bright as before and constantly brighter still. Then from all sides began to gather the hum of people awakening from their slumber, and here and there the not always deadened footfall of more early riser. A waiter tripped along with call-book in his hand, looking for No. 85; which being found, he rapped loudly at the door and sum-

moned 85 to arise and take the early train.   No. 85
remaining asleep or willfully obstinate, the waiter
rapped the louder, greatly disturbing all the neighborhood ; whereat, No. 87, alongside, cried out in
wrath, and No. 86, opposite, appeared and assisted
in the loud expostulation.   The waiter, taking it not
kindly but rather as an infringement on his vested
right to make a noise, answered profanely; upon
which, other doors on all sides were thrown open,
and Christmas being a day devoted to frolic, the
several occupants of the rooms took up the matter
in exceedingly lively spirit of jest and overwhelmed
the waiter with bitter sarcasms and threatened fell
showers of boots, causing him to swear the louder.
Just then, a porter coming down the nearest flight
of steps with heavy trunk upon his shoulder, turned
around to watch the contest, and doing so, swept
off the glasses from the nearest chandelier ; whereat
he grew afraid and nervous and his foot slipping he
and the trunk rolled down stairs together.   Upon
this, a bevy of chambermaids hearing the noise
gathered above to see what might be the matter;
and one of them leaning too far forward lost her
balance and tumbled over the banisters onto the floor
below.   Whom, then, a crowd of waiters at once
surrounded ; and finding her somewhat bruised, sat
her upon the gong and carried her off to her own
room.   In fact, it became evident that this portion of
the Bon Ton Hotel was being pretty well awakened.

   " Yes, it must surely be time for us to go," murmured the Gnome, a little frightened and thinking
for the moment that though the world was very

beautiful it was perhaps unduly noisy. "But let us step in here and wait until the tumult all is past."

He pointed to an opening beside the hall — a little space scarcely six feet across, adorned from top to bottom with carved and polished wood of different colors and upon each of the four sides a plate glass mirror. In the centre was swung a brazen chandelier with cut glass shades. There were no chairs, but merely a cushioned seat that ran around the little recess, close against its wall. Into this recess St. Nicholas and the Gnome retreated, to tarry until the passing by of the group of waiters with the bruised chambermaid. But scarcely had this happened when there came a sudden new wonder. For from the further end of the hall, slowly approaching and visible only to St. Nicholas and the Gnome, there appeared a single figure. Taller than St. Nicholas and not as stout — with dark fur coat brought partially over the face with deep hood — not so closely though, but that it let a grave saturnine face be seen, half covered with long gray beard. Over one shoulder a small pine tree and in one hand a heavy bunch of colored candles. A well-filled pack, also, strapped upon the back; but seeming somewhat, in its make up, unlike the pack belonging to St. Nicholas. Here and there a doll or a colored toy, indeed; but for the most part books and portfolios and whatever might be considered most useful.

The Gnome almost groaned aloud. Recognizing Kriss Kringle, he feared disturbance between him and St. Nicholas upon their meeting. It must necessarily happen, indeed, that when these two beings went upon their several rounds, the time would at last arrive wherein they would have encountered. Now that it had come about, who should answer for the consequences? But St. Nicholas, when he saw his rival, merely smiled — watched him composedly and unruffled as he slowly stalked past, seeming not to observe the lookers on and finally disappeared with his pine tree through a doorway at the other end of the long hall; nor all that while did the Saint lose one line or curve of his own now pleasant expression.

"An hour ago," he said, "I would have been very angry at meeting him. But now I know full well that there are enough to satisfy all my desires and aspirations among such as love me and cannot be turned aside from me. Kriss Kringle can never be to people what I am. Who ever heard of him a generation ago? But now there are old men who knew and waited for me in their boyhood. What can he do but strive to conciliate with his gifts? But I, standing beside old friends who have fallen from their once generous faith, can touch their souls with sparks of their olden sympathy and surely guide them back to the better and holier nature of their youth. His gifts are calculating and soulless — looked forward to as the mere reward of months of endeavor, — rewards, indeed, not spontaneous benefits; my offerings fall like Heaven's sunshine upon both the wicked and the good, not as payment for any past services, but as happy acknowledgments of a bright and pleasant season that all should alike enjoy. — And who is he, after all?" the

Saint added, in vein of earthly pride. "He comes we know not whence, and goes we know not where. When he is through his labors, he fades away or departs on foot, while I — We will return, Gnome, to our sleigh and six."

With that they attempted to step forth from the little recess, but before they could do so, it began slowly to ascend, passing through an aperture in the ceiling above. At first sight, the whole building seemed sinking down from around it; and the two occupants sat tightly holding themselves upon the seat, and gazing about in evident uneasiness. Nor was it until they had passed upward for a long space that they solved the mystery and regained composure.

"It is certainly a very pleasant method of ascent — far more so than a chimney, I should judge," the Gnome remarked. "How many novelties I am seeing this night, to be sure!"

Thus, almost noiselessly, they ascended, story after story seeming to fly downward past them and at last they stopped. A wire door, which had closed of itself in front, again opened in the same manner and the Saint and the Gnome stepped forth. Looking around, they found themselves once more in the plain uncarpeted hall beneath the roof. Could there be any doubt about the matter, the open scuttle from which they had so boldly descended would have reassured them. From one of the rooms came quick sounds of mingled thumps and scraping; it was the Head Waiter executing an extemporized double-shuffle in celebration of the just discovered California breast-pin.

Not stopping now to add any congratulations of their own, St. Nicholas and the Gnome passed by, climbed up the scuttle ladder and so at last stood again upon the roof.

The little sleigh was safe where they had left it and the reindeer lay dozing and blinking in front of it. So motionless had they rested that an inch of snow that had fallen during the night lay as yet unshaken from their sleek hides. The snow squall had passed over and the sky was clear again. Red now in the east with the rosy dawn — in every direction brightening with the coming of the new Christmas Day. Down in the city streets the lights were all extinguished and already the movement of population began to be plainly visible. Far out in the distance still glowed the revolving light-house beacon but it was paling before the coming day and its gleaming gold was turned to silver lustre. A few stars still shining in the sky, but soon to be extinguished — white caps upon the river and bay below — a long black steamer puffing in from distant port — the further hills beginning to grow brighter against the increasing blueness of the horizon — truly, as the Gnome now again exclaimed, it was a beautiful world and he longed greatly to remain in it.

" And why not then remain ?" inquired the Saint. " What can there be, indeed, to hinder ? "

" Nay, I cannot tell," said the Gnome, " except that I seem to have some duty belonging to me where now I abide and it must be right that I should perform it to the end. When or where I was born or whether I was ever born at all and have not always existed, I cannot tell. I only know that for more centuries than I can remember I have lived in the dark bowels of the earth guarding that treasure. Who committed it to my charge or for what purpose — whether I shall always guard it, or whether some time it will come into a destined use, — whether the griffin will one day try to steal it from me or whether griffins are really extinct — all this I cannot tell. It is enough for me to know that I have been placed in charge for some good purpose and in some spirit of needful trust and that there it is my duty to remain."

"You teach me a lesson, Gnome," St. Nicholas cried, "and it must be far from me to reject it. If you, in your life of silence, darkness and monotony do not repine, why then should I, whose life is one of moving to and fro among the beautiful scenes of this upper world? If you, who know not the reason for your task, remain content, why should not I who recognize the value and purpose of my duty, seeing how it is to make others happy, feeling so well that in doing this I cannot fail to add to my own pleasure as well? Nay, I am offended with myself that ever I let myself be downcast or troubled with my lot. Never again shall voice of undue complaint or despairing thought come into utterance through me."

Saying this, he looked once more so well pleased and happy — so thoroughly again did the olden expression of jovial serenity and peace diffuse itself upon his face — so cheerily did he take from his hat-band his long neglected pipe and send forth upon the morning air the fragrant incense of his content and thankfulness, that the little Gnome felt impelled to clap his hands with spontaneous outbreak of admiration.

"And forget not, furthermore, to think of this," said the Gnome, "that if I, who am so small and thin and dark, can forbear repining at my unloveliness, how much more easily should not you, so handsome in your plumpness, so beautifully tinted in the very center of your features, so graceful in all " —

"Let us now go, " the Saint interrupted, perhaps not altogether as well pleased with the ingenuous compliment to his personal appearance as he might have been had it come from some one of more enlarged experience and observation. "See, already the sun is close at hand and we should no longer tarry. "

He pointed towards the east, where now the clouds that had hung about the horizon were brightening in the radiance of the coming orb. Like courtiers left deserted and clustering in subdued and mournful raiment outside the king's gate, the clouds had rested through the night upon the distant hills in darksome tints. Now the king was coming forth; and they put on again their festive robes of gold and purple and with the freshening breeze, sailed away in joyous brightness to herald among all lands his majesty's approach.

Feeling the tightened rein, the little reindeer now scrambled up from the roof, shook off the light coating of snow, spread out their tiny hoofs and sprang merrily into the air, upon their homeward route. Rising thus invisible to men below; though, perchance if human ears had been held attentive and alert, the pleasant tinkle of the sleigh-bells might for an instant have been heard. For a moment only, however; so rapidly did the sound grow faint and then become altogether lost in the increasing distance, so speedily was the joyous tinkle overpowered by more sonorous clashing.

For at that instant the Sun appeared, lifted in regal state above the horizon, with thick battalions of spears of golden light advanced before him. And as though his coming were the expected signal, lo! there was heard at once the clanging peal of many bells from the great city below — rising at first far off in single note of praise, then taken up hither and thither in harmonious concord — chime answering to chime and tower to tower — all in pleasant unison of joy ringing down their sweet salutation to mankind below. To the poor menial, who listening to that glad acclaim, the meaning of which he could scarcely half comprehend, yet felt his uncultured soul stirred with something of the true spirit of the day and thenceforth moved with unwonted alacrity upon his ceaseless round of toil. To the rosy child, which aroused from its visionless sleep by the joyous peal, sprang at once into laughing and exultant wakefulness and hastened to possess itself of the various treasures the good Saint had left behind him — hurrying with rapid feet, lest the bright array might prove an unsubstantial vision and vanish before attainment, — dreaming not in its innocence that so

far from being a chimera this was one of those happy
moments that would remain a gilded memory
through life. To the lovelorn maiden, who now
with quieted heart could dreamily lie still and listen
to that pleasant clangor in the upper air and feel
that her perturbed spirit had regained those joyous
utterances that could vibrate in sweet sympathetic
accord with the merry metre of the bells. To the
worldly man, long worn and tossed with sordid aims
and ambitions, who, under newer impulses now giving his stifled fancy its natural bent, could let his
imagination flow back to olden times and feel that
he was a boy again and seem, amid the swinging of
the chimes, to hear those other bells for which, when
young, he had been wont to listen as token of the
coming of the good St. Nicholas, — that kindly Saint
who, though deemed a childish fancy had of late
stood so near him and with gentle influence had led
him into that line of purer thought which had brought
his better nature forever out from the rust and
mildew that had so long encrusted it. To all,
indeed, of every name and nature and to whom
want or inquietude or sorrow were not unknown;
that they, also, might lift up their voices in sweet
acclaim and rejoice alike for the blessings of peace
and comfort now brought to them by the gladden-
ing spirit of the bright Christmas festival.